Two Hills

George Axiotis

FORWARD

Cecilia Payne was fifteen years old, living with her father on Doctor Wunder's farm in Alexandria County, Virginia in the shadow of the nation's Capital when the Civil War landed on their doorstep. What had been a budding and affable community of farmers, war heroes, businessmen, and workmen nestled between two hills near their Mount Olivet Church, was now split with Virginia's secession and invasion by Federal troops in May 1861. What were once neighbors, almost overnight became either enemies of Virginia, the Federals, or both living in constant fear. Separating those two hills was a wonderful spring that fed a small creek where young boys and girls escaped their parent's prying eyes. Their little place of refuge paid witness to celebrations, romance, and later marauding scouting parties, skirmishes, and death.

When Alexandria County was returned to Virginia in the Retrocession of 1845, it did much to free it from Washington's ire, but it also set the stage for its occupation, becoming a key staging point for the war fifteen years later. Cecilia and her father struggled to survive by hauling goods to the many Union Army camps that sprung up on their lands, becoming witnesses to the injustices of war and learning to live within a sea of strange men. The war tested her family, friendships and even her love; shared with a young Union Army deserter. Yet, before the last year of the war she would lose nearly everyone she loved vowing to leave up-county and never return. Now seven years after the war, Cecilia and her daughter were back to settle her family's affairs with the Southern Claims Commission.

Although this is a fictional story about a young Cecelia growing up quickly in a suburb of Washington at the start of the Civil War, these are real people, experiencing actual events in our history.

CONTENTS

ACKNOWLEDGMENT

I want to thank all those who helped me thread these real stories and events into a Civil War experience as seen through the eyes of a young Cecilia Payne. I stayed true to the original accounts and events, though had to bridge some when they conflicted. A special thanks to the Arlington Historical Society whose magazine articles by local historians capture wonderful events and characters of Arlington's past and the property maps that allows us a glimpse into where these people lived at that time.

To the staff at the Arlington County Public Library's Central Branch, Center for Local History as well as the Alexandria City Library's Kate Waller Barrett Branch who helped with county maps, census accounts, slave, marriage and death records that helped put the key characters in their proper place. To the Arlington County Courthouse staff helping me sort through land and court records, providing insight into the business and property dealings of these characters. To James Russell, a renowned authority on the Civil War with significant roots to wartime Virginia, who was invaluable in his expertise, perspective and his extensive collection of reference material.

A special thanks to the staff at the National Archives for making rare documents available to amateur historians, as well as to staff at their annex in Silver Spring, Maryland, with their original maps and diagrams that helped put written accounts of camps, forts, and roads in Washington and Alexandria County into perspective. To the Library of Congress for putting old newspapers online allowing us to gauge the people's sentiments at the time these events happened.

Finally to my wife Marty, daughters Connie and Gia, and my friends who helped me edit this book with the hope of bringing a bit of our local history to everyone.

1 GOING HOME

The sudden jolt and the awful clatter startled me and woke Tommy as the train switched tracks in its final leg into town. I was exhausted even though I had slept through our crossing over the Long Bridge that separated Washington and Virginia. We had just passed Jackson City and were now on the last five miles or so to Alexandria City. Our last transfer in Washington had been such a trial; the city had grown seemingly four-fold since I last saw this place seven years ago. Then, I was desperately making my way out of here in the spring of '64, but now I had returned to settle Papa's affairs. Things had changed so much. Even that bridge across the river which linked our county to the rest of the District proper was now two; the original only fit for wagons and trolleys, and another beside it strong enough for trains. Both carried a steady stream of folks coming in and out of Virginia. Tommy had a worried look from the commotion, but quickly sat up and gazed out the window, thinking maybe our long journey from Pennsylvania was all but over. For a girl of nearly eight, she acts way beyond her years and has been my rock during the rough years after the war. I had hoped to reach Alexandria station early enough to catch the next train to the village of Falls Church on the final leg of this long journey. It has been six years since the war ended, and yet, I'm now seeing reminders of those awful times.

We rolled past the remains of two forts, Jackson and Runyon as I recall, both built in a hurry those first few days of the invasion to protect the Long Bridge from the rebels. Now those once formidable places are heaps of dirt with most of their timber gone, picked over for scrap, I suspect, when the Union Army abandoned them. Looking up the hill, I pointed out to Tommy the grand home of Confederate General Lee, now with a large federal flag flying above with thousands of grave markers circling his land. How such a thing could happen to a man's home was beyond me, but there were many such travesties during the war. Then, Jackson City, where once there were warehouses and stockyards filled with cattle, horses and wagons for war, someone had built a resort for gambling and fixed up the horse track. We were now just north of where Mama and Papa lived and where I was born which brought a wash of emotion from the memories as a young girl there before the war.

Within a few minutes, we were slowing down as we began passing city blocks, squares as they called them in the South, passing homes and businesses of Alexandria, rolling past once sprawling holding pens, hospitals and warehouses. It was as if I was looking in a picture book with its pages quickly flipping before my eyes, almost too much to take in. A tear came to me as we passed the remains of the large Sickles Hospital and barracks which had caused me so much grief. Tommy squeezed my hand, as she looked up and asked why I was crying. It's nothing, just memories of Papa, I said, hiding my feelings of anger toward this place. The view was much different from what I remembered. The city, which had been the hub of Federal wartime work, seemed now like any other, without all of the soldiers on every street or the trappings of war in the large camps and forts that dotted our land. That suited me fine. I was here to settle family affairs and find out what had become of my home. I dreaded making this trip. There were just too many bad memories; however, I did have acquaintances that I wished to see, and I wanted to show Tommy where Papa and I had lived during those years.

Tommy and I had come down from Pennsylvania where folk saw the war through the eyes of battles won and heroes made of young men whose youth was spent in faraway lands. Most had pretty much put the war behind them as best they could, but for those living south of the Potomac, it was much more different with the Federals running things. I didn't know what to expect coming back home to Virginia. For most of us who lived in the shadow of Washington, the vote for secession in '61 became our calamity.

The Federals were doing what they could to put the war to a close, giving pensions to the veterans and even passing its Claims Act in May of '71 looking to make things right to loyal residents for their losses during those four years. The Commission looking at such affairs around here was in Alexandria City and let it be known that claimants had to testify and present articles of note to be considered for any redress. Their work had barely made a mention in rural Pennsylvania where I only learned of it in a letter from a dear acquaintance that helped Papa and me during those hard times. Barbara, or Miss Barbara as I called her then, still lived in up-county and said I was welcome to stay on the farm while settling Papa's claims. It was up to me, Cecelia Payne, to tend to what was left of my family's affairs since Papa succumbed doing the Union Army's bidding. Since the fall, Barbara had been sending me what letters and Army chits she found around the old place that I could show the

Commission. Yet I had to get back to our old home, on that farm in up-county to get those who knew Papa best to vouch for my claim.

The train eased into the busy depot and just beyond sat the large railroad roundhouse with no less than eight rail spurs coming out of it. I had seen it during the war, a marvel built to parse soldiers and supplies all throughout the south. It now looked as if it was being torn apart having outlived its usefulness. We gathered our bags and Tommy her pillow doll, whom she named Eveline after one of my childhood friends, and clambered down with everyone else. I'd forgotten just how hot Virginia could be this time of year with the humid air almost unbearable. No sooner had I gathered my bearings than an awful fear came over me, one not felt since I had come with Papa hauling war goods to and from this city. That fear of suspicion and of being accosted outside every war place or at guard stops along the road. Gone were the soldiers and the trappings of war that had been everywhere, the flags at almost every street corner and the harried, fearful looks of people who hadn't abandoned the city wondering what was next to befall them. The large remnants of that awful war, its sprawling camps, endless lines of troops and wagons, and warships all along the Potomac were gone. Looking closer, though, there were still reminders.

Alexandria City seemed to have grown by half again as much since the war. Before the war days there were only about fifteen-hundred families or so with a tenth as many slaves throughout the county. Just before secession, many folks packed up and left for the countryside leaving the city pretty much a ghost town fearing the invasion everyone said was coming. Those few that remained, mostly Unionists but some secessionists with nowhere else to go, got lost amongst the thousands of Union soldiers, profiteers, brigands and other outsiders commonplace since the spring of '61. Locals were always weary of losing what little they had and fearful of being accosted, or worse yet, arrested.

The soldiers were now gone since the city had been returned to civilian rule just two years ago. Folks had come back to the city but those that came seemed different. They were men with business interests, more families, and many more colored folk than I remembered during the war. Amongst the bustle at the station, I saw men standing, some purposeless, some wearing the tattered remains of the loose, woolen uniformed trousers and others with their worn out, easy to recognize war issued boots with hobnailed bottoms. Yet, on this day, there was a certain freedom in the air, replacing the dread the average folk endured for fear of being rounded up for one offense or the other or worse, just for speaking badly about the Union or the President.

We were late leaving Washington so we missed the Manassas Gap train that would take us to Falls Church village before it made its way west to the Shenandoah. The next train was not for five hours, much past supper. I dreaded the delay, but Tommy, ever so inquisitive, wanted to see the city that she had heard so much about from my stories about Papa. It's been six years since the war ended and thank the Lord she was not around for the devastation and fear we felt living in the shadow of the Nation's Capital, trapped between those two hills. Tommy begged me to take her into the city to see the sites Papa and I saw. I had come back to Virginia to settle Papa's grievances with the Claims Commission which would occur in just three days from now. But a little tour first would be good for both of us. Although the bustle had changed since the war years, the city itself looked very much as it had then and it didn't take long for me to regain my wits on where to go.

We were at the edge of the city just before the steep hill climbs to the county farmlands. I took Tommy to a bluff just above the station to show her a splendid view of the Alexandria City's entirety. She was so excited, as was I, now at the same spot where I came with Papa. The city's edges had grown from those days and just off the station, I saw nearby King Street, one of the main roads through town from the station down to the wharfs. It was on that road that Papa and I hauled supplies from Meyenberg's Mercantile and the many Army Quartermaster warehouses back up-county via the turnpike road. To the east, you could see the Potomac River and upriver five more miles you could see Washington City, the white dome of the Capitol and the still unfinished monument to General Washington. A few squares north of us sat the old Sickles Barracks. Who could miss such a place with its large imposing hospital and a stockade for Union deserters and Confederate prisoners that stretched across many city squares. From what I could see, the place was no longer being used by the Army and was now filled with squatters. It was there that the last injustice was heaped upon me, speeding my departure from the up-county hills that I had called home.

I stopped to speak with a young mother holding her son's hand firmly lest he run into the path of the many wagons on the streets. I asked whether she knew if Meyenberg's was still in business. She told me that she, like many, was new here herself but she did believe it was near the Marshall House Inn, maybe a dozen squares away on King Street. I thanked her kindly as Tommy and I continued our walk. We left the train station when I caught a glimpse of an elderly man standing on a corner that I was sure I knew. I barely recognized Mr. Caldwell, an acquaintance of Papa's who helped him with supplies at the mercantile. He was older than Papa, and like him, was dependable and of good stature. Mr. Caldwell was kind and always made me laugh, giving me licorice as my reward for reading the manifests for Papa. He knew what was what and always which troops and supplies were moving to where. This wonderful, gregarious man was now a ghost of his former self, bent over and much greyer than I recalled, wearing the tattered remains of the long woolen Union army trousers. The war, it seems, had taken its toll on him as well.

He paused, seeing me stare at him, so I walked closer and immediately apologized for my rudeness. I looked him straight in the eyes and asked, "Are you Mr. Caldwell who worked at Meyenberg's during the war?" "Cecelia, my dear." His eyes began to water. "You are a gift from God and a sight for tired eyes". He touched my face with his hand all aquiver. Speaking in a low voice, he said that I was but a young girl when he last saw me with Papa a year or so before the war ended. He seemed so thankful to see me and asked how Papa was. I told him he had passed on in late '63. Caldwell stepped back, almost unbelieving and said he was sorry to hear that. He looked down at Tommy, who did not quite know what to make of this shell of a man, and asked if she was my own. Before I could speak, Tommy piped up, "Yes sir, I'm Thomasine, but everyone calls me Tommy, and that's my Ma." "You're a fine young lady. Did you know your grandpa and I go back many years together?" saying as he bent over to be eye to eye with her. "Your grandpa was a good man who always looked after his little girl, just as I'm sure your Papa looks after you." Tommy's smile disappeared as she hid behind me. I explained that Tommy's papa had died in the war as well.

I asked Caldwell what became of his wife Mary and daughter Abigale. He said sadly they were gone; as with so many during the war, they had just left, never to return. Caldwell paused for a moment and said that war had taken much from many and gave little in return. He had always wondered what had happened when he didn't see us around and figured we had moved on into Washington at the end of the war like everyone else. I told him that I left for

Pennsylvania late in the war after Papa passed on to be with acquaintances. The truth was that I'd left this wretched area after everyone I loved was taken from me, vowing never to return. But here I was, back to where it all happened, though only to testify at the Claims Commission to make right all of Papa's losses. He looked at me and said things had changed around here. Alexandria was no longer the little town we once knew. It was going places everyone said. He had heard the farms upland where Papa and I had lived now had all sorts of people settling there from the north. Alexandria County he said had been ruled by a military commission throughout the war and stayed on for five years after. Only a year or so ago had it been turned over to civilians and they had big plans for the city. The folks around here now have a different character.

We had run out of pleasantries and time was short. Tommy and I bid Caldwell farewell and told him that if I met up with any of the families up-county, that I would let them know he was still of this earth. Holding my hand, he whispered "God be with you two" and so Tommy and I just turned and walked on. Caldwell was another lost soul of the war, a hollow shell of his former self in the tattered remains of an old soldier.

Making our way toward King Street, at the edge of the station we came upon a three-story brick home that I recognized from many years ago when Papa told me it was an old Negro jail. I asked Papa when I first saw the odd house, with its tall stone wall that surrounded its courtyard, if the Negroes committed more crimes than others given the size of the place, but he never answered and warned me never to come here. This wretched place as I came to find out was the business of the Price-Birch & Co. slave merchants whose name was painted in large letters on its wall until the invasion. I guess a jail was less of an offense to some for the awful business that was done there. This unassuming home in this little city, a stone's throw down river from Washington, was the largest company of its kind in Virginia, and possibly the country, responsible for nearly half of the slave trade between New Orleans and the Virginia-Maryland area. Yet in some sort of justice, it later became a jail for secessionists when the Union Army took over the city. I recalled there was a courtyard with a high wall and a barred gate hiding the six or so pens with large steel doors that we could see when we drove the wagons along Duke Street. Before the war, this place held slaves being readied for trade to Louisiana and Mississippi to work the big cotton and sugar plantations. Just days after the invasion, the Union Army turned it into barracks for contraband slaves who fled the Confederate states and sought refuge with the Union troops. Within a year or so, it became a military prison for soldiers found in the city without passes, civilians caught selling alcohol to soldiers or anyone found jeering at Union soldiers. Later on in the war, it served a nobler role as a hospital for Negro soldiers and other free coloreds. For me, this home, like this city, was everything the war was about. Sinful business done behind walls that later split, then like punishment, consumed us all. Now, this place, and this city, looked like nothing ever happened.

Alexandria City had been a thorn in the District's side before the war, since it was a large trading port for slaves. The city, with its railroad and wharfs on the Potomac, was a suitable place for selling Maryland and Virginia slaves to cotton or sugar plantations in the Deep South. I was surprised that this home, the source of so much Union angst those few days after the invasion, hadn't been burned down to purge this city of its deplorable deeds. The high stone wall surrounding its courtyard was now gone along with those pens. The home, where slaves were kept in its basement, now appeared as any other. Although the Price & Birch sign was now gone, the evil that came to be there can't be erased by mere whitewash. How someone could live on grounds where such cruelty prevailed was beyond me.

Tommy and I continued for a bit passing all manner of merchants, many more than before the war. The city looked almost as modern as any I had seen up north. Plank board and even stone walkways with gas lamps were now common on the streets and the roads were filled with wagons hauling goods here and there. There were even omnibus wagons, like those I saw in Washington as a young girl, taking passengers up and down King and Duke Streets.

Once on King Street we made our way to the courthouse and if time allowed, down to the waterfront. After a few squares we approached Meyenberg's to see it still busy. The war it seems had not affected Solomon and Wolf's business in the least. There were now all manner of wagons and carts outside, almost as busy as it was during the war. Papa knew both men for many years and it was there where I often read the manifests. Early in the war Papa made most of the runs by himself or with Caldwell, but he did bring me there a few times. The place was always filled with merchants, traders and solders of all sorts and was easily found being next to the Union Army Quartermaster headquarters, itself with the tallest flagpole I had ever seen just outside its front door. It was there that Papa would cashier his chits and pay notices from the up-county camps and forts. Many of those chits had fancy wording attesting to Papa's good character, so after a while we felt at ease going there to get paid.

Papa brought me along on occasion to help him with the manifests, though he often made me dress as a boy in trousers and loose fitting shirts to appear as a farmhand so as not to attract the attention of any undesirables along the roads, taverns and storefronts. It was at the mercantile where Mr. Caldwell helped Papa load his wagons and would give me licorice every time for doing such a fine job reading the manifests. I walked in ever so quickly to look and see if anything had changed, but there was such a commotion and recognizing no one, I quickly got to the counter and paid the clerk for some licorice. Tommy and I both smiled as we savored our sweets; such a small thing brought such good memories to me.

At the door I paused a bit looking across the street at the Marshal House Inn. The red, white and blue bunting on the front windows that had been there all during the war was gone. Everyone knew of the place, more of a boarding house really, being a fixture in this city that it even made its own tokens to use as money throughout Alexandria City until '59. I remember Papa being anxious as the war came, with folk hoarding their gold and silver and even copper coins, so he always kept Marshall Tokens with him. It was at that inn on the fateful early morning in May of '61 that the cauldron boiled over, when the war came to our shores. Papa told me of the tale whenever we came to the Mercantile. It was there that the famed Colonel Ellsworth and his soldiers came to tear down a large secessionist flag that had waved so boastfully from its roof days before the invasion. As if thumbing their nose at the Federals, one could see it from the Capitol and no doubt from Mr. Lincoln's home. It was there where the war's first martyrs were made, Ellsworth for the Union and Inn keeper Jackson for the secessionists.

The Inn was a stop for all manner of soldiers, dignitaries and visiting northerners during the war looking for souvenirs of that fateful morning. Colonel Ellsworth, commander of a New York company of troops, called the Fire Zoaves, named so for their red pantaloons, fez caps and fearless demeanor with most being firefighters before the war. These men sailed from Washington and after landing at the wharfs, Ellsworth led his men up King Street that early morning in late May of '61. Upon seeing the Confederate flag waving defiantly from the Inn's rooftop, he rushed in with a few men to correct this dishonor. James Jackson, the hotel's proprietor and a hardened secessionist, raised the banner during a rally just after the vote of secession, saying to all who would hear that the flag would come down only over his dead body. His boast came true that early morning when the Colonel having taken down the offending flag, was killed by Jackson's shotgun blast to the chest. As the Colonel fell, a private killed Jackson and in an instant each had become a martyr for his cause. Papa told me that all through the war, relic hunters raided the Marshal House stripping it of furniture, carpeting, window shutters, stairs, handrails, floorboard and even the flagpole, anything as keepsakes of this now sacred place. Now as Tommy and I gazed at it, gone were the many flags that surrounded this shrine of war that brought such suffering to us. The fateful staircase had been put back together and there was little reminder now of the horrors on that frightful morning.

We kept walking to the waterfront as Tommy whirled her head around trying to take it all in. I told her how Papa used to bring me to the wharfs where the many ships docked during the war unloaded their cargo of goods and food stuffs for the Union Army to be stored at the many warehouses in town. Downriver a bit, to my surprise, still stood the shanty houses built on river barges where Papa said women of ill repute lived. They were known as "Hooker's girls", from the Union General who controlled such things in Washington for a while. Such scandal, but apart from that, there was little else left to remind folks of the war. It seems this place had moved on.

We had already taken too much time sightseeing and it was time to make our way back up to the court house to see where I was to appear before the Commission. Outside the place were groups of people of all sorts waiting to do their business. So many were about in fact that I could not see in a window. Had these souls come here for the same reason I wondered? What did they know that I didn't? I was determined to find out, asking a few gathered whether this was where the Commission was meeting, but most were too busy to answer me.

I made my way toward the front door to speak with a clerk. By chance, I met up with Mr. Jackson, a freed colored man from up-county some bit away from our place near the Chain Bridge. Papa and I had come to know of him and his wife at the Mount Olivet Church just as the war came. My dear, it's been many years, as he stumbled through his words. I'm seeing the commission again to tell about the timber the Union Army took from me when they built Fort Marcy up near the Chain Bridge. He was a friendly man, though not well spoken, and I suspect had a hard time making his thoughts clear, and being colored, they probably paid him no mind. I was wondering if you could speak to them as I don't have any Union Army papers, he said nervously staring at the floor. I was terribly sympathetic, but since he and Papa didn't have business dealings, I would make a poor witness I said. I dreaded having to tell him so, but I couldn't risk the Commissioners thinking ill of me before my own day with them. With that I bid him farewell and quickly rushed away with Tommy across the street to gather my thoughts. Here was a land owner, though not well-spoken, one nevertheless, with a legitimate claim struggling to right the wrongs done to him during the war. If he faced such trials, what was to be my fate?

I began to panic, was I being naïve? How was a young woman, without husband or land title to fare before the Commission? I needed more help and that was only to be found in my old home in the up-county hills, with those neighbors and friends who knew of Papa's good works and more importantly could attest to his and my own character. The time for sightseeing was over and I had to put my thoughts to the task before me. I lost all track of the time during this sojourn which brought back so many memories, but had to tend to more important matters. We had only an hour before our train departed and a long way back through town to reach the station. Tommy was too tired, and frankly I as well, to walk back uphill through town so we took the omnibus giving us much needed rest. I was now filled with purpose, to see old friends and find out what happened to our little community. As Caldwell said, much had changed since the war, and there was not much left here for those that stuck stubbornly to the old Virginia ways. The plantation way was being taken over with a new breed of folk tied to business and less concerned with old family ties. The city had indeed changed, and likely the rest of the County as well.

We got to the train station, exhausted from our day's foray in the heat. The train soon arrived, and Tommy and I settled in for this last leg of our trip. Not soon after we pulled out of the station I got my first real glimpse of the county proper, a few forts remained, but the camps which stretched for hundreds of acres outside of town were now gone and in their place farmers tended the fields. Alexandria brought back many memories and reminded me just how fierce and independent this county was before the war. This fierceness, borne of Washington's indifference before the war and outright animosity during it, became the downfall for some and their families. I was more curious than ever of what became of those firebrands up-county.

After nearly two hours of seemingly endless stops we pulled into the Falls Church station. Other than the sounds of the train pulling away, there was barely any commotion about except a few men and women milling about and merchants loading wares on and off wagons. It was a rather pleasing welcome to the upper reaches near the county line, far from the bustle we left back in Alexandria. Tommy and I gathered our things and stepped off yet another platform for the last time. Except for the winds whistling through the pine trees and the whirring of the cicadas it was peaceful, quite a change from where we spent our morning. The last few miles home were either to be on foot or, if heaven allowed, a kind soul would favor us with a ride. I asked a trackman if he knew of anyone heading east along the Little Falls Road that could give Tommy and me a ride, but he just pointed to the rear of the station where freight men and merchants were loading their wares. After a few pleasantries and a bit of pleading, a man offered us a seat on his wagon. It seems God was with me, as he was heading to the Glebe Parish which was less than a half mile from Doc Wunder's farm, my home during the war.

Glebe Parish, now that did bring me back. It was seat of all the parishes in the County since colonial times and where pastors were assigned to tend to God's affairs in these parts. The lands it held were granted from the King of England himself in exchange for taking care of religious affairs in the colonies and tending to the few churches including that of the Falls Church itself, where George Washington himself had been a vestryman. After the war with the British, the parish sold some of its lands to those who came to live in up-county. There were few, if any, lands in these parts without some tie to the Glebe and it was there that early county business was held. I had only visited it a few times in all my years recalling it a splendid home amongst the small farm houses in the area.

It took some time, but our driver finished loading his things and I quickly hurled my bags onto the wagon. He was surprised by my brashness, but I figured he wasn't too eager to load my bags anyway. So off we went, I at the driver's side and Tommy behind me for the last few miles home. Tommy settled atop the burlap bags to take in the sights while I tried to speak to our teamster. He was in no real mood to talk so I soon found myself drifting off trying to recall all the things Papa told me about these lands that became our home all those years ago. He said many times that this county was full of firebrands and that one day it would bring trouble. As I settled in I began to remember why.

.

2 A LITTLE FIREBRAND

This spit of land across the Potomac, had always played second fiddle to District proper which made up Washington City, especially so since Virginia, took it back in the retrocession of '46. Back then, Alexandria City was a bustling place of five thousand or so just five miles downriver from Washington that connected it to the railroads in Virginia feeding all points throughout the South. Alexandria was a bustling port and railroad stop in its own right, even in the shadow of Georgetown just up river, where the Chesapeake and Ohio Canal barges unloaded their goods to the wagons that crossed over the Long Bridge into Virginia. For that reason alone, Alexandria had a say in the District's affairs, yet was always its backwater, even more so with the rest of up-county where I grew up.

This county was my home where my folks, Blair and Elizabeth Payne, put down roots and where I spent the war years with Papa scratching out a living. At one time the county was the southwest part of the District land-grant when the capitol was moved here to placate both northern and southern states after the revolution. Yet by the time of my birth in '45, our land was well on its way to being its own as a new county in Virginia. Though our businesses were tied to Washington, our county pretty much ran things on its own. Papa talked many times about how Washington merchants and even the United States Congress paid little mind to us just across the Potomac, yet depended on us so. Though it was part of the Capital since the borders were drawn by Washington himself, this side of the river was never really part of it or of Virginia for that matter. Until the retrocession, men on this side of the Potomac couldn't even vote in the state and national elections as could the rest of the District.

Papa, as with most of the families he did business with, had few if any slaves. While some clergy and the abolitionists held strong beliefs on the issue, as with most, Papa did not much care for the radical abolitionists either. Yet, as a good Christian, he felt there would eventually be an end to this injustice. With the fall of the once mighty Virginia tobacco years ago, farmers sold their slaves to middlemen in Alexandria who either shipped these poor souls to the deep south from its wharfs, or more often marched them in chains a thousand miles to Louisiana and Mississippi to work the large plantations where cotton was now king. The largest of these anywhere was in Alexandria City, sending nearly a thousand slaves a month to the South until the war. This little city across the river from the Capital had made a name for itself, and none too pleasant as far as the District proper was concerned. Though Virginia was a slave state, the abolitionists were powerful and were none too fond of Alexandria City's pro-slavery representatives.

Our county was not large, about 25 square miles or so. In the south along the Potomac was Alexandria City, from there northwest nine miles to Minor Hill about a mile from Falls Church village. From there eastward nearly along the Little Falls Road, to the Potomac's falls at the Chain Bridge with its fisheries, mills, warehouses and the Fendall brother's distillery. Papa was prone to history lessons whenever it suited him and said to me many times on our trips to Washington that it was in these old Peterson warehouses where Dolly Madison, wife of the then President, hid the federal city's government books, valuable papers and even the Declaration of Independence when British troops burned the city some sixty years before. Back then I didn't pay much mind to our lessons, but after he was gone I came to yearn for them.

The Chain Bridge was the lifeline of the up-county across the Potomac. Papa said it was at one time the largest and tallest bridge in the nation, built in '01 with large chain links, that gave safe passage to most of Washington's merchants when the British came. The bridge had been rebuilt many times, now made of timbers on rock piers rising high above the river. Its height made many men, women and horses fearful when crossing it. It was, as its name said, a link in the chain from all cities up north to those in the south, and all of them through our county. Yet during the war, that bridge would also be one of many keeping us locked up.

From there the county ran south along the Potomac past the stone cliffs and palisades to the edge of General Lee's plantation called Arlington. It was near there where the Aqueduct Bridge from Georgetown spurred into Virginia off the Chesapeake & Ohio canals that ended in the District proper. It was this spur where Papa was to make, and lose, his fortune with the Alexandria Canal Company. From there further south along the flats, the Lee plantation ended near the end of the Long Bridge, itself the longest bridge in the world that Tommy and I came over. Such a wonder, it was nearly a mile long connecting the North's rail lines to those in Virginia using big wagons teams. That bridge was the Union Army's artery of war, pumping its blood of soldiers and war goods during those horrible years. At the Virginia end sat Jackson City, a seedy place for horse racing and gambling. From there the County ran down river back to Alexandria City along the swamps and flats, through factories and shanty towns that fed Washington City's growth.

Papa was a young man when he and Mama moved to Washington City in '40, eager and looking for his fortunes. He was a not a boastful man, not of large stature, with strong hands that I held often, lovely eyes, a kind heart, and true to his word. Papa had worked the mills in Pennsylvania but believed his future was tied to the new capital city. In a short time he became a trusted teamster hauling goods from the waterfront using a heavy wagon that he brought down from Pennsylvania. It wasn't long before larger interests squeezed out small teamsters like him so he and Mama crossed the river to make a go of it in Alexandria. The Potomac River was like a moat protecting Washington proper from those of the county, with Alexandria a place of exile, and for some, refuge from the Federal city. Those of us across the river, with its backwater of swamps in the south and difficult hills in the north, were not seen as befitting the same class as those in the District proper. That sentiment to those across the Potomac created its own firebrand. Alexandria City and its county, did pretty much as it pleased and was left to fend for itself.

Mama and Papa lived in a small cottage in a rundown area just north of Alexandria City. Between their home and Washington City sat Alexander Island, an easy to forget spit of land just at the base of the Long Bridge which sat Jackson City, itself a lawless place of gambling and men of questionable character working the nearby kilns that supplied bricks for Washington's growth. Its cornerstone was laid by President Andrew Jackson himself many years earlier hoping for riches in yet another port town, but the riches never came. When business interests pushed Congress to open a canal spur into Virginia from Georgetown, Papa like many others put what money they had into Alexandria Canal Company bonds for the roads and docks to unload goods to Alexandria City. He even speculated on a few plots near the end of the Aqueduct Bridge hoping to raise his stature as a businessman on the outer circle of local financiers, figuring maybe in a few short years he'd be on the verge of wealth. Mama was making ties within her circle of ladies, hoping someday to move from the rundown cottage into a fine house in Alexandria City proper.

But it was not meant to be and by '42, with the whole country in distress, Congress voted against the roads and docks off the spur and instead paid the excesses from the canal work on their side of the river that didn't benefit us a bit. Alexandria City was left on its own to improve the canal works with County businessmen working in earnest to find banking interests outside the District. In a bit of pique, Congress then banned outside banking interests across the river, leaving local banks to partner only with those in the District at shamefully high interest rates. Without proper banking, finishing the spur would be too heavy a tax burden for County folk. If that weren't enough, the canals were doomed anyway as Northern railroad interests had already laid tracks to the Long Bridge, and it was only a matter of time before Virginia extended theirs from Alexandria.

Later that year the Canal Company collapsed. Papa's dreams of success and Mama's of a beautiful home in the city were gone, as were those of many of Alexandria's businessmen. A year later, strong talk over the abolition of slavery in the District became yet another concern for Alexandria, seeing its livelihood suffer further should it be outlawed. The injustices were just too much, so concern became action in early '45 to right Congress's injustices and buffer itself from the growing abolitionists.

I was born in late May of that year during those trying times just outside Alexandria City proper. We lived there with other small clapboard homes of those who couldn't afford to live in the city. Mama told folk that we had to live there on account of Papa needing room to pasture his horses in a field across the way, but in truth it was all he could afford. That place made Mama fret as we were close to the poor house and the Four-mile Run creek where I often played as a child just ahead of where it emptied into the Potomac. Mama groused at being seen as lower stature than her lady friends in the city proper. She was a striking woman who kept herself prim in her manner of talk and dress. I'll tell you, Mama was better dressed than most of the other women in our neighborhood and because of that we were never quite welcomed in their homes. It was best that way, as Mama preferred to spend her days with me in and about the city proper when she could, making her way home, often near supper time. She had a weak demeanor and when we got home, took to sleeping often and sipping laudanum to ease her *ills*, and I suspect to ease her shame. Mama was sick quite often in those days, which left me to fend for myself. Papa was beside himself when he would come home after a long day's work looking for supper, but on many days he would tend to Mama suffering from her *medicine* as she called it. I would try to cheer her up with pictures of flowers and animals that I drew with charcoal from the fireplace on stray bits of paper.

When Mama was sleeping hard and the weather was good, Papa and I would go outside, and I'd sit on his lap and hold his hand. His were so strong and they made me feel safe holding on to them for what seemed like hours. We'd watch wagons roll by and I'd try to guess what was on them and where they were going. Barrels of pitch, boxes of nails, hemp rope, sail cloth, toward the docks, for the trains, rolling up-county, I was able to pretty much pick them right, and all the while he'd tell me how good I was at it. Maybe he fibbed a bit, but Papa made me feel smart and needed. He told me many times that he and I would make good teamsters when I got older. I was so looking forward to being with him on the road, but for now my place was to tend to Mama.

Most of my friends lived at the Poor House just up the road a bit. It was a large home with sheds and such all about. I never went in the home on account of Mama telling me it was not a proper place for a young lady but I had many friends there, and we would play often in the fields behind it when we were all done with chores. There were two girls my age that I was especially close to named Clarisse and Jessie. Clarisse was of fair skin and long, black hair which was always in a long ponytail stretching down her back to her knees. She was always laughing and never had a mean thing to say about anyone. Her father was a railroad track ordinary, who was crippled some years ago and now they lived in the home. She spent little time at home except to eat and sleep on account of her Pa and his bouts of yelling the cruelest things that scared most of the children. Jessie was mulato with light brown skin, curly hair and beautiful brown eyes. When she was around the elders, she would be as quiet as church mouse but would open up with stories of all kinds when we three were together. She loved to laugh and between us three, our hoots and hollers could be heard everywhere. Jessie lived with her Ma in the home and spent the days playing outside while her mother worked somewhere on the wharfs of Alexandria City and would be gone most days and nights. We played with our dolls and ran around the fields, seemingly without a care in the world as you'd come to expect from little girls.

A bit further up river, and up wind, was Jackson City where no self-respecting family would live. It was dirty and the soot and smell from the nearby brick kilns for Washington's building boom reeked something awful from the dried manure used for the fires. During the long hot summer days when the winds would disappear in midday and the stench of that wretched town would waft our way, many would stay in their homes nearly all day. Papa warned all the young ones not to venture too close to that place as there were many bad folk around there. We heard tell that there was a nearby gulch called Hell's Bottom, where bad men and those that couldn't pay their gambling debts were shot and hung regularly. Looking back, our home just outside the city was our world, full of adventure and sometimes danger. Yet, it was not all fun. Papa's failed business dealings had put him in debt and hardened him. Mama's loss of stature with her women friends and troubles from my birth took an even greater toll on her. Papa had always said that she was a fine woman, stern and proper looking on the outside, but frail within, someone who could never handle much stress. Mama had longed to return to Pennsylvania to be near her family, but Papa would have none of that leading to many words between them. I would just go outside to get away from it all.

Mama and Papa were caught up in a whirlwind that would come to shape our lives forever. The retrocession, as they called it, was all that was on everyone's mind and by early '45 city leaders successfully petitioned the Congress and Virginia lawmakers to return this land to Virginia. Their efforts bore fruit as President Polk signed the return of the part of the District on Virginia soil into law in July of '46. But before it became so, county men had to vote on it. The Alexandria Gazette wrote often of the coming vote which was all the talk that summer. For up-county folk far away from Alexandria City, passions were far less for such fuss as many were from Washington and other Northern states who had come here early on. For big landowners and merchants, up-county was a place of respite from the bustle of the city, land to pasture their horses and stone to be quarried for the city's buildings. Some ran mills while most others farmed the crops that were sold in Alexandria and the District. Their fortunes were tied to the capital city, so any loss in their status as District folk was seen as a loss for all. But for those families further from the Federal city and of long Virginia lineage in the west part of the county and beyond, having few rights and federal meddling in what were clearly State affairs was just too much and they made it known of their intentions in those weeks before the vote.

There were a few polling stations outside Alexandria City scattered about, but most were along the main north-south road known by many names; County Road, Road to the Falls or the Road to the Glebe. For folk of the Glebe parish, proper county work was done at the Ball's Tavern where the East-West Georgetown-Fairfax Road crossed the Road to the Glebe. The tavern was a typical one of log having one long room with a large fireplace at one end and a counter along one wall. It was run by Ball family kin who owned land about the county and had long established roots here. Men had gathered there to exchange news, do the county's business and send soldiers off to war. It had been where they formed a company of volunteers for the Mexican war and fifteen years later where militiamen chose sides during the war of the rebellion.

Everyone who was anyone came that day to vote, many with their families, all ten of the Birch and Ball families, three Donaldson families, the Minors and their kin, and others. So in early September of '46, two months after the President's decree, the vote passed with over seven hundred for and about two hundred against, with half of those against being folks outside the city. Alexandria City celebrated for three days on the good news that our county officially became one within Virginia, but that newly found freedom would come to haunt us all fifteen years later.

Though we weren't in the city proper, things around

here weren't without danger. I was no more than six or seven when Clarisse, Jessie and I were playing down at the creek near the Poor Home when a wagon pulled up. The driver was a portly man with a pleasant smile. He spoke to us in a low voice, as he rolled his large black mustache with his two fingers, asking whether we liked candy. Eagerly, we all said yes, and he went on saying he had a wonderful box of candy that he couldn't finish and was looking for young children which to give it to before he left town. This strange man got off his wagon and walked to the rear which was covered with canvas tied to the wagon sides. He lowered the gate and told us the candy box was at the front and if they could get it for him, we could take it free for all the children at the home. After hoisting Clarisse into the back of the darkened wagon bed, before I knew it, he grabbed both Jessie and me, shoving us into that cramped space. Clarisse began crying and Jessie just laid there quiet with fear while the man shut and pinned the gate on one side. As he ran around to get back on the bench, I reached through the cover struggling to lift the pin holding the gate shut. Clarisse tried to help too and just as the wagon pulled away the gate sprung open spilling Clarisse and I onto the road. We both ran across the fields too scared to scream. I remember looking back and didn't see Jessie anywhere as the wagon rode off quickly. Clarisse and I ran for who knows how long, until we collapsed. We both cried, not knowing what happened to our friend. Soon after we each went home to tell of what had happened.

When I came home, I tried to wake Mama, yelling all the while, and after a bit in her groggy voice told me to stop telling stories and drifted back to sleep. I was beside myself with fear and all alone. I was nearly taken by an evil man, my friend was gone, and no one seemed to care. I cried the rest of the night and didn't leave the house for many days for fear the wagon man with the mustache would come get me. I never went to the Poor Home again or saw

Jessie or Clarisse again. I never heard what happened the Jessie, not that anyone but Clarisse and I cared about a child of the streets. My world of friends and endless fields had shrunk to my home for the next few years taking care of Mama and fearing the return of the wagon man. I waited eagerly for Papa to return home every night and gave him a big hug when he came through the door. He would smile, and always asked if I had been guarding our home while he was away. I would smile and get to help fix supper. I never told him what happened.

Papa never gave up, working his mule teams hard and by '51 had nearly repaid the debts he owed to many. He did what he could as a teamster running supplies between Alexandria City and the Chain Bridge and up to the Georgetown ferry but it was never what he thought he would be. The long runs kept him away from Mama and me even longer, wearing out his horses and mules with not much to show for it. Yet, more and more of his hauls were taking him north along the Glebe Road through good and fertile land amongst the old parish holdings. This land was dotted with small farms typical of folks not born here and a few larger plantations of those whose families had some history. He had met many good people along the way and heard how many northerners had come to live in up-county. Papa became sure that this part of the county would be far enough from Alexandria City to raise a family proper, yet close enough to run his teams from there all about the county and up to the Little Falls. Things kept getting worse for us. The cottage was hard to keep warm, Mama was getting more withdrawn, and I was pretty much left on my own. Mama was growing weaker as the months went by and in the winter of '54 caught the grip and nearly died. Our family was being torn apart and only with God's help could we survive. Something had to change.

During Papa's runs up-county, he met many fine

folk, and a kind doctor and his family was to change our lives forever. Doctor Henry Wunder had himself come to this part of the county to live a simpler life from Washington City, himself a man from Germantown Pennsylvania. He practiced medicine and farmed on a parcel of land bordering along the county road just above the Glebe parish. He also ran a small store on Mason's Island near the Aqueduct Bridge that catered to folks coming and going from Georgetown. Wunder, or "Doc" as Papa called him, was a fine Christian man who had also run for the County Assembly having made a name for himself and his kin. Papa had come to know Doc after he hurt his hand something awful while unloading supplies at the tavern. Papa talked about us and his dreams of moving to the north while Doc talked about needing help to tend to affairs on his farm. With that came an invite to live at one corner of their farm in a small cottage. As if a gift from God, Papa graciously agreed. So a few weeks later on a cold day in the spring of '55, when I was but 10 years old, that we picked up and moved from that wretched place seven miles or so north to the county's Washington District to live at Doc's farm at the crossing of the Glebe Road and the Georgetown & Fairfax Road.

Doc's place was in a small community of farmers and a few merchants. Many of the homes were small, with a horse or two, a buggy, a wagon and maybe every other house a cow. Most didn't have too many dealings with outsiders as the roads weren't very good, barely wide enough for one buggy, becoming impassable muddy trials when it rained. About the only way to get to the District or Alexandria was along the toll roads. Around here were two kinds of families, easily known by the homes they lived in; Those mostly from northern states with some working government jobs lived in small story and a half farmhouses while the old gentry lived in larger plantation homes, some with a few slaves working the fields and the home. They were worlds apart in their manners, but this community got together when it needed to and did so to build and run the only school in these parts. With a parcel of land from one of the Birch family, a *Committee of Contributors and Builders of a School* as they called themselves built the only school in these parts near the Doc's place atop a small hill. I remember fondly doing my schooling there for a bit.

We would not be the only ones to benefit from the Wunder's generosity of offering us a place to live there with his wife Anne, daughter Aphelia and son George with his wife Ann. Another was a kind woman named Barbara Blogger, a few years older than Mama, who was the local midwife and helped Doc care for patients and there was an older workhand by the name of Daniel Turner. The Wunder's welcomed Mama and I with much kindness and even cleaned out the cottage before we arrived. It was a small place on the corner of their property that had been built to store supplies for trappers heading to the Falls, but we didn't mind as it was our new home. It wasn't long before we met other families in the area on account of folks coming to visit Doc. For me, it was a chance to play again with girls my age in the fields and creeks, no longer afraid of ungodly men and other miscreants that roamed the fields and roads near Jackson City.

Life with the Wunder's was more than we could ask for. They were good to us, and we helped each other. Doc was nearly seventy at the time of the war. He and Anne, could have passed for my grandparents, but they were full of fire. Papa and Doc got along real well and the only thing he asked in return was help with supplies on occasion and help clear timber from the land when needed. These were small prices to pay for the kindness his family showed us. He and son George were the calming sorts during those early days of the war with only Doc and another Doctor Locke who came by once and a while to treat sick folks around here and soldiers alike. Life on the farm was not easy for me with tending to the garden, Mama, Papa's teams and errands for George and Doc, but it was our home and I did my best to keep things orderly for Papa given Mama's condition.

George was married to a local girl named Ann and they had an infant son named William. Together, they worked the farm and the store and later he worked in the city for the Treasury Department shortly after Lincoln's men came to town. He traveled to and from Washington by foot a few days a week and when he wasn't there spent time at the store. George was kind, generous and affable, known in local county politics having run as headmaster of the school which we attended near the Glebe and having a good position with the Government. Folks asked him to run for a seat on the County Board, but one of the Minor kin had planned to make that job his own. There was a bitter election and George lost, which soured his feelings toward the Minor clan. The bitterness that followed was to haunt the Minor's during the war.

Though Ann was only about six years my elder by the time of the war, she acted older than Doc's wife always fussing over her William. While George was a friendly and outgoing man, Ann was the opposite, a proper and stern sort prone to outbursts about God and the Judgment day. George met her at a temperance lesson and fell for her devotion to the Lord. She thought many of us were on our way to perdition on account of not reading the Bible as much as she thought we should and cavorting with the other young folk down at the spring. Ann measured folk by their beliefs in God which set her apart from the rest. We didn't pay her much mind and tried to stay away from her when we could. Apbelia never warmed up to us thinking maybe we were after Doc's land. She pretty much kept to herself, and when not, preferred instead to read the Bible with Ann.

Daniel Turner, whom only I could call Danny, was quite a bit older than I, a kindly and gentle sort, pleasant to be around and always knew what was going on around here. He was as good with farm equipment as he was with needle and thread, not like most other men I knew. Many whispered behind his back, and some told him hurtful things straight to his face, of him being dainty and such. Ann was especially cruel to Danny, and I just didn't understand why given all the good work this man did. Danny taught me a lot about turning the other cheek, and being good to others no matter how they treated you. He often lent me his shoulder when things got hard or his ear when I needed advice, especially so when dealing with some of the meaner girls around here. He had a way about these things and rumors about him or not, he was my dear friend.

Miss Barbara was a few years older than Anne, and when not tending to midwifing or taking care of Doc's patients, taught me many things about how to be a lady, how to run a proper home and getting along with others. She would spend time with me on Sunday's teaching me to read so when I got to school I wouldn't be made fun of by some of the girls. Barbara felt girls could make of themselves as they wished and reading was how one got to be respected around here. She introduced me to the *Tales of the Arabian Nights* and of the *Swiss Family Robinson*, spending hours on those stories. For Miss Barbara, it was about hard work, not complaining, keeping to your word and always tending to family and guests. For guests, she would say, took time out of their lives to be with you, so it was your obligation to welcome them with open arms and an open home. Those words would help Papa and me through those long years. Miss Barbara had a sense about things like that. She didn't speak much about her own life, but over the years I came to learn of her trials at the hands of a wicked man who treated her much as a slave. She ran away from him and after a few days in the countryside was caught taking vegetables from the Wunder's garden. They took her in and taught her the ways of a midwife and she has been with them ever since. Miss Barbara was a kind soul who taught me many things a young girl should know, things Mama wasn't able to teach me on account of her ills. She always looked out for me and made sure no one bothered me. Barbara told me about the gatherings at the springs, where boys and girls would go tramping for berries, foraging for nuts and how to fit in with the latest style of dress making hoops for my skirts out of reeds gathered from the creek. She would come to be my savior for a while during the war. Miss Barbara taught me how to set a good hearth, work the wheat, bake the bread and prepare a proper meal. As Mama became weaker spending more time in bed, I became the cook for us all. Keeping the home just so and having a proper meal ready when Papa finished his runs was my chore, but I was proud to do them as he deserved it. Throughout that spring and into the summer, I finally felt as if I had purpose and the freedom to grow.

It was one day while fetching water where I met Eveline Vanderberg, by accident really, getting lost making my way to a spring that Miss Barbara talked about that was just over the next hill. I was crossing Eveline's property when I saw her on a porch. Sheepishly, I asked if she knew of a spring in the area, to which she just said that if I closed my eyes and turned one and a half turns, one would appear. I don't know why but I did as she asked and when I opened my eyes, sure enough there was a spring head that was right behind me all along. We both had a good laugh and got along splendidly from that moment on. Her family was well-known in the area and Miss Barbara spoke often of their kindness. Her father, Gilbert was a farmer and a businessman. Their 200-acre farm was along the Little Falls Road and sat next to his brother-in-law Gilbert Vanderwerkin's vast tract as he was a rich local businessman that ran the trolleys in Washington and used his lands to pasture his horses. Eveline became a fine rider on those horses and we would see her galloping about the county nearly every day.

Eveline's father and mother Sarah were good folk and always willing to lend a hand to others. They had come from Wisconsin a couple of years before we did and built a fine home, painted a warm blue, that sat on a nice bluff affording a fine view to the reaches of the county line. Their farm also had that spring surrounded by a small walnut orchard that folks would come by to fill their jugs. Eveline was tall, with long, dark hair and a fiery demeanor. Her two sisters; Charlotte, three years my younger and Maria, half as young as I was. Eveline and I became best friends and we saw much of each other when Mama was well enough to see Mrs. Sarah or when Eveline rode over on her own. They were kind and helpful during Mama's illness often making supper for us and giving me clothes so others didn't make fun of me. With them lived Johnny Day who was a year older than me. Johnny wasn't quite right in the head, but he was a kind soul who would never hurt anyone. He was a distant cousin of Eveline's that had been ill as a child when her family took him in. When he was made fun of by other children, Eveline would often snap back to protect him, shaming them all. Johnny was always polite to me, never missing a chance to tell me how pretty I was before Eveline would tell him to go and do his chores.

It was Eveline who first took me to the *spring* in the valley between the two hills just off the Little Falls Road nestled amongst walnut, maple and cherry trees. It was the place where boys and girls would take a break from their chores to meet, share a supper, sing and maybe sneak away from prying eyes with someone they fancied. It was a beautiful spot in the shade of those trees with a couple of large rocks to sit on as we enjoyed its cool, clear water, listening to each other and the wind coming off the hill as it rustled off the tall grass in the fields surrounding us. It was along that little creek that those of us that couldn't afford the latest fashions went to get reeds and make them into hoops to put under our skirts so that we would look like the more well-to-do girls. That summer I spent many Sunday afternoons there with Eveline and other young folk. We would arrange days ahead to go on a berry tramp to the spring with the other girls and boys. It was heaven. Danny even came with me on occasion to keep me company and *protect me* as he said from the boys. I didn't need much protecting, and besides, Danny enjoyed going there too, spending a lot of time gossiping with the girls about the goings on. The spring was my respite, though at times I felt awful for admitting that it gave me some time away from tending to Mama.

We would again be put to the test that fall as that unusually long and cold spring had taken its toll on Mama. Before winter she was bedridden in the grip of a cough that would not let go. She did her best to smile and wanted me to sit with her for many hours as she murmured about things I didn't understand. When her fevers got bad, she would yell out then fall into a deep sleep. I felt so helpless, but I was doing all that a ten year old could do. I had to run our home and help Papa with the animals and the wagons for the sake of us all. Doc and Anne did what little they could and thank goodness Miss Barbara and Danny helped me care for her when things got real bad while Papa worked his runs. Those were hard days for me and for many around here. We girls saw little of each other that winter, maybe when we ran chores or attended a funeral. What our little community needed was a place to call its own, to gather, pray and celebrate. That was to come with the building of the Mount Olivet.

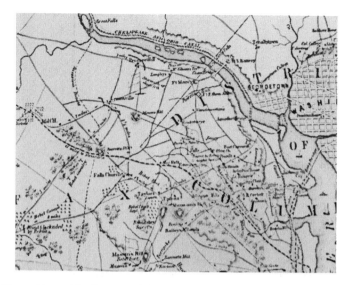

Upper Alexandria County and vicinity 1862 (Library of Congress)

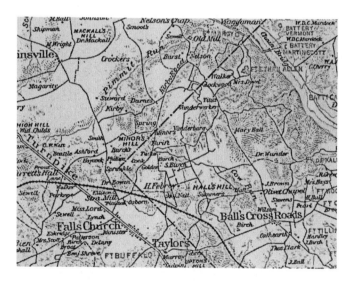

Farms about the Hall and Minor Hills 1864 (Library of Congress)

3 A GATHERING PLACE

In those years before the war, folks in our part of the county had few places to gather as a community for fellowship and to share news. The county was filled with many God-fearing folk, but what churches we had were too far away for farmers east of the main county road to easily get to. Though the Ball's Crossroads tavern was where county meetings were held, it was not a place for women and children and Papa reminded me of that whenever we rode past it.

Families up here were either Methodists like Mama and Papa or Episcopalians, though there were a few Catholics. There weren't many churches and even if there were, the roads weren't fit for traveling anyway. We held Service when we could in homes big enough to fit a few families with invites sent out weeks ahead. In those days' preachers on the circuit, as they called it, were told by the Parish where to hold service, mostly in farms and barns. One of these was north of us about six miles on Freedom Hill, but the one closest to us was at a small cabin near the tavern they called Birch's Meeting House. The

Episcopalians ran a Sunday school there, but it was too small for proper services. Most preachers around here were taught at the seminary near Alexandria City and put on the circuit for a year or so. Our preacher was the Reverend Edward Drinkhouse who stayed at a home near us owned by Sam Titus as he ran the circuit. The closest church in those early days was over three miles away at the Fairfax Chapel at the east end of Falls Church village over poorly tended roads, far too treacherous for Mama in her condition. The land for it was given by the Minor clan where locals put up the small chapel which was sadly torn apart for fire wood by New Yorkers during that first winter of the war. The Episcopalians held their service west of us at the Falls Church, built many years before the war against the British, whose members included George Washington and George Mason. That church saw men sign up for every war, but later on it too succumbed to sacrilege when Union troops destroyed much of its insides.

A year earlier in '54, at the behest of Reverend Drinkhouse, the Methodists came together to find a place for a new church, preferably on land near the County Road for those of us in the up-county. There were never many quarrels as families had bought and sold land to each other for over 100 years. When things did heat up, they were usually settled by the Deputy Sheriff or if there was a real quarrel, a committee of land owners was brought together to settle the matter. Our salvation came in the spring over a slight between two families, but one that ended up bringing our little community even closer. Bill Marcey and John Brown both laid claim to a small spit of land barely an acre in size, just off the road to Brown's farm. Marcey felt his land stretched some two hundred feet further to the creek along property owned by a Bazil Hall, while Brown disagreed.

Marcey, Brown and Doc got along as good

Christians should, but Hall was not a man to be messed with as he was prone to fits of anger, especially so after his wife's murder at the hands of one his slaves a year earlier. When he could, Bazil stoked the fires between the two hoping they would give up and hand the land over to him. Things got pretty heated for the rest of the year and come the next spring, everyone knew something had to be done as it was threatening what good feelings there were in our community.

It was during an Easter Service outside the Glebe Parish home where Reverend Drinkhouse, along with the handsome and affable Reverend Oliver Cox from Freedom Hill, shamed all four men into agreeing to build a new parish and a school for the community on that land. That fall, as George told it, laid down his *shucking peg* - that tool you put in your hand to work the corn - and led a committee to settle this mess, asking both Marcey and Brown for rights to the ground for the new church. In that spring of '55, Brown gave title to that small parcel for one dollar and a couple weeks later, Marcey was paid $25 for his parcel to build a Methodist Protestant Meeting House and burial ground. Soon after, the cornerstone of our future gathering place was laid with much fanfare as the energetic Reverend Cox presided over us.

Building our church forged a community from what was once scattered farmers. Everyone, no matter their faith, got involved. George, who was a Presbyterian, contributed the first $100. George and Doc became trustees and so did Bill Joe and Smith Minor who were Methodists. Nicholas Lemen, a Methodist pastor and a Minor relative by marriage, who hosted Cox many times at his home, also joined the first trusteeship with a local named Lipscomb who became its first elder. Other families donated what they could, but as money was scarce in those days, many donated supplies and their own labors. At Gilbert Vanderwerken's prodding, the Libby Company in Georgetown discounted its lumber and let Papa and other teamsters haul it back to get the church built by the next summer. Those who couldn't build helped where they could, when they could. The women folk around here, the *Noble Band of Women* as they were called, held fish and oyster fries nearly every week with Reverend Cox now very much leading efforts and blessing those who came to help. This man was not an ordinary preacher. He was handsome and very tall who carried his head to one side and spoke kindly but with a pronounced lisp. When he did speak, he gazed into your eyes and like a magnet, brought all those around him closer with his every word. And it wasn't just the men either. Many times I found myself falling for his spell when I should have been praying to the Lord.

There was a real fury to get the church under roof those first few months. When it got under roof with a good solid floor, we would celebrate with a great feast and everyone was going to be there. At the opening, to great fanfare, Reverend Cox announced that we would begin the schooling of us girls and others in the area that next week. We were so excited as we were now going to have a school to call our own and not some old shed on Vanderberg Hill. All the girls got fancied up in white dresses with pink or blue colored sashes. The older girls curled their hair with irons while the younger ones wore pig tails. Everyone came, bringing what they had to eat, chairs to sit in, and long tables built by the men with lumber meant for the church. That church was big and beautiful at two stories high set on a fine stone foundation, fifty feet long and nearly forty wide. On the main floor was the classroom with two large stairs on either end leading up to the auditorium for worship fit for over three-hundred. By the time it was done, the Olivet cost us all nearly three thousand dollars with most of that through donations and funds raised from the fish and oyster fries. Through the next spring until its completion in the summer of '60, raising the Olivet became God's mission for us, helping this community to come of age. Reverend

Drinkhouse's vision and Oliver Cox's passion gave our little community of fifty or so landowners and their families a place to gather, learn and pray.

Throughout that fall of '57 through the summer of '60 was where I made acquaintances with most all the young boys and girls of this part of the County and their families as well as learned of their politics. It was a community like any other. A few of the girls became my closest friends, while others were not worthy of much attention. And some men like the tall and handsome Oliver Cox, with this long black hair, his impassioned zeal for the Olivet and his way with the ladies would feature in my life as well. Though we were part of the community, we were not all the same and how the girls thought about things began to matter. Events in faraway lands began to scratch at our Nation's fabric and it was only a matter of time before it affected us, testing our community and these friendships less than a year later.

Up-county had its share of colorful folk, some obsessed with class and status. Folks like us tried to fit in where we could, but for many, we were only welcomed when it benefitted them. For Papa, his work as a teamster hauling their goods gave him a glimpse into their world and sometimes a nice welcome in their homes. But for me, their daughters and sons saw to it with regularity that I was not their kind. I didn't fret too much as my true friends cared not a lick of how much we had. In those years, leading up to the war, things like money and politicking mattered, but that all changed in '61 as class and status meant little if you were on the wrong side. For some the war was to pay off handsomely, while for others it was to be their downfall.

Of those that fared well was one Mr. Gilbert Vanderwerken from New York. He and his wife Jane had two sons; Charles, near 20 as I recall and handsome, Johnny who was my age, and real quiet and young daughter Ella at the time just before the war. They were the wealthiest family around here that we had come to know here. Gilbert was the largest landowner in this part of the county, with over 1300 acres, much of it stretching along the Little Falls Road across the Glebe Road nearly all the way to the Potomac at the Little Falls. They lived in a large home on a hilltop in a grove of fine trees called Falls Grove off the Glebe Road. Gilbert's nieces Cornelia Golden and Sarah Oaks also lived with them as well. It had been built extra-large originally as a summer retreat for his family and other prominent folks. His fine home served the Union Army well during the war as Union General Hancock's headquarters and the lands around it a camp and a hospital.

Vanderwerken was a shrewd businessman who owned and operated the Omnibus trolleys in Washington from the Navy Yard all the way to Georgetown along Pennsylvania Avenue through M street. He had run wagons in Mexico hauling silver for the Government and later omnibus lines in Newark, New Jersey and when the business went bankrupt, brought it all to Washington DC in '50 or so. He was connected in Washington circles managing to keep anyone else away from competing with his line. By the time of the war, he charged an unheard of twelve and half cents to ride knowing it was the only way to get around town. He often boasted of his place in Washington society and how his omnibuses were the most modern, fit for twelve passengers and that each was painted with the names of persons, historical events, trains and steamships on their sides. Gilbert owned stables in Georgetown and used the county lands to pasture his horse that he herded over the Chain Bridge.

Gilbert had his finger in most every business dealing around here. He had mining interests in a company called Potomac Bluestone on the banks of the Potomac River to supply Washington's building boom. Some of that dark stone was used to build parts of the Georgetown University that you could see when you crossed the Chain Bridge. Vanderwerken also owned a home in Georgetown on M Street and ran a mercantile and warehouses as well. He was known throughout Washington as a difficult man to do business with and was in court many times over the years. Papa said he was ruthless in his business dealings with a temper not to contend with so I didn't see much of Cornelia or Sarah unless it was at the Olivet. I heard it told that at one time he shot and nearly killed his neighbor in Georgetown in a spat over storing things in the cellars that they shared and even had a man jailed falsely accused of thieving from his property.

Papa's livelihood depended on a good feelings with Gilbert, so he was always cordial to him when we saw him and his family at the Olivet. His wife Jane, though cordial to me when the family came to the Olivet, was never one to shy from telling you your place. Papa never felt comfortable approaching her, both on account of Gilbert's temper and their social status. Though our farms were only within a half mile of each other I never went to their home to visit with Cornelia and Sarah. Our families were not in the same social circles so the Olivet was where we girls made a very fine friendship, getting together as often as we could. Gilbert gave handsomely to building the Olivet, though I couldn't recall them lifting as much as a finger to put in a board or nail.

As difficult as Vanderwerken was, no one was more colorful and trying to our lives as Bazil Hall. The property on which the Olivet sat was along the low side of his land. He and his wife Elizabeth were from New York and came to the area about ten years before the war, as he told it, tired of being a whaling captain. Hall bought over 300 acres from the former mayor of Washington City who used much of that land as a summer retreat. He built one of the finest mansion homes in this part of the county, second only to the Glebe parish home, with all the modern furnishings of the day, costing over $3000 dollars to build. About 30 acres were filled with fine pine, chestnuts and hickory surrounded by a clover pasture. Part of his land had a beautiful orchard of about five hundred apple, pear and other fruit trees bordered by a beautiful nine rail high wood fence. Yet by the fall of '61, this idyllic setting would be nothing of the sort, stripped of its beauty to become the home to one of the largest Union Army camps in the area.

Bazil had been active in New York Whig Party politics, and now here as a staunch Unionist. He was a cantankerous man, prone to fits of anger uttering obscenities for all to hear from his home atop the hill. Folks wanted little to do with Hall on account of his demeanor and he was known to treat his slaves even worse. Papa told me that he had heard that Bazil had shot a Negro man simply out of bravado. Though he was near 60 at the start of the war, wife Elizabeth was much younger at twenty, barely five years older than I. Papa said she was a good woman from the few times they met. They had three children; a son named Ignatius who was about 12 or so and two daughters, one named Celina who died a few years before the war and one named Elvira who was about seven. I saw Elvira often at the church fish fries, always laughing and wanting to be with us older girls. The Halls were respected in the community, though known to be hard on their slaves Alfred and Jenny Fair and their four young boys. His harshness may have come from, or been cause of, some of his barns being burned down the year before and the horrible murder of Elizabeth on a cold night in December of '57.

Papa and Doc got to know Bazil real well on account of that mess as it affected everyone around here so. We had never had a murder like that around here and the newspapers even wrote about it. The story read like frightful novel to hear that Elizabeth was brutally murdered by her slave Jenny. Old man Hall was walking over his farm while the rest of the whites of the family were at church. Mrs. Hall was home tending to affairs with slave Jenny and as told to us, on that particularly cold day, Jenny put an arm full of dry plank on the fire. Elizabeth, fearing the flames would get out of control, demanded Jenny to take some of the wood off, which she did. Maybe it was the cold of that night, but Jenny quickly put those plank back in the fire which started a fight between the two. Jenny caught hold of Elizabeth's head and put it between her legs and backed her into the fire. Elizabeth fought bravely and broke loose, but Jenny pushed Elizabeth again and again and the final time on her forehead with such a force, that Elizabeth fell into the fire. Her screams were so loud that everyone, including Papa, rushed over.

When Papa arrived, Hall's lumber man, Thomas Merchant was holding back Master Hall who was beside himself with anger, yelling, and carrying on about his wife. Others were in the house doing what they could for Elizabeth, tending to the horrible burns to her face, legs and arms. Papa then helped put Elizabeth's horribly burned body on his wagon to get her over to Doc's when Sheriff Minor arrived. While Papa took Elizabeth home, Sheriff Minor stayed back to question Jenny and those holding her. Jenny told the sheriff that there was no murder at all as it was only a little scuffle where Madame Elizabeth fell into the fire. She even said it couldn't be murder as she sent her daughter who was in the room when it all happened to the spring for water. Sheriff Minor had heard enough, arresting Jenny and putting her in chains.

The men then made their way to Doc's where he and Doctor Locke did all they could to calm her suffering. Yet not much could be done, and by early next morning Elizabeth succumbed to her burns but not before she told

Sheriff Minor of what Jenny had done. Bazil, now in a fit of rage, ran back home to shoot Jenny before she was taken to jail and in only a moment from being shot, the men stopped him. The next day, Elizabeth was laid to rest in the family cemetery in the corner of their property nearby where the Olivet was to be built. As Papa knew the route well, Sheriff Minor asked him to take Jenny to the county jail in Alexandria, to be held for trial.

Many of the men at the house that night were at Jenny's trial just after New Year's including Papa who was a witness. A lawyer for Jenny, named Beach questioned Papa and had Jenny tell the same story that Papa knew was not the truth. The trial adjourned later that day with Bazil, George and Thomas staying there overnight. Judge Dixon ruled the next day, convicting Jenny of murder and sentencing her to be hung on the last Friday in February of '58. Many up-county men, except Papa who was not prone to watch such things, were there to see Jenny Fair hang. Once she was dead, Bazil went and got the $500 that Judge Dixen awarded him for the loss of his "property". Elizabeth's death had done much to change old man. He remained angry and bitter for quite a while, then for some reason, maybe the good Lord's hand, or on account of a new wife, that he began to soften up. It wasn't until months after Jenny's death that I saw much of Elizabeth's sons, peering at us on the fence-line when we were at the Olivet gatherings.

Bazil had a wealthy sister named Mary Anne Hall who owned a fine farmhouse about a mile from his, next to Vanderwerken land. Papa told me she was quite the character known in many Washington circles, but for what reason, he never really said. She convinced her brother to move into the area in '53 where she had bought over seventy acres from the Burgess estate and built a fine and stately summer home with grand colonnades and dome over the front porch which she called Maple Grove. When I was old enough I found out that Mary Anne made her fortunes running one of the biggest and most elegant brothels in the District just steps from the Capitol in a four story brick building surrounded by a large walled in courtyard. I heard that eighteen *"Pleasant"* girls lived and worked in that home and that she ran the best such place in the city before, during, and after the war.

Stories about Mary Anne made for scandalous talk at the Olivet and rarely did Madame Hall come to the church fish fries. But when she did, it was in grand style in elegant dresses, and beautiful lacquered buggy with her a very beautiful colored help named Rosanna Gordon. For all the gossip and scandal, Madame Hall had a good heart and donated handsomely to building the Olivet, many causes for the poor and all the schoolhouse furnishings. When we did see her, she was always kind to us girls, giving us licorice to share. I recall her at Bazil's marriage to his second wife in the finest silk dress and veil that any of us had ever seen and Rosanna in fine linen herself. Stories about Madame Hall made the Washington papers every so often and when they did, she would retire to Maple Grove to ride out the storm. Those that knew her said she was most proud of buying slaves to work in her home, then freeing them after Congress freed the slaves in Washington and compensating their owners for their loss. The shrewd Madame took the Nation's generosity and bought more slaves only to free them, too.

The hill that made up mostly the Hall, Vanderwerken, Vanderberg and Wunder lands was one of the two that cradled our community. The other was about a mile west, just on the border which was the highest point in Alexandria County. On that hill and its surrounds lived a number of the Minor families. The Minors came from a long line of landowners having settled in Virginia for over two hundred years, acting as though they came from royalty whenever the occasion afforded it. The family patriarch Captain Nicholas Minor had done much of the earlier surveying of the Virginia countryside with George Washington. He passed the land onto his sons with a notable five-hundred acre tract to his son George which included the highest hill in the county at over four hundred fifty feet. Minor's Hill as it came to be called, was known for its fine springs with water of such excellent quality that people came from all parts of the county to fill the jugs for their home use.

George Minor, or *Colonel* as he wanted to be called, was a gregarious man fond of wearing older clothing of the colonial times of white linen and black broad cloth. He was married to a stern woman named Catherine who always donned white caps and somber colors. They lived with their slaves in a fine plantation home called *Springfield* on the northwest side of the hill surrounded by fine gardens of yellow roses, snowball, firebush and spirea bushes that were the envy of all around. Colonel Minor was well respected in the county having earned his reputation during the second war with the British, in 1814 commanding the 60th Regiment of the Virginia militia. He often told all who would hear, how his militia was summoned by President Madison's Secretary to defend Washington from the British invasion but couldn't get there in time before the city was set ablaze.

When the gunpowder from the Navy Yard was hurriedly moved across the bridges to the Falls Church for safekeeping, it was entrusted to Colonel Minor's militia to guard it. The President's wife Dolly, who had stayed behind to see to the nation's most important papers and artworks, fled to safety with those precious things across the Chain Bridge, storing them in the warehouses on the Virginia landing. She then made her way up the Little Falls Road trying to make it to the Salona plantation some five miles away, home to the Revolutionary War hero Henry "Light

Horse Harry" Lee, where she planned to meet her husband. But the road was long, and fearing British patrols, Dolly being a close friend of Catherine, spent two nights at Colonel Minor's home. From atop Minor Hill she was no doubt able to see the fires as Washington burned. After a few days of searching, President Madison came to the Minor's farm where he met up with Dolly and from there they made it back to Salona until the British left Washington. From then on, Colonel Minor and his family became something of celebrities in these parts, often entertaining his extended family and other well-healed at Springfield.

The Minor's had three slaves; Mary and Jane whom Catherine loaned out to neighbors, and a farm hand named Ugly Uncle Joe for his big face and nose that we would see on occasion. That name he gave himself as he was fond of scaring the little ones at the Olivet gatherings. By the time of the war, the Colonel was an old man of about eighty or so and had lost much of his charm. Over time, the Minors bought many plots of land in the area and sold parcels to others like Hall, Birch, Febrey and Vanderberg. Generations of Minors married into many other families creating strong ties in and about that hill.

Colonel Minor had five children and most lived on or near the hill. One son, John West Minor, lived nearby and had married the granddaughter of Lord Fairfax, who at one time owned nearly all the lands in this area. A daughter named Sarah Ann, a great beauty, married one of the signers of the Declaration of Independence and lived out in Fairfax County. Catherine Anne, a strong woman of determined character, married a weakly Reverend Lemen, a trustee at the Olivet, who preached at the Freedom Hill chapel. Lemen hosted Reverend Cox at their home on occasion when he was on the circuit. The Minors thought so much of Cox that they sent for his ill mother from Philly to live with Smith Minor and the Belles. There was something odd about having a young Reverend staying in the same house with six young women and it was cause for all manner of talk at the Olivet. Colonel Minor's grandson, William J. or "Bill Joe" as he liked to be called, helped settle the Olivet land tiff. He lived in a fine brick home nestled amongst all the other farms just east of Minor Hill over the ridge from the Vanderberg's. William was well dressed, fun to be around and a highly respected veteran himself. He had grown up in the area and played with President Tyler's sons and made a name for himself in the military. He lived there with his mother Catherine, who herself was quite the matriarch. Bill Joe owned four slaves, with Catherine lending them out to others to curry favors. She was a stern woman who would not wince at using a switch on anyone who misbehaved and did so to her slaves on a few occasions.

Smith Minor was Old Colonel Minor's half-brother who lived on a farm next to the Springfield plantation just off the Georgetown-Fairfax Road on the road to Minor Hill. Smith had made a name for himself as a courier for the generals in the second war with the British. He was an affable sort and a wiry man, with snow white hair and a beard but a clean shaven upper lip. When we heard him speak at the Olivet, he would pronounce his words very carefully and look you sternly in the eye, pointing his trembling finger in front of your nose. Smith looked mean, but that was just for show as he always made folks laugh. Just the opposite was his wife Polly, who was stern and clearly the one who wore the pants in the family, always making sure everyone knew their places in society. They lived in that home with their six daughters, two sons and a few slaves. These six ladies were the *Belles of Alexandria County*, and would be the source of endless grief for me, Danny and anyone else who they saw as not fitting or of their class. From what I saw, they rather liked their title as it made their place, and mine, known whenever the need arose. They were the cattiest in these parts and when they set their sights on you, their wicked tongues would be merciless.

The eldest was Marietta, six years my elder, a sparkling brunette and striking in her appearance. Marietta was a true southern woman and made her sympathies to the secessionist cause known early on and often. She saw herself as a well-healed young maiden, fit for any young well-to-do suitor, though not many came a-calling, I suspect because she had her sights set on Oliver Cox. She was the leader of the Belles, never missing a chance to offer her opinion on things and pretending to be well learned, though I heard she was not much on schooling. Marietta was an odd sort who was prone to fits of despair and was rumored to tell the future in her dreams. One time, before we moved up this way, Marietta dreamed of a dead slave girl beside a log at a creek near our place and when a posse of Minor's went to see, they did indeed find one of Lemen's slave girls dead behind a log right where she said it would be. From that day on, many feared to be around her or cross her in any way lest they be in one of Marietta's dreams. She and Cox were really close on account he was living there and would always be seen riding in a carriage, and everyone thought they would get married.

Next was Elizabeth, who was my age and very much the old maid of the hive. Somber and seething, she agreed with Marietta's every word and was no less biting in her tongue against others when the mood suited it. The next youngest was Cornelia, at a few years younger than I. She was the nicest of all and would confide in me on occasion, but would clam up when the elder girls were around. Finally, there was Mary Jane, Mollie as they called her, who was much younger but felt like she was as old as we were and never shied away from getting in everyone's business. There were no drones in that hive. Their mother, always worried on how others saw her Belles, would dress them well and twice a year she would buy fine silk cloth from which to make lovely hooped dresses for them. Cornelia and I would talk often at the school and at church socials and on occasion would meet other girls in the orchards and down at the spring. We got along fine when Marietta and Elizabeth weren't around, but when together, they would talk of the raciest things with the boys and often make those less fortunate feel worthless. Things got scandalous when Marietta was often seen at the spring or when we all got together to tramp for berries in the company of Oliver Cox. They took to going to church parties together and everyone thought they would get married, but Oliver had said many times he would not get married so long as his ill mother was alive. While he swore to others nothing was going on, their closeness was all the talk amongst the young folk at the spring. The Belles were to have their day of reckoning testing the resolve of the Union Army.

The Olivet was finished in the spring of '60 and was cause for much celebrating. Reverend Cox had done his duty splendidly, and with his replacement on the circuit by the Reverend Hoblitzer, he was free to socialize with the young ladies and did so often much to Marietta's dismay. I recall a splendid affair when the Olivet celebrated its first nuptials between Hall and the young Miss Francis Harrison. Most of the community was there, having a grand time helping to put aside those horrible events of the prior year. It was a fitting celebration for all the fine work put into building our gathering place. Francis was much younger than Bazil, just over twenty as I recall, and the daughter of Robert Harrison who owned a farm nearby. They were related to President William Henry Harrison and had come to know Hall well on account of his Whig party politicking. The Harrisons lived nearby on a five acre farm just across from both Doc Wunder's and that of Mr. Hall. Francis, soon after their marriage, bore him a daughter named Lorenza.

That summer between the hills was a fine time as we

spent many festive days at the Olivet, the spring and even on picnics. Besides Cornelia, Sarah and Eveline, there was the kind Joseph Titus who lived close by, and John Vanderwerken who were both about my age and always sweet to me. There was John Birch, all of 18 and always talking things going on with the militia. Margaret Newton, a relative of his who was twenty and always seen in the company of Charles Vanderwerken who was the same age. The Minor Belles aside, together we made for fine summer gatherings and twice the community got together for a big picnic at the Great Falls just north of the Chain Bridge. I still recall fondly the boys fishing for rockfish and broiling them in butter on the rocks that we had heated up with a fire. All summer, long we ate well with a plentiful bounty of shad, crabs and oysters.

Before the war, I rarely accompanied Papa on his runs, looking forward to the Sunday gatherings as we worked to make the Olivet the gathering place it needed to be. It was at those many fish and oyster fries where we worked, made small talk and talked of young boys. This place became our spiritual and social anchor and Papa helped any way he could with bringing that vision to life. Doc was firm in his beliefs that Christians should do all they could to help fellow neighbors which Papa and I admired. I recall him many times at the Sunday church fish saying just that. For Eveline, Sarah, Cornelia, myself and even the Minor Belles, it was if we had our own meeting hall, yet it was things far beyond our little place that was to turn things upside down.

4 STORM CLOUDS

Papa was hauling goods in and about the county, doing odd job here and there, and making runs into Washington about once a week. He was getting well known, much more than I ever thought he would be as Papa usually kept to himself, but always kept a pleasant demeanor in company. Yet, I knew deep down the pressures of those last years had broken him and he lost much of the zeal for life, with dreams of a big business, and a large family on a farm of his own gone. Papa blamed himself for the stress over the Aqueduct spur venture that weakened Mama. He saw himself a failure, broke, living under the graces of others in the remote county farmland; but to me, it was a simpler life on Wunder's Corner away from the highbrows of the city who had always looked down on us.

By the summer of '59, Papa was making steady work as a teamster with his two wagons and a few of the local boys to haul freight up from Alexandria's piers and the train depot to the working farms, taverns and merchants throughout the county and even to the Falls Church. Those hauls took me to all parts of the county and even on occasion across the Chain Bridge to Georgetown and Washington City. I remember fondly when Barbara would look after Mama, joining Papa on long journeys to haul goods from Vanderwerken's mercantile and other such places in Georgetown across the Chain Bridge to the farms in our area. It made for a long day beginning way before daylight, but Papa made it a point to stop at the soda parlor in Georgetown across from the sheriff's office for my favorite iced cream. I preferred vanilla, but Papa fancied his with strawberry. These sojourns were his way of making everything seem right. For me it was a chance to look after Papa as a daughter should, accompanying him on his stops, reading the manifests making sure we weren't being cheated. Just as he said many years before in those seedy streets outside Alexandria City, we were a team and we were bound to hold it together no matter what. Yet, a storm was coming that would test us and our faith in God.

It was on those grueling runs of heavy loads, rough roads and steep climbs leading to and from the Chain Bridge that I became a witness to County, and even Washington City, politics. Wherever we stopped to tend to our business, county merchants groused on the injustices, the burden of supporting Washington City's follies without real benefit and the indifference towards the wellbeing of those of us across the river. Men would ask Papa for his thoughts and to sit a spell and tell what he sees', but Papa, long since stung by failed business ventures, would rarely speak forcibly, preferring instead not to be labeled as "for this" or "against that".

I heard the County's true sentiment about most things and witnessed the injustices to daily life in the county on those roads in the years before the war. There were many, but Washington City's refusing to support the canal spur and docks into Alexandria city leaving that enormous cost to the locals to bear was especially harsh. With

Congress's failure to heed the cries from Alexandria's merchants, its loathing to repeal the prohibition against banking south of the Potomac, and the growing abolitionist sentiment in Washington aimed at Alexandria's profits from the slave trade; most of the city's prominent men were reaching their ends. With the retrocession vote of '45 Alexandria County believed it was sure enough to chart its own destiny, but given its ties to Washington, it couldn't distance itself from its gaze.

During that fall, an abolitionist named John Brown tried to start a slave revolt in Virginia at Harper's Ferry out west in the valley, which was broke by a Virginia militia commanded by the County's own Robert E. Lee. The treasonous act was the talk of the town and even through the winter of '59 after Brown's highly reported trial and execution in Charles Town in December. Those events brought home to many the abolitionists' cause with talk about slavery. Papa knew better than to take a side too quickly not knowing whose character would be upset. We didn't pay much mind to the abolitionists; Papa called them anarchists, and most around here supported the putting down of that revolt. Yet for Papa, he believed the scourge of slavery would eventually leave our community as many of us did not own slaves and with fall of Virginia's tobacco fortunes, many slave owners had sold off their stocks in Alexandria for points down south in the growing cotton trade.

Sometimes during our many get-togethers at the spring, we'd get to talking about the abolitionists and slaves which didn't take long for some spirited arguments. Clearly, where one stood about these things depended on whether their families owned slaves. The Belles and some of their ilk paid no mind to their slaves' plight and were downright harsh on those of us that didn't believe as they did. One day Marietta and Reverend Cox were riding past us all at the spring, she heard some of our talk and quickly stopped her carriage. She stood up, pointed her finger at me, yelling "Slaves were living proper lives amongst good Christion folk as their property and they knew what was going to happen if they got out of line" as if she was scolding children. Cox just sat there, looking away, while Marietta went on with her diatribe. The abolitionists, she belted out, were rabble rousers that had to be dealt with sternly. Around here, slave owners did not see much cause for concern for the matter and I'd best be careful with such talk, lest someone set you straight! I knew then that Marietta, and her Belles, had me in their sights.

One early fall day at the spring after a wonderful tramp with the boys, we girls sat at the fire eating cracked walnuts and burnished red apples. The boys had gone off for rabbit and Marietta had gone off with Cox on one of their many carriage rides, when we began talk of slavery. Many of us only saw slaves with their owners when out and about, seeing them more like house servants. Most didn't know what to think about Abolition, but Papa had said slavery was wrong and that was good enough for me. Others whose folks didn't own slaves tended to feel the same way.

We wondered aloud how slaves were going to celebrate the Lord's birth in the coming months. Elizabeth had heard enough and got so mad, that she started yelling, telling us that their slaves were happy, celebrating the season in their own way and having a right fine time of it. They'd have a whole week of merriment before Christmas Day every night around the fire she said. They had their own customs and we allowed them to do as they wished so long as the work was done. Why, things were so good, they would be allowed respite from working the farms so long as what they called a *"Yule"* log burned. The slaves, crafty as they were would get the biggest log they could find and soak it in the creek for weeks so it would burn for many days on end. She said the slaves did games of other sorts, playing what they called *husking bee* where as they shucked corn, whoever found a red ear would be allowed to kiss whoever they wanted and would dance around their homes and do prayers for the dead and such.

With her hands on her hips and a finger pointed our way, she yelled that we couldn't expect them to be like us because they weren't. The slaves, she said, believed in a lot of spirit stuff that God fearing folk wouldn't dare hear of, saying that the reason they wore their hair in tight pleated rows was to keep the witches away. I didn't know anything about that, but I said it was wrong for one to enslave another. Both Elizabeth and Cornelia stared yelling that folks not born in these parts had no business telling others how to live their lives then both turned and stomped away.

I didn't know what they meant as I was as much a county girl as they were. We had many such arguments and they would get more heated as slavery became the talk of the nation. Papa and I had more pressing concerns that November of '59, Mama's weakened condition made her prone to illness. Just as winter set in, she caught a severe grip of the cold and was bed ridden for many days. With all the chores and caring for Mama, there was little time to rest, much less talk with the girls. Those Sunday's at the Olivet were my only respite and I cherished that time so.

In early December Mama's conditioned worsened. Mrs. Barbara and Danny spent many days helping me care for her. Papa was beside himself, and wanted to be there every day to care for her as well, but he had loads to haul and would leave every morning sad, at times blaming himself for our misfortunes. I didn't accompany him much during those days not wanting to leave Mama's bedside. Papa took fewer jobs during that fall and into the winter to get home sooner to be by her side.

Folks around here were very kind to us with the girls stopping by for a bit every once in a while to help me with chores while I tended to Mama. Mrs. Hall and Mrs. Vanderberg helped as well and even Mrs. Minor from across the way sent her house servants on occasion to bring us some food. Eveline would ride over every few days bringing me some much needed respite. Mama perked up a bit when the ladies gossiped about all the local goings on, which brought comfort to Papa. He was so thankful that he would haul loads for them without pay.

Christmas came without much merriment. Mama was coughing something awful and Papa and I were just exhausted. Eveline came a calling and took me to their home for Christmas supper, more so to give me a respite from the months at home. There was not much to celebrate, but being in the company of my friends that day was a gift I would not forget.

Just before New Year's Day, Mama passed on quietly in her sleep. Papa's heart was broken, and I could barely stand to see him so distraught. I was exhausted myself with no more tears to shed. Mama's long ordeal, with the loss of their savings and social place after Papa's failed business dealings, still without a son, bouts of malaise, and her weak demeanor had come to an end. On a bitterly cold Saturday morning, with most everyone there, we laid Mama to rest under an oak tree on the corner. Papa now felt all alone, believed this to be his fault. However, he wouldn't be alone. I was not much more than a child at fourteen, experiencing more heartache and despair than one should at my age, but there was no time for giving up. It was my duty to be there for Papa and help keep his teams running, and maybe over time help find him a nice woman.

Our community came of age in March of '60 when Mount Olivet was finally completed and it soon became the hub of up-county life. I often prodded and helped Papa gussy up a bit for church hoping to give him something to look forward to and maybe, just maybe, someday find another good woman. Alas, he no longer had interest in such things, putting all his strength on a better life for both of us.

For many men it was whispers of secession and war, for others it was concerns over the price of crops that had dropped last year, for others it was endless talk of the government and the coming election for president. For the women it was a respite from housework, a chance to talk of goings on with other families, temperance and such. For us girls, we talked a good bit about each other and the young boys who always seemed to come a calling whether true or not. Folks were cordial in their meetings, yet all throughout that spring and into the summer, men of like minds gathered separately to discuss the abolitionists and the like. Papa had no interest in such words reminding me that slavery, though allowed in Virginia, was a moral corruption and that no Christian should enslave another. He couldn't understand how many at the Olivet could profess themselves as good Christians with the freedom to practice our faith, yet accepting of this abomination. Not that it meant much for Papa as we, and most of those we knew didn't own slaves. What few there were in these parts belonged to larger farms like the Hall's or inherited by families over long times like the Minor's. Across the county, I think the largest slave owner was at Arlington House with well over forty slaves before the war, so I'm sure things didn't sit well with them on talk of abolition.

Slavery became more a part of every Sunday's sermon and folks would gather in groups to talk and sometimes things would get quite excited and angry over the issue. Some would even get up at church and begin preaching to others about the evils of slavery. The newspapers were eagerly read and talked about so much so that the new Reverend Solomon Hoblitzell got barely his sermons out. By the end of summer, most of those who favored or were indifferent to slavery had had enough of such talk and we would see less of them at church. Many of those in the community with long Virginia ties felt the government was treading on things that they shouldn't be. What was cordial talk on the outside, masked hard felt feelings that were not so easily dismissed. There was now open talk of war and for some, the sooner the better. This was a tragedy in the making.

The fabric of our little community had begun to strain, like a quilt that was being stretched to the tearing point, though all the patches were together, one could now see through the seams. Papa didn't pay much mind to all this as he was too busy working to keep things going teaming his wagons all about the county. But it was clear to many around here that we were headed to a place that we weren't sure we could come back from. Concern had grown to action as the Minor men and others who felt as they did, had been patrolling around these parts looking for illicit slave activity for a year or so, making sure slaves stayed in their place. Robert Minor was patrolling twice-weekly almost five miles around his farm while another son who was in the militia cavalry began his day and night rides over six miles from Benton's Tavern. There was a tempest in the making, while most others dismissed such talk and went on with their daily lives, one could not ignore all that was swirling around us that within six months would consume us all.

The vote for President in early November '60 came and went like a whirlwind with endless talk and eager readings of the papers over slavery in the Border States and the territories which Papa said were of no real interest to us. The talk and bluster was everywhere and it was as if no one had any work to do. Mr. Lincoln's Republicans won the election and some were none too happy about it on account of the Democratic Party being split on protecting slavery in the territories. His election riled some around here, believing that Virginia's ways were being lost to Northern thinking. Most paid little mind as Mr. Lincoln had not campaigned much over slavery even vowing to protect slavery where it already existed. It would be months before Lincoln would come to Washington.

That should have been the end of it, but radicals in the south had threatened talk of secession and while most folks here were none too happy about such talk, others like the Minors kept stoking the fires. Most of those on our hill agreed that Virginia had a proud heritage and was a solidly Unionist state and any talk of bending to radical demands of South Carolina was unfounded and likely treasonous. Yet these radicals were coming into their own and in late November the Virginia Governor called for a secession convention to keep the Union whole. Save the union? My god, what had happened in this short a time for this talk to even be uttered from anyone's lips was beyond reason. I kept asking Papa many times but all he would say was that States that made such talk were treasonous and all this would soon be squared away. Folks, he said, were fretting over issues they had no business being worried about.

Yet, South Carolina did the unthinkable and declared their secession from the Union just before Christmas to the howls of many around here, and cheers of those west of the spring. As far as up-county folk were concerned South Carolina's brash act was a faraway concern as Virginia was solidly Unionist with no intentions of being that cat's paw. Yet, the papers reeked with similar talk of secession by other states in the Deep South, with calls for Congress to save the Union. President Buchanan and the Congress had called for committees to settle on something called a Missouri compromise dividing Slave from Free states to preserve the

Union before Lincoln and his men took office in January, but we heard these meetings accomplished nothing. Papa said the mood around the county was souring, and though he had not been to Washington for some weeks, he said the mood there was souring as well. It seemed passions were taking the better of some, with the Gazette and other papers writing all manner of words about what was to be, stoking the fires of the most passionate. Christmas Service at the Olivet was particularly heavy with angry talk about secession by Reverend Hoblitzer threatening to spoil the festivities planned by many of the families.

The New Year of '61 was not much cause for celebrating for Papa and me since Mama's passing a year ago. Our friends had been very cordial to Papa wishing him well and with kind words about Mama, but the mood around here had changed much with heated talk over secession. During the winter, Papa's work slowed quite a bit, and the pace of this part of the County did as well, which left more time for folks to grouse about all the goings on. We saw less of the Vanderwerken's as they spent more time in Washington tending to business interests. For others like the Minor's and those of like mind, their time was spent now at the tavern with traitorous talk of secession. Folks from the two hills rarely saw each other and when they did gather for a burial, there was angst in the air. Folks were tight with their words lest someone spoke ill, setting off angry talk.

We heard tell that in mid-January, the Congress called on the six free and six slave Border States to resolve their differences at a Peace Conference in Washington the first Monday in February. But to the dismay of many, before the conference could meet, Mississippi, Florida, Alabama, Georgia, Louisiana and Texas had done the unthinkable and joined South Carolina in passing ordnances of secession from the Union forming what they called the Confederacy. It seemed to Papa and others that their true intentions were shown with no interest in peace. Yet, the Conference did meet with Vanderwerken telling the congregation that following Sunday of fourteen Free and seven Slave states meeting at the elegant Willard Hotel in Washington. He himself had seen the newspaper reporters gathered there to hear if this group came to agreement on how slavery would be treated in new territories, laws over slaves where it already was and the ever vexing issue of what to do about fugitive slaves. We all prayed that Sunday, with God's help this nasty affair would be settled soon.

In the days before Mr. Lincoln's swearing in, Washington's papers were writing all sorts of horrible things about him, for his personal demeanor, intentions on the slave states, and the manner by which he skulked into Washington for the inauguration. On this side of the river, the Gazette and other Virginia papers were even more visceral, writing that the Federal Government had overstepped its role in what were clearly State's issues and there wasn't much the new President could do to stop the inevitable. They all reported what they could, inflaming the passions of one side or another and it seemed anger with this man grew every day he made his way south to Washington, yet there was great hope that cooler heads would prevail.

But alas, it was all a farce, as by the end of that cold February the so-called Peace Conference had failed. Seven states had ordinances of secession and were further looking to sway others into their treasonous ranks. Virginia itself was now caught in the tempest as well. The county was all ablaze with rumors of Virginia's own secession much to the dismay of many businessmen here. But most were hopeful as Virginia was to hold its own convention in April on the matter where Unionists clearly outnumbered these radicals. "A tidal wave of treason that God must intervene to stop" cried Reverend Cox to those few that had come to church on that first Sunday in March. Folks didn't pay him much mind and a sense of dread was felt by all. Only one last heroic act could prevent a mighty cataclysm. The new President's speech was hoped to settle these issues once and for all so folks could go about their business.

Mr. Lincoln's swearing in day was rife with rumors of riots and shootings, so much so that troops were sent all about the Capitol to quell any trouble. Vanderwerken went to Capitol Hill that day to witness the event but folks didn't hear much from him until days later when he returned. The papers reported the next day on what happened. George and others read the President's speech calling for compromise, promising not to start force to maintain the Union or interfere with slavery in the states in which it already was law, toward state rights and even talked about amending the Constitution. This seemed to the many gathered at the fence rail to be a fine speech and should have settled all this angst once and for all, but it wasn't to be. The President's words angered some as he also pledged to keep any property and places that belonged to the government. He also declared that the Union was un-dissolvable, that secession was anarchy and taking up arms against the United States would be seen as rebellion. The speech struck deep with some who had now become more vocal in their support to the southern separatists. Lincoln's words stoked fears that property would be taken and for some, that meant their slaves.

Though Virginia was solidly Unionist, most wanted no limits on slaveholders' rights. All winter long talk here and around the Olivet was all about the dissolution. With the sad outcome of the Peace Conference, Unionist sentiment faded with every vote of the Virginia legislature. That Palm Sunday we all gathered at the Olivet to celebrate the finishing of the church proper with a wonderful fish and oyster fry the ladies had been planning since Christmas. The girls and I stood our places at the serving counter as usual, expecting everyone to be there, but many of the families west of the spring never came. The uneasiness that had set in since January and especially so after southern secession, had grown to fear and mistrust. Following the service and lunch many men went off separately to talk about the latest news from Richmond and Washington, grouped alike in their leanings. The more vocal and angry of the Minor, Ball and Birch men and others of like mind were near the old oak that bordered the county road, while others gathered back behind the church. By Easter Sunday, it looked as if only a miracle could save Virginia from a treasonous fate so the Reverend asked for a special prayer that day.

Sure enough Virginia did its duty to the Union four days later on that first Thursday in April and rejected secession by two-to-one and we celebrated our good fortunes on the beautiful spring Sunday at the Olivet, though only the Unionists came this time. Yet even with that vote, angst between the confederate states and those proudly in the Union never waned and it looked more and more like folks were itching for war. Congress had even seen fit to free slaves in Washington by proclamation and even pay their owners for their loss. Many took advantage of this and began cashing in their slaves, including Mary Hall, then buying more and freeing them too.

There was much talk of troops being called up and we learned that by the end of April thirty-four companies of men from all over the North had been sworn into United States service for three months to come and defend Washington. All that was needed was a spark to unleash forces that could not be controlled. What was to be of this county with its fortunes so tied to Washington? Who would have thought that within three weeks our community would be on war's front lines.

Before that week was over that spark came upon the tinder that had been strewn about these last six months. As we had come to learn, the fort guarding the entrance to Charleston harbor, by the name of Sumter needed to be resupplied and Mr. Lincoln refused to leave it. The General in command of the Confederate forces there demanded the surrender of the garrison at the fort on Wednesday and upon refusal by its Federal commander, opened fire on it two days later. The men on that island endured a merciless bombardment, and by some miracle without a man killed, surrendering the fort the next day. The Federal commander had already evacuated when we heard the news at the Olivet on Sunday. The first treasonous blow had been struck as Virginia and the rest of the country waited to see what happened next.

On Monday morning, true to his words of just a month earlier, President Lincoln called for over forty-thousand volunteers to serve three-year terms and for one hundred fifty thousand militia troops from Union states to join the regular army to right the wrong. This was the last straw for many in Virginia. In what had been a firmly Unionist state a week ago, the moderate's support quickly waned and the legislature hastily voted to secede two days after Lincoln's demands. We learned the Federal navy began its blockade of Virginia's port at Hampton Roads and other places along the Chesapeake so the Potomac was now closed. But seeing the matter of such grave importance, the Governor called for a ratification of the secession by the citizens.

By mid-May, the Washington was filled with thousands of loyal men within its borders. Troops were quartered in many office buildings including the Patent Office. The Capitol itself was a citadel with troops quartered in the meeting halls and supplies stored in its basements. Bakers had set up ovens outside the Capitol steps for the tens of thousands of loaves that would be needed each day to feed these men. The smoke from those ovens billowed every day being seen for miles, covered the city in a soot something awful. Washington was now a fortress and we were across the river with no protection of our own as there were over twenty-five thousand troops from Virginia and other states loyal to the Confederacy milling about. The insurrection had become an all-out rebellion.

For us, May of '61 was the defining moment for our community as the next two weeks would forever change us all and little of it for the better. What had become a peaceful community anchored at the Mount Olivet was put under to the test. With the ordinance of secession on that first of May, the ratification vote was to follow soon after. Some folks thought it was their duty to support the acts of their state leaders whether they believed in secession or not, while many others talked of not voting at all for such a treasonous proposal. By the 5th of May, Alexandria City was all but abandoned with streams of folk heading for the Fairfax countryside which began after the fall of Fort Sumter two weeks before. Papa said the turnpike and all the roads as far as he could see, were filled with wagons of all sorts with women and children and goods of all kinds, men on horseback and on foot, almost all looking as forlorn as if going to an execution. Slaves who were not taken with their owners were sent to the city jail. Most of the city's merchants and shops had closed and Papa had little business to do. By the end of May, nearly seven of every ten had left town rather than live under the fear of the Federals. Our county was being carried on to the horrors of a civil war.

The week before the vote carried a string of troubling news about secessionist affairs. More and more, the papers had talked of war, but not a real war of conquest, but to assert the rights of the passive majority being held by desperate minorities they reasoned. This was not about subjugation, but of liberation, the Editorials opined; and they said that the federal city needed to be protected and that preparations were only for its defense. Virginia should not be invaded, but that all could change with the result of Wednesday's vote. More and more troops were arriving from all points north seemingly turning the capitol city into even more of a federal fortress. There were so many troops that their camps quickly became unsanitary and disease broke out. Washington's residents were being warned to keep away from Capitol Hill as the conditions had gotten so bad around the capitol building over these few months and with the pending work to the capitol dome itself, federal troops there were to be moved out by the first of June into camps in the countryside within short marching distance should the alarm be sounded. Not a day went by without newspaper reports of troops coming into the District from points across the northeast in special trains, with details of their officers and men and armament as if to show others they were ready. It's as if the whole north had come armed to rush to this city's hour of need.

If Virginia's Ordinance of Secession passed, it would spell doom for Alexandria as far as the Federals were concerned, given the State had all but seceded and its grounds were already filled with troops from southern states. But it didn't matter as the vote was seen as a farce. Though many of those left in Alexandria City were for secession, given to their long held feelings over Washington and strong slave trade interests, most county folk outside the city harbored no such demands. The up-county's vote to affirm the State's call for secession was to be at the Tavern on Monday the 20th. Those weeks before the vote were filled with all manner of anger and angst, with the Gazette rallying its readers that it was Alexandria's civic duty to vote for the secession and not to do so was treasonous to Virginia, while papers from Washington said secession was treasonous to the Union. To make things worse, Arkansas had joined the confederacy and there was talk of North Carolina joining as well. Ordinary fork were caught in the middle of things that were larger than themselves, and most of the less passionate, like Papa kept to themselves until the vote.

A sense of doom fell over all of us that last Sunday before the vote. The Olivet was not as filled as in the past, but those that were there sang more loudly than other times, so maybe God himself would hear over the nation's furor. Reverend Hoblitzell did his best to bolster people's hopes for peace and calm, though in his sermon he chided those anarchists on their perilous path to calamity with a yay vote. Few paid him much mind as people had already made up their minds one way or the other. No one was in a mood to celebrate and for the first time since the fall, no one stayed after service to celebrate as a community. The Belles quipped, knowing how Papa felt about things, on the coming storm and how those not loyal to Virginia would get their up and comings. Men had gathered about the Olivet grounds split into their groups talking this and that about military affairs, the President and the Confederacy.

Men gathered at the corner nearly every day to read the newspapers aloud saying how many regiments were being raised and celebrated in northern cities and other reports deriding this *drunken monkey* in the White House, with his mercenary armies, and fears of the Government pillaging our homes. They read long lists of men resigning their commissions in the Federal Army and Navy to include our own Colonel Lee. Papa told those gathered that on one of his runs to Alexandria, he saw that Federal troops now blocked the Long Bridge and had posted troops on both ends to prevent any damage by secessionist elements and that there were Navy steamers of all types arriving at the Navy Yard and patrolling the river. Navy ships had also blockaded ports at Savannah, Charleston, and the Hampton Roads.

Of complete shock to all was a report that Federal

troops from New York marched all the way to the Mount Vernon home south of Alexandria to inspect the revered President Washington's tomb reporting that all was fine. How it was that anyone would consider defiling that respected man's final resting place was beyond words. On their way back to the Federal city, these New Yorkers took down a large Confederate flag in Alexandria and brought it back to Washington, further fanning the flames of secession to those within the city. Men, it seems, were already dying as the papers had made something out of the sudden death of a Colonel Vosburg from illness who commanded a regiment of New Yorkers and how many of the military and the President had come to pay their respects, even lowering flags around the city. Why such a ruckus over this man was not clear to many around here, but he must have been of great importance to the Federals across the river. Soon, there would be more loss on both sides of the river.

From his daily trips into the city, Vanderwekin told the congregation that Federal workers, including those of the Post Office, had taken oaths of allegiance and those that didn't comply were dismissed from their duties. Shockingly, some reverends in the District had also been dismissed from their duties for not including a prayer for their president as was customary. How could this be that clergy had to be careful when they preached? The Washington papers reported of telegraph offices in northern cities being raided by the marshals to confiscate dispatches heading south. Papers also reprinted stories from Southern papers deriding the Federal troops, *Yankees* as they called them, as poor undisciplined soldiers without the heart for military life. They also reported about plans to move the capitol of this new confederacy to Richmond. How was this possible given Virginia's long history of defending the Union? Papa was beside himself, that our state was drawn further by the secessionist siren's song. We came to learn that more shots were fired as the Navy had broken a blockade of a

Government Fort in Hampton Roads and that cannon fire was exchanged by both sides. Were we already at war? No one knew or believed it could be.

It was getting harder for us girls to keep such talk from bringing fear and splitting our group of girls, especially the young ones; but the Olivet, and most of the trustees were against secession. Even for those with kin in the militia or the cavalry, family ties were beginning to fray. The Belles weren't talking to us anymore and instead to the boys who were in the Virginia militia, meeting with them at the spring when it suited them. I was able to catch Cornelia on occasion and talk, but things were now just getting too personal depending on what side of the spring you were from. We socialized for a bit, but that week had no fish fry or much celebrating at all for that manner. The church's front stoop had been completed two weeks before but there was no stomach for pleasantries. Folks were now consumed with talk about the coming vote and rumors of turmoil in Alexandria city; so the girls went home with their families to sit out the night, thinking about what was to happen the next day, or week for that matter.

Wednesday's vote was all important for Papa and others of his leaning if nothing but to solidly affirm their allegiance to the Union and to once and for all paint this county with the brush of Unionism which it deserved. Yet a sense of dread set in as the vote was seen as worthless with Virginia already in the secessionists' grip. For many, the vote made little difference. Confederate flags had already been flying from high points in Alexandria within days after the surrender at Fort Sumter last month. No more so than the twenty foot flag atop the Marshall House Inn put there by its secessionist proprietor. With the loss of Fort Sumter, Washington City began flying the Federal flag from its highpoints in a show of Union solidarity. Word had spread that on that Tuesday, a couple of days before the vote, the

President himself would raise a large Federal flag over the post office at about ten in the morning. The girls and I made plans to make a day of it atop Minor Hill to see it unfurl and before long the hill was filled with folk doing the same. From what we could see, there were large flags flying all around the capitol city, and folks were yelling with excitement every time a new one went up. An especially large one, even bigger than that put up by Mr. Lincoln, was raised on a very tall mast on the hills north of Georgetown. And those on the hill of strong secessionist leanings were none too happy about the whole affair.

To the fear of some and the joy of many, on Wednesday of that fateful week, the papers talked of occupying Alexandria regardless of the vote, this out of military necessity for its rail lines and port, but also to rescue Virginia from the clutches of traitors who traumatize over their soil. These were fighting words to some and had begun preparing that week for armed conflict. That day of the vote was the flint that lit the fuse of war. Most were now under no illusion that a miracle would come to prevent war. North Carolina passed its ordnance of secession on Tuesday with reports of troops as far away as Louisiana sent to Richmond. Secessionist elements were in almost every county and the Richmond convention allowed the military, even those troops from South Carolina and Georgia already camped about the state, to vote. The Sentinel reported that our own Colonel Lee, hero of the abolitionist rebellion at Harper's Ferry a year and a half ago, now had resigned his commission and had ordered the Virginia state militiamen to ratify the ordnance as a precaution.

That Wednesday, Papa hoped to get to the tavern early so as to not to run into secessionists. That morning he was not feeling very well, and it took him much longer to get going on account of he had caught the grip. I warmed a biscuit and some hash and set him a good cup of tea. He had a worried look on his face that he could not hide, but he knew he had to do his duty. By the time he was done, it was just past sunup and by then the community was likely up and about. I had bridled the horses and brought the wagon around. He and George were to ride in and pick up others along the way.

They headed out on the short trip down the county road, he saw many headed the same way, some a hollering some celebrating, but most others were keeping thoughts to themselves. I knew Papa would speak his "nay" vote and we knew many from the Olivet that lived east of the spring would do so as well. But it was not to be so easy. By the time they arrived, there were many carriages and horse about and to their surprise about twenty armed men. George and Papa saw Caleb Birch and James Tucker there too still sitting on their wagon not knowing what to make of this spectacle. This was now serious business as outside that tavern stood Virginia Cavalrymen of Lieutenant Johnson's Second Company, mostly made up of locals who knew most everyone. There were also armed men that Papa recognized as Minor kin. As men waited their turn to vote, cavalrymen snaked their way through the crowd with threats for anyone against secession of taking their property, being run out of Virginia or worse. Some armed men even said that those who did not vote to ratify would be hanged the next day at 10 o'clock. These were bold words and not ones easily ignored.

George, Papa and Smith Minor got to talking. I'm really worried now as a vote against secession could be like signing my own death warrant. I know said Minor, and I'm in the Unionist party and own slaves, but this is too much. Passions were high, and it was clear that if one didn't vote for secession, their lives, families and their livelihood would be in danger. Once inside, Papa heard others cast their votes aloud then put an "X" by their name in the register. The threats were making their mark he thought, and with every increasing 'Yay' vote the county's fate was being sealed. How about we not vote for either side on account of so many foreign troops already on Virginia soil George stammered? No, I didn't hear many men say "absent" and besides, we aren't cowards. Papa's turn came as he nervously stood tall in front of the table. Nay I say! Loud enough for others to hear, turned and walked out. George did the same but stayed outside to watch more of the spectacle. Papa would have none of it and took the wagon home. He felt worse now than he had before he arrived; for in doing his duty, his mark on that roster, right or wrong, prior good deeds or not, would forever define our place in this community. He came home visibly upset, knowing that the vote at the tavern would forever split this community apart.

By the end of the day, even with such threats, we learned that most of the men in this area had not supported the secession, and there was hope this nightmare would finally be over. Again, it was not to be. The next day, North Carolina had voted to secede bringing the number of states in the confederacy to nine; and Virginia let its leanings be known as well. The Fort Sumter affair and the President's calls for troops, tipped the balance from 2-to-1 against less than three weeks ago to now 3-to-1 in favor of secession. All day and into the night, through telegraph and word of mouth, we learned though joyous yells and rancorous lament that Virginia had joined the ranks of the Confederacy and to add further insult, Richmond became it's new capital. No one knew quite what was going to happen next; but as we were to soon learn, the wheels of war had already begun to turn.

The War Department had not been idle in those weeks before the vote, having already decided that should Virginia join the Confederacy, Washington could not be protected unless the heights across the Potomac were taken.

They named a General Mansfield, whose men were to feature much in our daily lives, to protect the Federal city. Virginians had begun to stir for war themselves as the Governor ordered militia officers to recruit and train volunteer companies and regiments throughout the state. By Wednesday night Virginia volunteers began manning their posts up all up the Potomac and an artillery battery was organized in Alexandria with cavalry men on patrol all day.

Papa hitched his team early Thursday morning for his monthly run to Alexandria city. He came home that evening, shaken but eager to tell all who gathered at our corner what he saw. The county road just beyond the Columbia turnpike was clogged with folks making their way to Alexandria city to get on trains out of town. Just above the train station, cavalry units had gathered waiting for what, no one seemed to know. It seemed the whole city was celebrating Virginia's excise from Washington's tyranny and not much work could be done that day, as further down near Washington Street men were signing up for the Militia. Troubling to many were reports Captain Ball's Fairfax Cavalry riding all around our area and taking up posts on our side of the Chain Bridge to keep watch on the District militiamen who were now guarding their side of the bridge. The papers wrote that President Lincoln drove out to view the spring scenery and, coming to the bridge, was stopped by a sentry warning that Virginia cavalry were nearby.

Others like Vanderwerkin with business in the capitol, were now told they weren't allowed to across the bridges thinking they might be insurgents. Folks were shocked when they heard what Papa was saying. What to us had been joyous news of a new presidency six months ago had now become preparations for war. No one knew what to expect when Virginia left the Union, but it didn't look good. The naïve believed that things would just go on, and nothing would really change. Papa knew better and by the time he came home there was a certain unease that couldn't be shaken. Most of the fortunes of this county, except those of the slave traders in the city, had been tied to Washington; and many around here stood the most to lose from this folly. This backwater of Washington had now become the aim of the entire Federal Army. The storm arrived on our doorstep and the savagery that was to go on for the next four years was set to be bestowed upon us.

5 INVASION

That third week in May was as if we were entering an abyss of the unknown. Naively, we believed cooler heads would prevail and all would come to their senses, but we were on the road to perdition. Reverend Hoblitzell preached that we were not going to war with anyone, but rather he had it on account that those Federal forces were not about conquest, but about freeing folks from secessionist subjugation. He said that God would see that peace prevailed; but Papa knew better. On his trips to Alexandria, he had seen for himself the wheels of war beginning to spin ever faster over the past month with the march of states to the Confederacy and northern troops spilling into the capitol and even to Alexandria city proper. Things were swirling around us and for us in up-county, it's as if we were merely ants floating on a log in the Potomac.

There was now real fear amongst many, especially those that voted against secession. We heard that nearly all the Alexandria militiamen voted "Yay" and that a few thousand troops from all parts of Virginia were in Alexandria city preventing any "no" votes. Yet some militia men from our area refused to take the oath of hostility toward the Union. There was anger in Washington as well as the papers reporting that ordinary folk were being arrested by Federal troops for seditious talk. District militia were at their armories and told of their duties. Those men who had regular jobs during the day had to endure night duty guarding the public buildings, roads and bridges. Troops from Michigan and New York were drilled daily being readied to march on a moment's notice expecting orders hourly to leave. Other reinforcements from New York continued to arrive as well as troops from Ohio into the city in special trains. It's as if some believed anarchy had truly taken over the city needing so many men in uniform to quell it. What were good folk to think about all this? There was an inevitable dread that gripped many as word quickly spread that Virginia had too cast its lot with the anarchists as predicted it would. Who would have thought our community was now seen as enemy territory.

The machine seen by many of liberation, and to some of subjugation, was put into motion as Mr. Lincoln gave the orders to take Alexandria across the Potomac River once Wednesday's vote was approved by the Secession Convention the following day. The papers were full of stories of troop movements and such. More Federal flags were raised in the city that day, with a large one above the Northern Market just north of the President's house. Mr. Lincoln himself was there to present a flag to a New York regiment that we would come to know all too well in the coming year. Another New York regiment led by the famed Colonel Ellsworth, took the first actions against the secessionists by stopping war supplies on the Potomac headed from Baltimore to Alexandria City. But there were unsettling reports unrest in town, of fist fights, and even a stabbing amongst District militiamen and other troops of the North. What would become of us should this unruly lot come across the river? Folks were getting rightly concerned, but it wasn't long before we would feel the might of the Federal Army.

Friday morning came and went like most. I was preparing Papa's meal for his journey and then to help get the teams ready then later seeing Eveline and the girls at her orchard. Papa was still anxious about yesterday's goings on and the closing of the bridges leading to and from the city, but there was work to be done to finishing yesterday's hauls. He left that city in turmoil with most now abandoning it in fear of a coming invasion, when and by who was a guess, but Papa had no time for such things, he had done his duty on the vote along with most others in these parts. He was getting the mules ready for the day's run when we heard a commotion toward the Hall home. A man on horseback, from somewhere down at nearby Riley's Hill, had just come from the Glebe parish bringing news to anyone who would hear that the train from Leesburg had been stopped by mounted cavalry and that men were herded off and some were arrested. Papa and George rushed to the fence rail to hear more, as the excited man paused for a bit, he said that he heard of hundreds of Federal troops east of the tavern on Ball land and for what, he didn't know. I hurried over to hear more, but by the time I got across the field, the man galloped away, hurriedly yelling that Federals were coming.

Papa and George didn't know what to think of this man's ramblings thinking it likely that he had seen the Virginia cavalry from Fairfax and got confused or that marshals were looking for secessionists who were out and about causing trouble; but if true, if mounted troops were stopping the train and arresting folk, that was another matter. Something was up, and it wasn't clear what. Not more than a half hour later, the ominous dust cloud and the rumble of many mounted men could be heard to our north along the Falls Road from the Chain Bridge and it was getting louder. Men had now come to gather at Wunder's corner to hear what was going on. Some had heard rumors of an invasion while others heard of treasonists going house to house looking for those that voted against secession and were prepared with their rifles at the ready. Before long, the two long columns of riders reached us, both a frightening and impressive sight and they appeared almost ghostlike in their long formation. We knew they were Federal troops on account of their uniforms and the federal flag as their standard. Papa told me to get inside, but I wouldn't go. He warned me again sternly, more so than he had ever since Mama's passing. I left doubly quick but hid behind a wagon to hear more.

The troops came to a halt at the fence, staying in formation with their rifles at the ready, some with their barrels pointed at us. Their horses were skittish, breathing something fierce from their long gallop. The uniforms on these young men were crisp and clean and there were markings on their standards that I didn't understand. These men were looking around as if fearing an ambush, from whom we weren't sure. An officer and his second approached and with a stern look informed us that they were the District of Columbia Militia under the command of Colonel Stone. He said "That under the direction of General Mansfield, Commander of Military forces of Washington, Federal troops had arrived in northern Virginia to ensure the security of Washington itself and warned of any interference in their hunt for secessionist elements".

Papa was surprised by the tone and demeanor of this young officer, but settled the situation with a few pleasantries and offering to water their horses which the captain and his men gladly obliged. It was then that I got my first look at these soldiers as I hauled pails of water. I was uneasy as many looked to be sizing me up as I was likely the first *"southern girl"* they had seen and some even caught my eye though none dared to make a notion lest their commander see it. Many of these troops were boys not much older than I with a few barely a whisker on them. They smiled at me and I exchanged some light pleasantries with a few of them.

Through those talks we learned that indeed Federal troops had arrived in the county securing all the bridges from Washington and that Alexandria City was now closed to all but the military. New York troops were on their first patrols and had indeed come as far as the tavern. I didn't know half the things they were talking about, but words like "Regiment" and "Company" kept being repeated so I figured these were big groups of soldiers coming to fight and I had to hear more. The rumor of arrests were true as District Militia cavalry stopped the train coming from Leesburg arresting some three hundred fifty armed secessionists. We also heard that cavalry from the President's Mounted Guard arrested many men as spies near the tavern, one named Nevitt, another named Porter, an elderly man named Quinton and young man named Cluite who was in uniform. This secessionist business was becoming all too real for us as we listened and there would likely be much more to come.

For how long these troops would be in our midst, the Captain didn't know, but he did say this was far from over. Papa and others asked whether there would be any trouble getting around the county as they posed no threat on account they were good Unionists. But they were warned to stay put today and for now to travel only in daylight and not stray too far from our homes. Once the Army got settled in, then they might attend to requests for passage. This was bad news for Papa, but what could he do? Their Captain warned aloud for all to hear that the Army would not be too kind to folks harboring secessionists and hoped they would give full cooperation to the Federals. That threat was none too veiled as far as Papa was concerned. I spent the rest of the afternoon peppering Papa with all sort of questions on what the Captain was talking about. Papa indulged me as if we were back near Alexandria sitting on his lap. He told me all about how the Army was put together, how a Company was about a hundred men led by Captains and Majors, a Regiment was about a thousand men of ten companies each led by Colonels, and a General was the leader of many Regiments. It was all so fascinating to me and wished he would tell me more, but Papa had other things on his mind and before long I put myself to finishing my chores.

On Saturday, the invasion was all the talk, with most folks gathered at the Olivet to get the latest news from the Gazette. Vanderwerken had copies of the National Republican and the Washington Star, to learn more of what was happening to us. Many of the men gathered about and I struggled to hear their words. There were gasps from many of the women and hoots and shouts from some as the details were read aloud. We come to find out that on Wednesday, the Federals made up their minds to invade this sacred soil based on reports General Mansfield got from watching secessionist officers scouting for fortifications atop the heights at Arlington House and that confederate pickets were seen on its heights and near the Virginia landing off the Long Bridge. We heard the details of military movements across the bridges from Washington in the wee hours of Friday to positions all along the Arlington Heights from the Chain Bridge to Alexandria City. The city was indeed closed to all but the military. Having been warned by Federals landing under the flag of truce from a Navy frigate the previous night, the Virginia Militia and the radical secessionists for the most part had left town and residents shed tears of joy over their deliverance.

The papers were filled with reports of the first martyrs of the conflict. During the invasion, that New York Regiment commander, Colonel Ellsworth, a popular man in military circles in Washington who had been the subject of so much talk in the months leading up to this, was killed himself by none other than the secessionist proprietor of the Marshall House Inn named James Jackson, cousin to Minor's wife Catherine. It seems Ellsworth didn't know about the earlier warning, unloaded his *Fire Zoave* troops from two steamships and led them up through the city proper. He was on a mission to take the telegraph and railroad stations when he saw the secessionist flag that Jackson had raised the day before which could be seen all the way to Washington. Ellsworth charged in with five of his men and a reporter from the New York Tribune, climbing the steps to the roof, he cut down the offending banner. He was heading down the steps with his prize when Jackson fired a shotgun blast into Ellsworth's chest killing him. At the same time, a Private named Brown turned and fired at Jackson, killing him. The dead Colonel, beloved by his men, was taken back to the Washington Navy yard in a grand procession on a gunship along with the blood soaked flag.

From all the reporting, it seems the loss of this beloved Colonel was not just a tragedy for the 11th New York, but the nation as well. Ellsworth was well loved by his men, popular with the officers in Washington and even the President himself as he had known him personally having clerked for a while at Lincoln's law office in Illinois. The papers talked about him often as he was a regular at the President's house having dinners with Mr. and Mrs. Lincoln, hobnobbed with his Secretaries and played games with the two Lincoln boys, Willie and Tad. He now lay dead as a Union martyr; his body under guard at the Navy Yard for a few days to a stream of mourners including the President himself.

The Sunday newspapers said Alexandria City was quiet since that Saturday night under the watchful eye of nearly a thousand troops from New York, Ohio, Pennsylvania and Michigan. Those same Ellsworth's men were marched back to Washington for fear of them taking vengeance upon the city for the death of their beloved leader. But there was still more bad news to come as North Carolina had sent a thousand troops to Richmond. The Federal advance on our shores early Friday morning fascinated us all, reading like a war novel. It seems that on the Thursday night of the vote, Washington campsites were all a flutter as troops from New York, New Jersey, Michigan and others assembled with orders for extra provisions. Shortly before midnight the Federal patrols marched across the Long and Aqueduct bridges into Virginia without a fight. At 1 o'clock in the morning, District volunteers followed in long blue columns through the moonlit Washington streets toward the Potomac. By 4 in the morning, seven regiments from New York and New Jersey, nearly eight thousand men, marched across the Long Bridge scaring away secessionist pickets. This mass of men made positions all along the Potomac from Roach's Spring, half mile from the bridge, near where Mama and papa first lived, up river past the Aqueduct Bridge. Three other Federal regiments and cavalry from New York and Massachusetts, to the delight of District folks who had gathered, crossed over the Aqueduct Bridge in a silent march with bayonets a glistening taking up positions on our side of the bridge and all over the Arlington Heights including the Lee's plantation home. It was just after sunup that those troops from the President's Guards stopped two train cars returning from Leesburg, arresting the spies. Other Federals troops destroyed six road bridges to keep rebels from heading to Alexandria and by mid-morning, got to less than a mile away from the tavern before making camp. How could this be that Virginia was now at war?

Being from Virginia, the Gazette was a bit less gracious in its words with a more fiery tone saying that troops entered Alexandria city intending to subjugate the people of the South to the control of one Abraham Lincoln, the first sectional President ever elected by the people of the

American Union. It said the invaders met with no resistance; but the "frown of the citizens gave unerring indication of their feelings" and something about this infringement upon their rights. It seems the Virginia militia troops in Alexandria took the agreement to heart and left hours before the Federal troops crossed the Potomac rather than risk a bloody skirmish in the city. Yet not all got away as a company of Fairfax Cavalrymen were captured by the first Michigan infantry as they rode out Duke Street.

The Washington papers told it a bit differently saying the President's Mounted Guard, and Artillery men arriving from land, surprised an unfortunate Captain Ball and thirty-six men of the Fairfax Cavalry bedded down at John Cook's Negro pen near the Negro jail. It seems the cavalrymen mistook the 6 o'clock in the morning arrival of the Federals as forewarned for 8 o'clock. Papa and others knew of this Ball and were none too fond of him on account of the demeanor of men under him at the Tavern during the vote and in the days later as he and his men patrolled our area. These prisoners, the papers said, in their lead colored jackets and grey pants were marched to the river and taken by steamer to the Navy Yard. Of the thirty three men that were captured in addition to the officers, two were from the Ball family and one from the Bell family much to the dismay of some that were listening.

We came to learn of news a bit closer to us on that Thursday night that the District Militia cavalry that Papa saw on Friday morning, was sent again across the Chain Bridge to disperse the Fairfax Cavalry and their pickets on our side lest they set fire to it. Following them later in the evening, a Captain Rodier led his District Militiamen called the "Anderson Rifles", after Fort Sumter's famed commander, across the bridge to finally secure the Virginia heights. In a bit of pique to Papa, this Captain we heard was the son of the Chesapeake & Ohio Canal engineer who nudged Congress to take funds from the Aqueduct spur crushing Papa's hopes for riches some years ago. The *Anderson* men captured John Ball and a George Kirby of the Fairfax cavalry, who were under the same Captain Ball who himself had been captured in Alexandria with the rest of his men. Besides those two, a third man named Smidt, belonging to the same troops was arrested a little later. These men were taken to General Mansfield who, strangely enough, swore them to loyalty and let them go. All told, over forty-five other men, committed to Virginia's cause, were arrested that day.

On that Saturday the first of many edicts and proclamations were read. They had been posted by cavalry at all the churches, taverns and other gathering places stating that "no one peaceably inclined should be molested and told fugitives to return to their homes". It was not until Sunday when we learned about how the vote went at the tavern, but the newspaper reported nearly 3 out of 4 landowners of the over hundred who voted from outside the Alexandria city were against the ordnance. It seemed to Papa that our community had done its part to keep the Union whole. But this was not to be enough to quiet those at the tavern or families west of the spring. While the county folk stayed loyal, the same wasn't true for Alexandria city where those few left in town voted with 20 to 1 for secession.

By Friday sundown, Federal troops stretched from the Chain Bridge, across the Arlington Heights to Alexandria city proper. Before the weekend was over, New Yorkers were posted at Arlington House and once Lee's family left, they turned it into General McDowell's headquarters for the new Department of the Northeastern Virginia. The commander even sent word to Lee that he would look after the place. As for us, four more New York Regiments crossed the Chain Bridge, from their camps in Georgetown to occupy the heights surrounding Washington. Many of these troops we came to learn were now quartered on

Vanderwerken land. By the end of that weekend, our county saw fortifications arise from its pristine hills, camps housing thousands of men on its farms and trenches carved into its lands which stretched from Roach's spring on the Washington-Alexandria Road across Arlington Heights almost to Chain Bridge. New Yorkers were camped at Lee's plantation and on the road to Balls Crossroads, while others were building a fort near the Aqueduct Bridge. New Jersey men were camped at the base of the Long Bridge and all along the turnpike. By the end of the May, these men had built two large forts at the base of each bridge named Corcoran and Runyon after their commanders but there were to be many more. Timber for all of it was now going to be in great demand and many here, including Papa saw opportunity.

Reading the papers every day became an obsession with folks around here. Things were changing ever so much and it was clear our occupation was not to be a peaceable one. The Staunton papers were fanning the flames of fear saying the invaders were upon us to butcher, enslave and pollute our wives and daughters. How one could print such crass words was beyond me. We also heard Federals had taken over our Gazette paper when a Mr. Snowden, their editor who was kin to some around here, refused to publish some of the President's proclamations.

The following Thursday and Friday in early morning we heard the rumble of hours of cannon fire a ways in the distance frightening all. We came to learn that a Federal Navy flotilla on the Potomac fired on a Confederate artillery battery and secessionist fortifications along the Potomac and Aquia Creek much further south of Alexandria City and two schooners were also captured with fifty of its secessionist crew. On that last day in May, a large cavalry group rode by our home at night creating such a rumble across the ground waking us all and almost tossing us to the floor as they made their way west toward the Fairfax Courthouse. We heard later these Federals got into a gunfight with confederates killing twenty including Virginia Militia's Captain Marr who Papa had seen at the tavern days earlier. The Gazette called him the first Confederate casualty of the war. By the last day of May, Papa told me there were over forty thousand troops in these parts with more to come. As for us, it seems the flat lands around the Ball's Crossroads tavern was making for excellent Army campsites. Our guests had arrived, looking to stay for a while.

6 A SUMMER OF FEAR

The Federal Army's intentions were all that was on anyone's mind. Within a few weeks, the families and merchants of Alexandria City that left in such a hurry were replaced with thousands of troops, even more throughout the county. Having Federal troops on Virginia soil no more than a mile away of our home was unsettling. What were their intentions? How long would they stay? No one knew anything, not the Sherriff, not the jailors or even ministers at the Glebe parish. There was a real fear across the parish. Rumors abound of arrests and property taken with the many of those families that voted for secession not as boastful as they were two weeks ago. Folks stayed close to their homes and they were hungry for news with men trading stories at the tavern and church elders reading aloud the newspaper accounts. It was all the talk about the horrible events in Alexandria early that morning; the deaths of Ellsworth and the inn-keeper Jackson, the taking of the telegraph office, but not before the operator removed the equipment and months' worth of dispatches out the back door as Federal troops entered the front, militiamen captured at the Chain Bridge, the arrest of men off the Alexandria train and the forty or so

Virginia cavalry captured as they slept in their barracks.

These were not just stories of strangers, but of neighbors and kin now in jail or worse by troops from far away states under a national banner. Was this now to be the fate of all of us living across the Potomac? No one was sure. These reports were not of some far off land, but goings on less than ten miles away and some of it less than a mile away in the camps on our farms and fields. What were the Federal's intentions, and who was the enemy they sought? We all knew of men who were volunteers in the militia, but aside from ardent secessionists, most had either stayed home during the turmoil or had long since left for parts unknown. Were we now the evil the abolitionists feared? For us, there would remain an ever-present fear of being rounded up. No one wanted to confront these strangers who were now in our midst.

Suspicion was ever present and the rumors were running wild with home invasions, battles, skirmishes and manhunts lest we all be thought of as rebels. It was a week or so after that invasion, and we had no better sense of what the Federals wanted on our farms. Was it capturing some unseen rebels, or was the army pressing to fight near our homes. No one knew. It was going on the second week where Papa had learned from others that troops, mostly from New York, New Jersey and Michigan were scattered all along the Wagon Road with some as close as a quarter mile from the tavern. Others were now scattered about in Arlington Heights and more who had crossed the Chain Bridge had set up camp just beyond the palisades on Vanderwerken property; but they had not gone any further. I heard the sounds of horses, and axe with the snap of trees being felled some distance away all day and night. No one wanted to go near those Federal camps least we be shot at by nervous troops or arrested for being secessionist spies. Even more troubling, Virginia militiamen began riding through at night scaring folk outright. It wasn't going to be long before the horror of some conflict would be in our midst. That first Sunday in June was to be our baptism as just before we left for church, we heard shots in the distance, later hearing of a skirmish between men of the 28th New York and militia scouts just north of the Chain Bridge. This was the first in what was to be many such skirmishes in our midst that first year of the war.

The Olivet was crowded that Sunday but there wasn't that sense of joy as there was a few weeks before. Parishioners listened less to Reverend Hoblitzell's sermon as they were eager to learn what they could from each other. With all that was going on, we all thought it best to stop the fish and oyster festivities until things settled down. That Sunday, confirmed what many of us already heard, the National Army now had thousands, if not tens of thousands of troops in the county. More men from New York and Pennsylvania came by ship and over the Long Bridge, now camped and building forts in the Arlington Heights and Alexandria City itself, preparing to set for a while it seemed. Alexandria City was now under martial law with folks needing permission to come and go. Troops from southern states were also making their way north, with men from Carolina and Tennessee already in Falls Church. The National Army had made it known that it was to rid the county of rebels and arrest their sympathizers. The Reverend reminded all that it would be wise not to stray too far from home lest they be rounded up. Smith Minor piped up that his cousin, himself in the Captain Ball's Virginia militia was caught up in that fuss and was intent on getting him out of prison. Others spoke of troops from Rhode Island scouting the Little Falls Road making their way just this side of Fall Church. No one knew who or what to believe. Many others on hearing this news were down right angry and it was all Hoblitzell could do to keep the peace. Others knew nothing of friends and relatives elsewhere throughout the county. Were they rounded up as well and in prison? Was anyone hurt? No one was sure what to do or say. We all left church that Sunday more fearful than ever.

By the next week young folk were itching to get away from their homes. Word was passed that after church we would all meet at the spring and tell what we knew. Eveline and I told our folks we would be at each other's homes but we were warned to stay close by. What we thought was going to be a wonderful respite from all the goings on, became a shock for us both. Together we set out for the spring and just as we got to the ridge past her place, we saw two Union scouts slowly working the woods as if they were hunting.

We stopped to watch them across the ways from us wondering what they were doing. Both had rifles with long brass pipe atop their barrels that they would look through every once in a while. It looked as if they were spying on three militiamen who were at our spring. Fearing the militiamen would get us, we stopped and quietly watched to see what was gonna happen. No doubt having spotted the Union pickets, one of the militia men took off his jacket and cap and put them on his rifle. Then from behind the large oak, began waiving his gun hoping to spook the scouts I guess. The Union soldiers watched this game go on for some time and we stood there quietly not knowing what was to happen. I guess the Union scouts thought of a plan to root out the militiamen, so they waited until one waived his jacket again, then one of the Union scouts fired, scaring Eveline to nearly scream as I quickly put my hand over her mouth. When another militiaman peeked out to take his shot, the other Union scout fired felling the man. We both stood there in shock as a man was killed before our eyes.

The other militiamen skulked away leaving their lifeless friend there at our spring and before long the scouts left as well. Eveline just fell to her knees and cried. I quickly got her up and we left for her place never looking back. Eveline told her ma and word quickly spread of the calamity at the spring. Some of the men went to go get the dead soldier, but when they got there, found nothing but blood. No doubt the militiamen came back for their friend. Papa was none too happy with me when he found out, and we were both forbidden to go to the spring for a while.

Papa had supplies to haul and other business to attend to. He and others figured they would have to go to the closest camp to talk with the local commanders. They needed free passage through the county to do their business, and maybe just maybe, do business with the Army itself. Another week had gone by, and it was mid-June as I recall, with everyone just as eager for more news. Their initial shock of the invasion had worn off some and now folks were carefully going about their business. The Union Army, as they were now being called, was making its presence felt in this part of the County with more and more patrols, at least a few per day. Long columns of cavalry and once in a while troops from the camp on the Vanderwerken lands were making forays around us. Papa had come to know the guards and the chief quartermaster at the camp as they didn't know the roads and grounds around here. Papa told them where the nearest springs were for fresh water and the makeup of the community. He even brought Doc to the camp in case they needed help, but one Sargent, a bit too full of himself, barked that the Union Army had the finest physicians the North had to offer and were in no need of a country horse doctor to treat Army men.

Such insults were to be common, but Papa just ignored them and told many to keep their mouths shut and offer to do odd jobs for the camp, that maybe they would come to leave us alone and move on. Yet, Papa knew the Army was likely here to stay for some time and would need hauling done and saw himself as the man to do it. If it all went as he thought, he would get the passes he needed to go about his longer hauls back to Alexandria and maybe back to Washington. Papa told me the guards there were always asking if he had seen any rebels lately. Papa did not know what to think of such talk. Did they mean us? Or was there some other army that they believed we knew something about. We were simple farmers and merchants making our living paying no mind to such things. The camp officers had come to recognize Papa as a loyal regular.

Loyalty to the Union Papa came to find out was everything for business with the Army. If your friends and neighbors vouched for your loyalty, then it was likely the Union Army would trust you with more permission. If you or your family showed southern sentiments, then you were at best ignored, or likely to have property confiscated or worst yet, jailed for treason. How that loyalty was figured was never quite simple, but for many it started with the roster of votes cast for secession back at Ball's Tavern almost a month ago. Now that the Union Army was in our midst, being a sympathizer to the confederate cause came at a price with the first of many arrests including a local man named Major Nutt, from his service during the Mexican war. He had once worked in the US Treasurer's Office and owned property near Bazil Hall's. Nutt was a good man, though he held southern sentiments and twelve slaves, some thought his fine work for the Government could afford him some forgiveness from authorities, but we were all mistaken. He was arrested by New York soldiers with others, one of them being George Jackson, a relative of the Minors who had been a messenger in the Government Comptroller's office, and was the brother of the Inn keeper who shot Ellsworth on that first night. To be in the company of such a wanted man was to be guilty themselves.

One had to be careful who they were seen with or

the words that came out of their mouths. Within those first two weeks in June, we heard of many more being arrested. Lines of loyalty were being drawn with little mercy being shown to those on the wrong side. Union soldiers arrested one of the Veitch brothers and one of the Ball kin as they were herding fifty head of cattle toward the Confederate lines. Things got even worse when they searched Ball's home and found enough arms, bedding and cooking gear for fifty men. The slightest affront was now cause for arrest. We heard that one of the Minor kin, named John, who was the former jailor, was arrested near Benning's bridge for of all things thieving from the Vanderwerken farm some weeks since. This was an old spat over lumber that had been brewing for some time, but now with troops on his property, it seems Gilbert could have them do his bidding. This Minor was a good man with family. Thanks goodness, he was paroled within a week.

New Yorkers had settled into their camp on the Vanderwerken fields and were in the midst of building impressive fortifications. Others were making their home in and about the lands at the Tavern calling theirs Camp Union commanded by a Colonel Arnes, a good man of fine character who didn't mind meeting with locals and getting to know our lands. Papa had come a calling to both camps hoping to see if he could help with loading and after almost a week or so of trying, an opportunity of sorts happened. Virginia's summer heat had gotten to the men from their endless marching and making defenses. Many had passed out from the heat and weren't coming to. Papa, George and Doc had gone to the camp before, talking to the Sargent of the Guards hoping to pass a message to the camp commander offering what help they could, but now the Army came looking for them. Lieutenant Groves, the same one Papa had seen a few weeks back had given orders to fetch Doc, so George and Papa hitched the wagon and went over. After exchanging some pleasantries, Doc was taken to the infirmary to do what he could while Papa and George stayed outside to speak with others.

A Sargent told Papa how much they appreciated the help and with finding the nearby springs. It seems the Army was going to build large forts on this side of Chain Bridge and more camps all about this area maybe to the heights westward. To Papa and George this meant either they'd come all the way to Hall's Hill or even further to Minor Hill. It seemed the whole Union Army would soon be in our midst. It was late in the day as I was unhitching the horses, I could hear the thunder of cavalry heading as they came toward us. Nearly fifty men were riding hard kicking up a big cloud of dust behind them, like a biblical apocalypse. I was scared, not knowing if they were coming for us for some slight at the camp. Come to find out these men weren't from Camp Vanderwerken, but Captain Rodier's *Anderson Rifles* riding in from Georgetown across the Chain Bridge. They were an impressive sight, reminding me of that first day seeing the District Militia. These men were on a scouting patrol upland past Langley near the Salona Plantation, making their way to the Fairfax Court-House letting Confederates know that the Union Army was in their midst. We learned later that they were surprised seeing over seven-hundred secessionists there and had to make their way back double quick lest they be captured.

By the end of June, the fear most of us had eased a bit with folks going about their daily lives as best they could. Folks got used to seeing Army wagons all about our roads and cavalry on our trails and they were getting to know us. Eveline said an Army wagon full of saddles got stuck in the mud going up the steep part of Little Falls Road outside her place. The soldiers hauling them threw off nearly a dozen saddles to get the wagon free, then went quickly on their way leaving them behind. Her Pa went out and picked them up storing them in the barn, knowing the soldiers would be back. A week later indeed a Captain came by on horseback inquiring about the saddles, no doubt testing him and when her Pa led him to the barn to give them back, less one for his troubles, the Captain was pleased. Word began to be spread amongst the camps that the locals, at least on this side of the spring, were good folk and could be trusted.

Papa, with a good word from Vanderwerken, was now making more rounds throughout out the county with the pass signed by Lieutenant Groves. Camps had sprung up all through the eastern part of the county and the Union Army grew its reach like vines. Although Papa had his pass and was getting to be known, he'd be stopped by troops regularly asking him for his passes and even questioning his loyalty. In his travels, he became witness to how this county was turning so. What had been land of little note a month ago was now becoming a nest for all manner of war. Hundreds more troops arrived daily, mostly by way across the Long Bridge, up through Arlington Heights and back along the Fairfax road almost up to the tavern. At night we would hear buglers calls and the constant drone of axe and pick. It was clear the Union Army was up to something more than just building forts and camps to sit and wait. Men were drilling and practicing their shooting as if preparing for war and we were all hoping it would be somewhere other than near our homes. There was no enemy here.

Papa became known in these parts and now needed me to help with manifests on his forays south along the Wagon Road to the canal just off the Aqueduct Bridge. He was terribly fearful of bringing me along, but I told him that I was not afraid and that my place was with him. I remember him smiling, telling me how proud he was of me and how I had none of Mama's frailties. Making runs about the county was not to be easy. To keep brigands and other men of ill sorts away, Papa painted the sides of his wagons a deep blue with white on the wheel spokes to look more like those of the Union Army and made me dress "simply" as he would say, with britches, boots, a loose shirt and a hat of a boy so as to not draw attention. It was on that first trip that I saw for myself the might and wonder of the war machine that had come upon us. All along the wagon road, I saw sprawling camps of little white tents arranged in neat rows for many acres. Most were small tents, pegged on their ends with poles in the middle that made them look like a block letter "A" holding four or six men each while larger tents with canvas walls, held officers or four sergeants each on bunk beds. Their floors were of hewn plank with chimneys of mud and sticks built toward the back of the tents. Papa heard that these wall-tents could keep men warm even on the coldest nights. I found that hard to believe as I remembered just how cold our cottage that we lived in just outside Alexandria those many years ago got in the winter. Men were standing in lines of all sorts, or marching here and there in formation, at times thrusting their rifles with bayonets affixed forward in unison, yelling. Each camp had their own banner and their entrances were adorned with all manner of signage attesting to their home state and town. Each camp had pens for their horses and even larger tents for storage. Wherever there was a rise, at the top would be a flag post surrounded by cannons on heavy wagon wheels and men on small towers waiving colored flags to seemingly no one in particular. So much were the men and their wares it's as if multitudes of family arrived unannounced at one's doorstep reckoning to stay for a while.

On those roads as we passed the camps, Papa was very careful not to call too much attention to himself though always tipped his hat when he saw officers. It was his way of paying respect and fitting in, but for those who did not yet know Papa, there were looks of scorn. Maybe they saw us as some sort of traitorous beast, or as possible spies for secessionists that they had come to rid this state of before they went back to their homes. I do remember the dust, oh how thick it was, much more so than on the plow, as every so often on those trips a long column of cavalry would pass us kicking up clouds of dust that would choke us so, leaving us caked for the rest of the day. On reaching the heights, I was caught almost without breath as we gazed out over the scene below. Washington was dotted with flags from every high point, the white Capitol on the hill nearly blocked by smoke that was belching from camps surrounding them. The Potomac was filled with all manner of boats, traders and warships going this way and that. Most imposing were the large camps that had sprung up on the palisades and at the base of both the Aqueduct and Long bridges; each had their own flags, cannon with men, horse and wagon going in and out. How were we to make sense of all this commotion? Papa it seems had seen it before and knew where his place was.

We went along the last of the Wagon Road down passing forts with names like Cass, Woodbury, Corcoran, Story, Anderson and the like. Papa told me many of these were named after important commanders who built them or others of high note. I would come to know some of these well in the years to come. Before long we reached the Alexandria canal loading point which was now more of a lot for storing goods with the imposing Fort Runyon only a few hundred yards away. The Aqueduct Bridge from Georgetown had been drained for foot and wagon traffic in the months before the invasion, starved the Alexandria canal becoming nothing more than feted pools of stagnant water. It seemed a sad end to Papa's long dreams of riches. Rail now became the new way of sending goods through the county and Papa guessed it wouldn't be long before a rail spur was laid from the Long Bridge to it. We got through our business that day and maybe due to the heat or all the excitement earlier, I fell asleep in the wagon for most of the rest of the trip home. My mind was a whir with everything I had seen, but there was more to experience in those months.

Independence Day was always a time for celebrating, but on this month, it was not to be. Though many had started coming back to church, their mood was growing ever sour. Things were beginning to get more fearful with word of Virginia and Tennessee troops making their way closer to the Falls Church and we heard of big battles in Kentucky and the Ohio Valley. The Federals responded in kind with many more men, mostly from New York swelling the ranks at Camp Union. Folks with secessionist feelings stayed pretty much in their homes to grouse and that suited Papa just fine. They had brought this turmoil with them and what sentiments did remain were kept in private lest they'd be arrested. The Union Army meant business and was keeping discipline high for its men with soldiers arrested regularly for drunkenness, being unkempt or gambling.

The War Department sent out an Order that set a bad tone for us allowing the Army to do as they wished with any property, real or personal seized for military purposes and could pay blacks for work on the camps and forts. It was clear the Union was letting us know who was in charge. Within a week Union cavalrymen were making patrols throughout our hills and even at times to the Falls Church itself. They weren't just strangers across the next hill, these troops were along our roads and trails almost every day. Yet the Army was trying to get things regular and began allowing farmers to sell their crops in Alexandria and Washington. They had also eased up on their bridge passes to and from Washington allowing the merchants to get back to business. Even the canals were filled and reopened, having been drained for the invasion, to help get goods in and about our area.

Nearly every day Union troops made their way atop the Hall's roof on account of it being the highest point on our hill to stare through the spyglass at the *"rebels"* atop

Minor Hill and a little further south on the hill at Upton's farm. Union commanders and even Hall himself would be up there spying the enemy. The thought of being within sight of the rebels caused all sorts of excitement in Washington and almost every day important Government men and other officers made their way atop the Bazil's home to do the same. These visitors would be so bold as to wave banners and handkerchiefs at the rebels less than a mile away, only to have them return the courtesy. This sort of thing went on for weeks and many of the local men and boys would do the same later in the day when the visitors had gone. Some of us girls, and a couple of the Belles even got a chance to look a bit after church and to my surprise, yes indeed these rebels were looking at me as well. I dared not wave on account of being quite improper, but Elizabeth hushed me up and began waving her kerchief and blowing kisses at "our boys" as she called out. It was quite inappropriate and old man Hall, who was none too happy, shooed us off his roof.

By mid-July, what had been troops in our lands to protect the capitol had now begun to prepare for war. Few if any folk ventured far outside their farms. Papa kept to his rounds to Camp Vanderwerken and to the Aqueduct Bridge, but not much further. We learned that Alexandria City was no longer closed and there was brisk travel to and from Washington. There were over a thousand men being treated in hastily set up hospitals in Alexandria while five times as many in Washington. Through the papers we learned that Southern troops, were gathering further west toward the Fairfax Courthouse and their scouts were in our area almost daily. Folks were scared that all-out war would be upon us at any time. Musket fire was now becoming routine as there were skirmishes between New York troops and state militia scouts and pickets near the Balls Crossroads, Chain Bridge and just to the west of Minor Hill. Until now, no one believed there would be death, but as the skirmishes became more regular, the fear grew even more. For Union folks there was a rebel raiding your home and for secessionists, a Yankee behind every tree.

Less than two months after coming to our shores, the Union Army, no doubt goaded by Northern firebrands and the papers to do something about the *rebel* problem, went to war. At mid-month, New Yorkers at Camp Vanderwerken with other District troops who came across the Chain and Long Bridges marched toward the Tavern lands to meet up with other troops for what we all dreaded was to come. Rumors swirled, but Papa had it on good account that the whole Union Army, some thirty-five thousand men were going to advance on the rebels camped near the Manassas railroad Junction some twenty-five miles away. Danny was there with me, and before long Eveline came up to our place to see the sight. After a bit we decided to see more of the spectacle, sitting on the bluff overlooking the tavern fields at the wonder before us, a mass of men, horse, wagon and cannon.

Elizabeth and Cornelia were standing there on the next ridge, no doubt with less enthusiasm. The boys wanted a closer look, so they made their way down to the Wagon road, and against Danny's scolding, we followed them. We heard cheers from folks lining the road for the men on their noble cause as they marched to the county line and beyond. Could it be that this was to be the last chapter in this sad story? Were these secessionists getting their doings for all the mess this spring? Most of the talk was about how our men were going to whoop up on the rebels and put an end to this rebellion. These long lines of men were marched out of Washington to war along the Georgetown-Fairfax Road, with most in crisp blue uniforms and stiff flags with their marching bands playing.

It was hard to tell one group from another except for

the colors of their standards. I saw regiments mostly from New York, but there were others from Pennsylvania Michigan, Washington, and even a state called Wisconsin. From what we heard, these brave men were to meet up with others coming up from Alexandria to march westward to somewhere near the village of Centerville close to the Manassas railroad junction. All the roads through the county were jammed with men, horses and carriages of all sorts and so long that the precession ended up lasting almost three days.

It was mid-morning by the time the last of the troops and their wagons, some with lettering that said "Lowe's Balloon" had gone from sight. I wonder if the mere sight of this army would be enough to put this all to rest without a shot being fired. Only God knows I said. These men don't seem to be leaving for good on account I could see that their tents were still at their camps. We made our way back home to tell Papa what we saw, but by the time we did, there were men gathered at the corner talking about the troop march. Not a shot would be fired, someone quipped. The Rebels would just leave at the sight of this Union Army another said, but Doc knew better. Nothing good was gonna come of this and that folks itching for a fight these past months were soon to get it! I'm telling you all to be prepared for the carnage that would befall us all should the fight come our way, he said. Folks we no longer smiling like they had been.

A day or so later we heard the sounds of cannons in the distance. Papa, is that the war? Had the killing begun? Would we have to leave? Papa just stared westward. War is a cold, evil thing that never settles anything. We shouldn't fret as we were good folk and citizens of this State he said. We will pray for the best, but be prepared for the worst. If the fighting came here, it wouldn't be a good place for children and young ladies, so I'll send you across the river with the others until this all blew over. Nothing of the sort, I piped up, much to his surprise. My place is with you! Papa just smiled, but I knew he was worried.

That Sunday from atop Hall's Hill, we saw carriages filled with well-heeled folk from the District, no doubt wanting to see the coming spectacle, heading west along the Wagon Road and still others along the Little Falls Road. Papa heard that Union troops skirmished with Confederates at the Fairfax Courthouse and that there would soon be a trouble someplace near the prized Manassas Junction. There would soon be plenty more to hear about as by mid-morning, as we listened to Cox's sermon, we could hear the rumble of endless cannon fire which made the Reverend pause every once in a while as he collected his thoughts. Even in church the war couldn't be ignored. It was like the rumble that thunder makes when it was real far away, but in short bursts with claps every so often.

The rumble went on all morning as folks boasted of about what had gone on that week and the whooping the rebels were going to take. For us girls, it was a chance to meet and talk but there was such an air of dread over all us knowing that a battle was coming. Oddly, the Belles did not see fit to come to church that day. Did they know something we didn't? The cannon fire didn't die down until well past supper and started up in earnest by mid-morning and went on for nearly thirty hours. Then finally, on Wednesday afternoon around 4 o'clock, the thunder stopped. Doc told Danny and Barbara to stable the horses, fill the water troughs and prepare extra dressings. Dressings? For what? Barbara exclaimed. For those poor wounded souls coming home he said.

It began raining that day and it was long after supper when we heard the clatter as horses and wagon began coming back eastward along the Little Falls Road. Others had seen the same along the Wagon Road. By late night and all throughout the next day, in a pouring rain we saw men on foot, at first a trickle, but soon there was a streams of them, no longer in orderly columns, but staggered with worry on their faces as if they had seen the devil. Other groups were more orderly, but not in crisp step as they were a few days ago. As more passed the corner on their way back to their camps, I saw up close broken men with sullen looks on their faces. Some were without jackets or muskets of any kind, dirtied from some unknown ordeal.

Papa and George brought pails of water with ladles to the fence all night and all day the next, offering it to whoever would take. I had never seen such a sight. Many collapsed from exhaustion there as they drank, some crying, others angry and a few with bandages, stained blood and all soaking wet from the rain. I nearly fainted from the sight, but gathered my wits and went closer to help Papa and George care for these men. One exhausted soldier said that it had been nearly thirty hours of fighting with no rest or food. Few had water till they reached the Falls Church station at sunup. Another said the Federals had the rebels in their grips and were giving them a good whipping all morning and into the afternoon. Those Wisconsin boys of the *84th* gave it their all, then it all turned in a moment and our lines broke. He said that they were ordered to retreat and regroup later and by then it all fell apart. We weren't sure, but many said the rebels were right on their heels and that we'd all best get to the safety of the forts and let those heavy guns take care of those dammed rebels. How could this be that the mighty force we so happily saw off to battle return now a broken shell bested by rebel militia? We slept uneasy that night, but the rebels never came.

A day or so later the Washington papers, but not in the Gazette, reported the disgrace that took place near the Manassas junction by the Union Army at the hands of those rebels. There was now a deep fear that fresh from their victory, the rebels would come marching through our lands on their way to attack Washington. Those fears were put aside as someone said lookouts in some floating contraption kept a good eye on the rebels and reported that they weren't making any way toward us. This was good news as the Federals had fallen back to the safety of the camps. Before the Manassas affair, Virginia militiamen were camped just west of Falls Church, seemingly content with harassing the Union Army camped in our midst.

The Army outposts in our county it seems were merely a side show to bigger things as the Union was on the march to Richmond. Now the rebels were many, well-armed and fresh off their victory, with the Union Army busy licking their wounds and doubling their efforts to protect the capitol. There was no hiding it, we were now living in enemy territory. The Army made it clear to all that they would not tolerate locals giving support to the rebels and sent out another General Order to arrest all disloyal male citizens within or near the lines, and that meant the men around here. Folks could take the oath of allegiance to the Union and remain in their homes. Those that didn't would be treated as spies or those who broke the oath would be shot and their property taken. Any talk amongst folks living in the lines of the enemy was not allowed. These were serious words and no one wanted to test the Union Army's resolve.

That week we lost our gathering place as our precious Olivet succumbed to the war. As men slowly marched to the county, every empty home or farmhouse, anyplace that was just off a main road was taken by the Army to use as a hospital. Even Vanderwerken's place at Falls Grove fell victim and could not be spared. Late in the evening retreating troops rushed into the house to get out of the rain and to treat their wounded. Cornelia Golden and Sarah told us a week later that the whole family had to rush upstairs and lock their doors holed up with a shotgun until the next morning. Our beloved Olivet became a makeshift hospital for the sick and wounded. There were men laying all about its grounds and the worst were no doubt inside being tended to. The constant screaming and moaning could be heard all day and especially at night. It was horrible to hear and worse to think of the suffering as men were dying or having their limbs sawed off to save them. Doc offered to help the Army with those poor boys and stayed at the Olivet all night long. Our little gathering place had a new purpose, and the burial ground with what few locals were there was now being readied for many more New Englanders who were to make their eternal rest on Virginia soil. So about a year after its finish, the Olivet was no longer ours. After that third Sunday in July, no one around here ever stepped into the Olivet again.

That last week in July seemed to embolden the secessionists when about seven-hundred men of an Indiana Regiment were returning from a march west when they wandered into Falls Church and were all captured by Rebel cavalry. Such boldness was not so easily hidden and the papers made light of it bringing further shame to the Union commanders. With such a threat to its troops and to the capitol, the Union Army decided it was time to push to the major hills in the county. It was all too much for Vanderwerken. With two forts nearby protecting the Chain Bridge, hundreds of soldiers camped and milling about his home and fearing an errant musket or cannon ball, Gilbert decided to move his family to their home in Georgetown. Sarah and Cornelia would be gone, probably not seen again until the war ended. With so many troops in and about his farm and with the blood of Union men still fresh on his floors, to keep Falls Grove from ruin, he offered it to Union General Hancock to use as a headquarters. All he asked was for the Army look after his home and orchards and the fine grove of trees. The General, as I recall, used the two-story carpenter shop as his headquarters, preferring instead to keep the fine home as his own.

All that summer, it seems the secessionists and their southern protectors were itching for another fight, especially so after the rout at Manassas. All month, there were skirmishes reported whenever Union troops went out on patrol past the tavern, in and around Upton's farm Hill along the wagon road about a mile away and even Munson's Hill a few miles further to the south, those being the other two high points for rebels to spy on union troop goings on. It was only a matter of time until something more serious happened and it came that last week in August which put most of us in fear for our lives. Two companies of the 23rd New York Elmira regiment were sent out to put an end to the secessionist harassing beyond the tavern on the wagon road to Fairfax. To their surprise they found about six hundred secessionist troops waiting for them. Musket fire could be heard throughout the two hills. As Papa heard it told to him, the New Yorkers retreated orderly in the face of such a large rebel force with their one dead and some wounded. The dead New Yorker was a young man named Carroll from their home town, said to be so full of life and very popular with his regiment. Another soldier was wounded in the neck and had a finger shot off. I said a prayer for the young soldier that Sunday with Papa as we sat to supper.

We'd pass the Olivet often hoping that it'd be returned to us soon, but the Army had seen fit to keep the it and although we saw less of the Manassas wounded there, having been sent to larger hospitals in Washington and Alexandria, broken soldiers were now replaced with supplies stored in our school room. Weeks went by and nothing. The Olivet was gone. Reverend Cox, who was still seeing Marietta, was no longer preaching and instead was appointed to be the County Surveyor allowing him to travel freely all throughout the county. Oliver became somewhat the celebrity regaling us all with stories of all the goings on, as our little community was changing all around us. With the Vanderwerken's gone, others began to talk of leaving as well, but some things stayed the same. George kept working a few days a week for the Treasury and would walk the six miles or so to work down the Glebe Road passing the Olivet and seeing all the goings on at the camps then east along the Fairfax road to the Aqueduct Bridge to Georgetown or further down along the river to the store at Mason's Island.

There was no doubt about it, with the Union Army camped close by and rebels less than a few miles away, we were smack dab in the middle of a war and there wasn't a day that went by that we didn't hear of a skirmish or two. New Yorkers from the 14th, 23rd and 25th regiments skirmished and the rebels almost every day somewhere between the Chain Bridge to Upton's Hill and beyond. Shots could be heard somewhere on our lands almost every day with most before breakfast. Every day there was another such story, adding to the fear already in our hearts. The Chain Bridge was especially troublesome. Union troops captured rebels spying on the bridge and holding them at Fort Ethan Allen while a few days later rebel pickets captured a Union Lieutenant and a private after a skirmish with two other privates killed. It had gotten so out of hand that even "Abolitionists" with a penchant for killing were coming from Washington to the bridge with their long hunting rifles to shoot at rebel pickets. Even the tavern itself, the hotbed of secessionist leanings, was not safe having been occupied by Federals by day and Rebels at night.

It seemed the war was getting closer to us with Virginia regulars and militia under a General Longstreet now camped outside Falls Church only a few miles from us. From folks who told it at the Glebe parish, the village was now under secession control using its farms and homes to care for over a thousand sick and wounded and holding those

Union pickets captured throughout the month. This would not sit well with the Union Army and it was a matter of time before things got worse. Papa was right in his fear that there were more skirmishes to come. Most of us around here were afraid to go out lest we got shot as either traitors or Yankee supporters. I saw very little of the girls that month with both armies being so close, skirmishes became more regular coming to a boil with New Jersey troops exchanging fire with those from Virginia and North Carolina on Munson's hill, thank goodness without a death.

August was filled with endless talk about the war, here and afar, reports in all the papers. But most chilling was of men skulking about our homes late in the night. We had such a fright when we heard Eveline was *captured* by the Union Army. The way she told it, she had tired of sitting around the farm and as she often did, took her prized gelding named Ginger out for a ride all the way to the spring. Union men thinking she was a spy riding for the rebel lines stopped her with their rifles drawn. She had forgotten the pass that her Pa had given her so was taken under guard until he could vouch for her. Eveline, ever the head strong could have been killed that day. Her Pa forbade her from riding anywhere past her lands from then on. It was a wonderful story about my friend, the spy.

For the third time calamity was to befall Hall's home with it being the highest point on our hill, was a tempting target for the rebels. The raids and patrols, as frightful as they were, were nothing to what happened on a quiet night the second week in September when the war came to our homes. Seeing another poorly defended prize before them rebel troops at Upton's farm made a run for Hall's Hill. Troops from the Alexandria regiment under a local man Colonel Corse, the same men who had been had been chased from the city that first night of the invasion, had now gathered his rebels at Falls Church and planned to take our hill. Just after supper time on a Saturday, Papa was out on a long run while I was tending to chores hoping to see Eveline a bit later. I was in for a sight that no one, except maybe the Belles had ever thought would come our way. Most of the men had caught wind of the militia's plans from folks who were leaving the Falls Church. Cavalry from the Alexandria Militia regiment with a couple of cannons came east from Upton's Hill along the Wagon road toward the Glebe road firing at Union pickets until they got to the tavern, but they didn't stop there. Raiding parties then rode up the Glebe Road past our place, hollering and shooting at anyone with a gun in their hand or in Union blue. I ran to the barn to calm the spooked horses. I saw smoke coming from around the Olivet and just froze with fear. I was in the middle of a war.

These brigands bent on destruction, and like horsemen of the apocalypse, set fire to Mr. Hall's home, a few of his haystacks and one of his sheds all the while holding folks at bay with their guns drawn. I recognized a few of the men from gatherings at the Olivet, but things just were happening too fast. Their leader gave all a stern look and then with a shot from his revolver as quickly as they came turned and rode off headed north along the Glebe toward Mary Hall's house where they tried to set it ablaze. By the time I reached the hilltop the flames at Hall's place had spread with men and wagons making their way to the hell before us. Someone rang a farm bell to warn the rest of the community but it was for naught as all could hear the firing going on. Folks were helping get water buckets from the troughs while others grabbed shovels and rakes to work the flames and embers. It was quite a sight with everyone helping a neighbor in his time of need, not seen since the building of the Olivet itself.

Before long about a hundred Union troops and just as many cavalry and had come up from the crossroads and some from Camp Vanderwerken halting the rebel advance and now lent their help to fight the fires, but it was too late for Hall's place. How could this be? Were we to now witness fighting in our homes, too? Soldiers were rushing about with their officers barking orders I couldn't understand. Everyone else had left the roads, put their livestock into barns and shuttered their windows and I did what I could for our home. Barbara was yelling from her porch for me to come over, but I yelled back that I was fine and that if things got bad, I would be right over. A part of me wanted to bear witness to it all, to be the one telling Papa of how I watched over our home during all this.

I hurried over to the split rail at the edge of the farm looking over to the soldiers scurrying about the Hall property. Not more than five minutes later from somewhere near the spring in a grove of trees, a muffled rap of cannon shot rang out with men yelling to take cover. I didn't know what that meant or what to think, but within an instant the whoosh of cannon shot could be heard as these instruments of death made their way across our farms and a moment later a loud bang and a cloud of dust and smoke billowed up as the shot found its mark on Hall's property. The blast took my breath away and it may have been a second or a minute later to regain my wits as I watched the Union officers yelling orders to their men as if in a dream. And then another shot. This one whooshed away from the hill and not a moment later exploded on Vanderberg property. Oh my God..Eveline! None of us had done anything to deserve this. Soon there was another cannon shot which found its mark amidst men on Hall's Hill. There were screams the likes of which I had never heard. I tried to cover my ears but it was no use, the explosions forced their way through my hands and into my head. It was all that I could bear and ran crying back to my home, locking the door and cowering in the corner. All I could think of was Eveline, her sisters and her parents. What was to become of us?

The cannon fire soon ended and even as far as I was from the road, I could hear men barking orders, buglers rallying their men and screams from the wounded. Death had now come to our door steps. I couldn't take much more and ran to Doc's place to the comfort of Danny and Miss Barbara who were panicked with fear as well. I stayed there for a while hearing the sounds of men on horseback, wagon and of gunfire in the distance. George came in and said the troops were rallying and were moving out to confront the rebels from Upton's hill. There were wounded, and maybe even some killed at Hall's place and they would likely be needing help. Doc, George and Barbara got their things to go over and see how they could help, telling me to stay put lest I get killed and Papa be left alone.

They left and I began thinking about Eveline and her kin. I needed to know if she was hurt, so I ran out across the field to her place. When I got past the orchard and almost to the house, I saw Eveline and her mother sitting on the steps to the kitchen very upset. Mr. Vanderberg was not about and neither were the other girls. I yelled as loud as I could when Eveline looked. We ran to each other crying with both joy and fear in our eyes. Her Mama yelled to us to come inside to the cellar lest there be more shooting. She told me they had just set for dinner when they heard the cannon fire and were hurrying to the cellar when all of a sudden a shell landed next to her home in the woods cutting a tree in two. Her father then told everyone to leave the house and head for the orchards thinking troops were aiming for his house mistaking it for a target. There they huddled at the well protected by its stone until the shooting stopped. I babbled on like a dolt, my heart racing a mile a minute telling them how Federals had come to Hall's home to fight off a rebel attack and now they were moving toward Upton's farm. I told them Doc, George and Barbara were helping tend to the wounded. I stayed there for a while to console Eveline, and myself really, and before long they told me that I'd best get back home before dark lest Papa be worried when he got home.

Rebel anger came to our homes that day as not only was Bazil's home set on fire, but also those of William Libscomb, Sam Birch and Mary Hall. Smoke could be seen from the ridge atop Hall's Hill attesting to the carnage. Not everyone was helping though, as I ran home to help and bring more buckets to fight the fires at Bazil's place. Thank goodness the backside of Hall's roof was nearly level with the hill which allowed men to climb it easily to get water directly on the fire. It wasn't too much time before the house fire was nearly out, but those at the shed and hay stacks raged on and pretty much burned up. I looked up the Leesburg Road and saw the Belles and some of their Minor clan in a wagon staring at the carnage before them. Not one of them had a worried look on their faces. In a fit of pique I yelled at Marietta, asking if she were going to help, waiting for a response I knew would not come. She looked at me with her arms folded and smiled, as if some sort of justice had come to punish us. Before long, they turned their wagon and left. I knew then that their anger toward the Union was more than just talk. They had turned their back on their neighbors and from then on in my mind the Belles were not to be trusted.

By the late evening, the Wunders had come home, their clothing a mess with dirt and blood, exhausted from tending to the men hurt at Hall's place and those across the valley as the fight moved south. Papa came to the Wunder's with such a fright on his face as he had been home and didn't see me there, now sobbing as we both hugged each other. We spent most of the night recounting the horrors of the day, all the while hearing horse and wagon taking wounded and able men back to their camps. The next morning we came to learn a Union officer and a few of his men were killed in the skirmish to push back the rebels. Two men from Virginia and Maryland militias were killed and the rest chased back across the Four Mile Run.

Our hill was safe for now and out of the reach of the rebel six-pounders as folks called them being what their shells weighed, that were probably back on Upton's hill. In the next few days the Gazette ran wild with stories of over a hundred Union and twenty Rebels wounded or killed in the fight but these were merely boasts, though men had been wounded, Union and Militia both. We heard from others of their dealings that day; the Febrey's said God must have been with them for as they sat down for supper, their table leg had been shot out by an errant musket ball, but it didn't stop them from saying grace and finishing their meal. For me it was to be another loss as, having seen enough and fearing for the girls, Gilbert was going to send them to live at their boarding house in Washington off I Street. Now I would be alone with no one around me my age to talk to.

We had all been told on first day of the invasion that the Union Army was here to protect us from the secessionists so long as we helped, or at least did not get in the way. Yet, our homes had been attacked and to us the Union Army seemed indifferent. The complaints piled up and before long a crowd of men came to Camp Union's gate yelling that this injustice would not stand. A few officers came to see them and told them "Rest assure, the National forces would take care of these secessionist elements in due time", and implored folks to go back to their homes. These were not comforting words to most. What was a problem between the Union and the secessionists was now ours and we were caught in this whirlwind with no one sure what was next. Papa was so angry at all this turmoil and the irony of it all. At the same time we were being fired upon by rebels, the Union Army had seen fit to issue a Special Order #17 from General McClelland himself calling on all forces under his command to not fire on rebel pickets lest for defense and to respect the Sabbath, halting work and warring, declaring this to be a holy war. One side it seems felt it more righteous than the other and from what I saw it was all evil pure and simple. For McClellan to order his troops not to fire on the rebels told us that wasn't gonna be a war around here, yet here we were in the midst of one. What were these Generals seeing that we weren't? The papers called our nightmare *"The Battle of Munson's Hill"* as if some glorious thing, but for us it was destruction in our own midst. The rebels soon abandoned Munson's hill, retreating for the Fairfax courthouse while New Yorkers of the 37th took their place on the hill. As if this rebel injustice wasn't enough, they ended up further embarrassing the Union by looting and pillaging homes about the hill in their own right much to the dismay of everyone. There was now plenty of shame to go around. Something had to be done.

About a week or so later, one of the two forts commanding the bluffs above the Chain Bridge, named after the revolutionary war hero Ethan Allen, was finished with the locals invited to join in the formal flag raising. Papa, myself, Danny, and George went by wagon for the festivities and get a good look at it. Before long the Glebe road was clogged with all manner of troops from the camps. We saw most folks there including Madame Hall riding in a beautiful black and red carriage. She had spoken to some about moving soon to Washington, "to better tend to her affairs there", but it seemed right to get away from this turmoil. I think most everyone wished they too could just get away. The fear of war and death made one grow weary, and it ate at our souls. Seeing the completion of such a war machine in our midst was kind of comforting to some, but for Papa and me, it was a trumpet call of things to come.

The fort was just off the Glebe Road before the bluffs to the Chain Bridge after it joined with the Little Falls Road. On the way there we saw what looked like thousands of troops camped on Vanderwerken land at Falls Grove. It was such an impressive sight with hundreds of troops arrayed in nice rows, but the fort itself was even more imposing. The land for nearly half a mile was cleared of trees in every direction from the fort affording a clean line of fire to the enemy. Civilians like us were halted just off the road to witness the ceremony.

The fort's commander spoke eloquently commending the men of the 2nd and 3rd Vermont and 79th New York infantry for its glorious completion. The officer went on to tell those gathered of its prowess to defend the approaches to the Nations' capital with nearly 800 yards worth of thick log walls and thirty-nine large cannon to more than match anything the rebels could throw their way. We sat for a spell staring in awe at this instrument of war with its large and imposing walls, deep troughs around them, large guns and men pacing along its edges. It seemed odd to me that such an imposing place would be needed in our midst. Until the home burnings by brigands, there were only a few skirmishes. I wasn't sure what enemy the Union Army felt the need to guard against, but clearly, the Manassas affair had spooked the Union leaders.

September proved to be another frightful month. After the rebel raid and the burning of both Hall's and Birch's homes there were almost daily reports of more rebel troop movements to our area. Folks were fearful of being outside, children were kept inside, but work had to be done and folks did what they could to get through the day. Thank goodness our farms were yielding good crops, but for many who had made their lives selling goods in Washington City, it was getting harder to bring those crops to market on account of the army closing so many roads and making folks get passes for even the least bit of travel. The Union Army sent out an Order #13 keeping all civilians and officers from visiting farms in what they called the occupied areas and started closing off wagon traffic across the Chain Bridge except for a few times a day. At night they had lifted boards from its roadway to keep rebel cavalry from making a run into the city.

Folks now looked to the camps to sell their wares and supplies, but this came at a price as most in these camps could only pay with script, and at much reduced prices. Papa was getting well known as a reliable teamster hauling goods between the camps as well as his regular runs to the river. There was no money to be had, except for the chits the Union Army gave. So folks didn't see much for their labor unless an officer paid with something other than these chits. Most of the enlisted troops had no money to speak of and what little they had was probably being sent home or spent in the camps for gambling.

The main rebel camp was just this side of Manassas but there were many others and some pretty close to our homes. Since the Manassas affair, there were many rebels camped at Falls Church and most folk there had fled their homes fearing a fight between them and the Union Army. And there were a few skirmishes as the New Yorkers camped at Upton's farm were chased off the hill by rebel troops under command of the Colonel Jeb Stuart. During the fight, we heard that two cannon shells were lodged in the walls of Upton's home, their fuses did not explode leaving these horrid weapons to sit in wait. By now there were many more groups of rebels west of the Ball's Crossroads along the wagon road across the Four Mile Run. The run became the line between the two though few ventured near the creek lest they become targets for each other's snipers. We told Papa that on our runs to the spring, we saw rebels perched atop Minor Hill likely keeping an eye on us and the troops at Camp Vanderwerken. Clearly the Minors had something to do with this and Papa warned me to stay away from the spring and not stray too close to Minor Hill lest there be trouble. The Belles even boasted that the militia was building its own fort atop Minor Hill bigger and better than anything Mr. Lincoln's men could do.

Things were getting more worrisome as militia cavalry even made a brazen raid on Munson's Hill just outside the county line south east of us on the road to Alexandria City chasing federal pickets from the area, killing six. The young folk got together a dared a berry tramp near the spring, when we saw Federal cavalrymen come up from Camp Vanderwerken scouting the area past the Little Falls road then heard gunfire coming from Minor Hill. We learned later on these were New York cavalry, calling themselves the Highlanders, had rode to Minor Hill seeing earthworks with cannon atop it as they headed west. They got into it with the rebels and were cut off by their fire, fighting their way back to camp wounding the horse of the commander's aide.

Papa told us that more Union men were coming across the Chain Bridge every day making the fields of the Vanderwerken land their new home, and not just New Yorkers, but even some from as far away as Wisconsin. This should have been of comfort to many, but no matter how many troops had come, the night was not safe for anyone to be about. Militiamen were making more raids into our lands and not afraid to capture anyone who they deemed disloyal to Virginia. One night we heard of a sergeant and a private from Massachusetts on picket duty were surprised and taken prisoner by militia men.

The two armies were like giants nearing to squaring off with Confederate General Longstreet's headquarters now just outside Falls Church not more than five miles away from General Hancock's headquarters near us at Falls Grove. Things were just too frightening living in a war zone. After that last tramp, folks rarely went out of their homes during the day except to tend to the fields or flock while children stayed at home locked inside. Worse was at night where folks slept on the floors of their homes offering some safety from a stray musket shot. I didn't see much of the girls that month and Papa was now making sure he was home from his runs well before sundown; and when he could not come home he would stay over at another's house or barn. Those nights when he was gone scared me the most not knowing if Papa was safe before seeing him the next day.

Papa had begun to shorten his routs a bit, making runs to visit the commanders of these new camps and offering his services where he could. It was hard at first, but word got around of Papa's good reputation so after a few visits, the quartermaster sergeants began to give him hauls between the camps. The Army it seems was here in our midst to stay for a while as it prepared for war. For many folk, these *"protectors"* from faraway lands were uninvited guests that we kept up appearances to stay on their good side, but at some point, their welcome just brought more trouble. We were not always seen as helpless farmers on the outskirts of Washington, but as Virginians not to be trusted and in their shoes I guess we would feel the same. That said, some of our neighbors, especially those west of the spring, seethed with the notion of these men on our lands telling us what they could do and not do. There was an uneasy peace amongst those of us that lived on these two hills, but it would only take a spark like a misplaced remark to light the fuse.

7 DEADLY SNAKES

By the end of September of '61, Papa had now become a staple amongst the camps near the taverns in the south and at Camp Vanderwerken by the Chain Bridge in the north. Though it wasn't much, camp supplies mostly like tents, cots, fuel oil, horse tack, linens and such; it did allow Papa to run his wagons through the upper reaches of the county and once a week to Alexandria City. Occasionally, Papa would haul items for the officers when they transferred. Much of this had no real military value for fighting a war, and that was fine with Papa lest he be stopped by *sessech* scouts. I would go with him on those where I had to read the manifests or to cash in the chits at the Alexandria City Quartermaster headquarters.

It almost became routine. Three days a week in and around the camps in the north, one day down to the Canal wharfs and one day to Alexandria city. We became witness to it all. The forts became larger with more guns and troops. Camps were decorated with fancy gates and fencing as if they were moving in permanently and the roads more traveled by troops and horse. The trains that ran out of the newly built round house in Alexandria were loaded with all manner of troops and war goods. On our trips Papa would learn about troop movements in faraway places no one had heard of. For good or for bad, folks were eager for news and Papa became somewhat the local story teller to an ever growing crowd of eager folk every week at the corner fence.

In the three months since the invasion, our county had become the jumping off point for the war. Every week, thousands of troops from all over the North would come by special troop trains and some by ship to Washington, be put into groups, regiments and the like, then marched across the Long Bridge to large camps in and about Arlington Heights, Jackson City, and Alexandria City. These men, boys mostly, would be disciplined and trained to fight, marching and drilling endlessly and then after some months packed and loaded onto trains to meet their fate somewhere in rebel lands. There were so many, that one could barely recognize them from the lot. A few months ago I would nary look up at them when I dressed in farmhand cloths lest they recognize me as a girl, but now we were amongst them day for day, almost like living inside this great beast. I could now look a few in the eye as we passed them on long roads. These were all Union men, but many spoke strangely making them hard to understand. Some still looked at us with scowls as if we were the enemy, others were of a tawdry sort trying to catch my eye when Papa was not near suggesting all manner of vulgar things. Most though were kind, bringing their good manners with them to our lands. These men were caught up in this biblical event, looking for adventure and hoping to make a name for themselves. For many, there was a yearning in their eyes and a stutter when they spoke to me, hoping that maybe they might find a belle in these southern lands to take home once this awful war was over.

Soldiers worked hard to make their camps feel like

home while their commanders were eager to get at the rebels after the events this month. Riding with Papa I watched as they drilled these men endlessly day and night. I felt pity for them, but Papa told me it was best they be readied for war lest they make poor account of themselves to the friends and neighbors they had signed up with, and to their families back home. Traveling through the camps made good and bad impressions on me. There were large camps with all manner of goods laid about. Tents were laid out in neat and orderly rows, rifles in groups neatly near the camp fires all attesting to might of this Army. Yet looking closer, one saw misery and despair amongst men far away from the comforts from whence they came. The beast of war would consume men in many ways. Most I come to learn were not at the hand of the enemy, but of things more dreadful. Nearly every day we heard word of men falling and some even dying of sickness or accident and there was sure to be more once winter set in. It had been a very wet September, and many were far away from the comforts of their homes living in small tents at the mercy of the winds, rain and the mud of the open fields. Mr. Hall told how he saw New York men steal a door and other good plank from his storage shed. He followed them to let their commanders know about their thievery, when he was taken by the sight. The men were living in damp and uninviting tents, patched together within with all manner of cloth, barely closed to the elements. Things had gotten so bad; they were using these stolen goods to raise their bed rolls above the muddy ground. The anger he felt went away as he could not see himself bringing these men to account and just turned and left.

There would be more such stories, but before long, there would be worse threats upon men than musket and cannon. It was all too much for many. Others were following Vanderwerken's lead and moving away. Mrs. Vanderberg, Cornelia and Maria left too for the safety of the District to run their boarding house, leaving Eveline and her

Pa here for a while to get things settled. We were in the midst of an armed camp and all of us were always under suspicion. Smith Minor, fearing for his family's safety, and with the Union knowing of his vote, moved his family and his seven slaves to Washington. We heard later that when his slaves were to be freed, Smith had the nerve to petition the Government for his loss of property and even called for George and one of the Ball men to testify on his behalf as they were loyal Unionists, but once the Federals found out about Smith's vote, they turned down his petition. At least there was some justice in all this affair.

There were other wonders of the new military wares that were all the talk. There was one that set the path to Papa's sickness, then his death, leaving me alone. In early July we were told that a large bag, bigger than a house, was raised in Washington to prove to the War Department the benefits of hoisting a man in the air. The silk bag was turned upside down filled with air that held a large basket below with a man inside it and raised it hundreds of feet into the air. Folks around here told us they saw it while looking from atop Minor Hill but at that time we didn't pay them much mind. The papers wrote of the President being shown this and it seems these "balloons" as they were called, had been to his liking and now he put them to use watching the rebel goings on.

A bit later, one of these balloons was raised again in the District and this time many could see it from atop Hall's home. We saw one of these balloons raised high near the Arlington Heights just after the battle at Bull Run near the Manassas Junction, no doubt looking to see if the rebels were advancing to Washington. On that last Saturday in August, we got word that the army was fetching to launch one at the field aside the tavern. Papa and I got the wagon to go see for ourselves and took as many as we could hold. Eveline and Danny joined me and we were going to make a day of it.

We saw for ourselves such a marvel. About a dozen wagons with soldiers and city men surrounded what looked like large silk blankets on the ground. Large baskets that could fit two or three men were at the side with much linen cord. Hoses, bigger than those seen in city fire brigades, were coming from the wagons to the bags. On the side of the wagon was written "Professor Thaddeus Lowe", the same name we had seen on some wagons heading west for that battle in July. Papa was told that this professor was the head of these contraptions, calling himself an *"Aeronaut"* and that this balloon was called "Union". The wagons made a special kind of gas that blew up the bags, like the kind that ran in the gas lamps in the city. It took three hours or so to fill these large silk bags to where they stood on their own taller than anything I had ever seen. Men were tugging hard at the cords to keep the large thing steady while others worked the basket.

Before long an officer and Professor Lowe himself were aloft to the gasps of all being raised ever higher than the tallest trees on our ridge. Not soon after they were so high that we could no longer see their faces. Men around the wagons shouted out a height of a thousand feet. How one could bear such heights was beyond me! Some said they could easily see all the way to the Fairfax courthouse some fifteen miles away. After an hour or so they were hauled back down safely to the cheer of all. The bags were pressed down until all their gas was gone.

That week, the "Union" went up at least once or twice every day and it had been fitted with telegraph wire to report on rebel General Longstreet's troops at Falls Church and beyond and every time one went up, rebels would fire on it, but none were ever hit. Within a week, there was another one named "Intrepid" that was brought in to do the same.

These things were mighty pretty to look at and we were told were made of the finest India silk with linen cordage for lightness and strength with each costing $1500. We got pretty used to seeing them being blown up and raised. Every once in a while these things would tear apart as they were being inflated to the fright of many with a loud whoosh as bags opened. One could only imagine if such a thing happened when one was in the air with someone in it. There were many stories almost daily about these things.

Vanderwerken told us how on a late October evening how one of Lowe's balloons was partly blown up in Washington and led to the Chain Bridge to come over to our side. But when Lowe got there the bridge was crowded with artillery and cavalry heading to the camps. Lowe did the unthinkable and ordered his men to haul that contraption over the top of the bridge trestle. To the amazement of all as they saw men guide the balloon perched on bridge works no more than a foot and a half wide, 100 feet above the river. We heard later that they lost that balloon in a gale and it ended up one hundred miles away in a Delaware field. That was to be one of many times we would deal with these balloons and Papa would come to pay dearly for it. Papa had gone on a run from the camp near the tavern when a sergeant asked if he could haul some supplies from up Georgetown for them the following day. Papa eagerly agreed as it would make for much more cordial relations in his dealings with the other camps.

The next morning, Papa hitched the horses early and was about to leave when I begged him to take me along. There wouldn't be much trouble since he was on official business for the Army, and this would be my first time in Georgetown since the Army closed the bridge to all but the military. It was less about the supplies as I really wanted to see Sarah and Cornelia since they moved there a few months ago. Papa at first didn't want me to go, but then changed his mind thinking it might be good for me to get away from home for a while. He had chores to take care of on account of locals finding out that he was going into Washington asking if he wouldn't mind doing them some favors. Papa could never say no to a neighbor in need, so he burdened himself with half a dozen or so of these *"favors"* and he would need all the help he could to get them done and be back home before the bridge closed at dark. Before we left as I was getting things in order, he said I didn't have to wear the farmhand clothes as he couldn't see me getting to the parlor not dressed proper.

We set along the Glebe Road north a bit then along the Little Falls Road toward Fort Ethan Allen on our way to the Chain bridge. Along the way Papa and I got to talking about all sorts of things and how proud he was of me taking care of things during these trying times while he was away on runs. He also said a few times how sorry he was for putting me in the midst of all this turmoil. I told him not to worry as I could take care of myself. Besides, I was looking forward to us sharing a dish at the parlor in Georgetown.

We passed the camps in and about the Vanderwerken fields and on the Falls Grove property itself seeing the large flagpole that they had put up at General Handcock's headquarters and then a bit later the formidable walls of Fort Ethan Allen. We passed a few guard posts checking Papa's pass and as we got closer I saw the most wondrous thing, the Army had begun cutting a road away from the fort south and east along the thick woods. To where was not clear as there wasn't much through those woods. We got to just the other side of the main gate when Papa asked a guard what he knew of the new road. The Sargent boasted to Papa that the Army was in the midst of building a corduroy road to connect Ethan Allen with the next fort, called Smith south a few miles away. They had begun this work a day or so ago with hundreds of men cutting down the trees and clearing the ground to make a wide road. They laid these cut logs across the road then packed them over with gravel and hard dirt to make it sturdy and smooth. This new *military road* was to stretch for three miles or so.

Papa talked with others about hauling wood from around the fort, but he was as surprised as I that they were nearly done. Papa and I gazed at this marvel, as far as the eye could see, there was a road winding its way to the valley below and then up again around the next ridge. It was made with a firm dirt ground and wide enough for four wagons abreast. Papa asked when the road would be open to haul supplies, but the Sargent told him sternly that this was a military road for Army use and that anyone caught on it without permission would be arrested or shot as a rebel spy. I was shocked at his tone, but Papa paid no mind to these threats, but it seems being left out of this fine effort after working hard to be friendly to the commanders there crossed him a bit and it showed.

Once we got past the last guard post that again checked Papa's pass, our wagon began the treacherous path down to the Chain Bridge. One now had to keep his wits about him to control of the wagon lest calamity befall. The road to the bridge from Ethan Allen ran north along the ridgeline above the creeks leading to the Potomac, snaking back for a while then turning steeply downhill. It was here that Papa had to be careful riding the wagon brake hard to ease the burden on the teams as they stutter stepped their way slowly down the path. Should the horses stumble or fall, or the wheels roll free we would slide helplessly into ditch, a tree or god forbid, over the ridge to our death.

We made it down the first leg of the winding path, soldiers in the rifle pits above us would caterwaul that we'd better be careful lest *Johnny Reb* get us or to bring them back some fine ale and other such nonsense. Papa told me to pay them no mind as we had to keep our wits about us on this leg of the trail. Once off the hill, we made the final turn and got to the bridge which was guarded by more soldiers. Before we got onto the bridge, yet another soldier checked Papa's pass while another kept staring and smiling at me, curling the tips of his thick mustache with his fingers giving me such a chill. My heart beat fiercely as thoughts of the wagon man and what happened to Jessie and Clarisse years ago raced through my head. I forced a smile to the soldier so as to not cause any trouble for Papa. As we sat there, soldiers began placing plank flooring down where sections had been removed to prevent rebel cavalry attacks and all along the bridge, men were posted to keep an eye on travelers lest someone set the bridge afire. Our journey across the bridge was quite a feat for me. I took care not to gaze too much at the river below on account of how high we were. We stopped at the end of the bridge for yet another check by the guards just below the imposing guns manned by District militiamen. After a few pleasantries with the guards, we turned south for the last three miles to Georgetown.

Oh the wonders of being in the District proper. We looked all about as we entered town, excited to be in Washington again as it had been over a year since we had last visited. I was hoping that if Papa had time, once we did our chores and maybe stopped by the iced cream parlor, we would try to visit Sarah and Cornelia. Mr. Vanderwerken also ran some warehouses and a mercantile in Georgetown where he and his family lived during the winters before the war and now they were there for the duration.

Things had changed with so many folks heading about with purpose and soldiers almost everywhere marching in groups and guarding street corners, wharfs and the bridges heading back to Virginia. The barges that once floated down the canals were now sitting still as the Aqueduct Bridge was again emptied of its water. From what I could see, the bridge having long since been drained was a bustle with men and wagons coming in to Virginia. Most all the favors set for Papa were in Georgetown proper at the local shops on M Street and along the waterfront. I was eager to make him proud and make better use of our day, so I pleaded with him to drop me off to get cooking supplies, food stuffs, a few medicines from the apothecary and some clothes items that folks wanted. After some words over my safety, Papa reluctantly agreed and gave me the money folks had given him wrapped in paper with notes on what to get and where. Papa dropped me off on the main road and told me he'd be back by noon to return home, and if there were time would stop at the parlor for a treat. He looked at me sternly and told me to keep my wits about me and never go off with anyone. Things around here were not the same, especially for a young woman. Papa drove off, turning down to the docks toward the warehouses where he was to pick up a few barrels and some other supplies for the Army.

I made it through my list quickly and within a couple of hours I got just about all the things, less a special kerchief Mrs. Wunder wanted that the linen store no longer had on account of the war. I came to see that things were a bit harder to come by and that the prices for some things had been raised as almost to be criminal. I made my way to my last stop at the apothecary to pick up some badly needed ointments, sedatives and ether for Doc and just as I made my way to the door, shots rang out. Folks stopped where they were then ran for safety where they could. There were screams and shouts coming from everywhere. I couldn't count them, but I cowered on the stoop hoping it would all be over soon. The police came out from their station across the street from me with rifles in their hands. They turned and ran toward where folks were pointing down M Street. Before long everyone began making their way to see what was causing all this commotion.

I was hoping that the girls were nowhere close to such madness on account of Cornelia's frailties toward such things. I left the apothecary not wanting to miss anything made my way the block or so to the crowd all about the Vanderwerken's place. I made my way to the front to see what was amiss, to my horror I saw one man caring for another who was bleeding. On the porch were the policemen with guns raised with one of them talking to Gilbert and my friend Charles. I looked up and saw both Sarah and Charlotte in the window looking down while others were scurrying about. I did my best but couldn't catch their eye.

Folks said the cantankerous Vanderwerken, who only last month moved his family to Georgetown on account of fear of being shot by rebels, was being arrested for shooting his neighbor and from the looks of things, pretty near killing him. Gilbert was a difficult man to deal with but shooting a man was another thing. It seemed the man was shot in the basement and made his way to the street before collapsing. Before long the wounded man was taken for help and Gilbert hauled off to the police station. With all the excitement, I lost track of time but not wanting to be late for Papa, I raced to get to the corner before he got there.

The papers reported the scandal the next day that Vanderwerken went before District Judge Reaver for shooting his neighbor George Hill Jr. It seems he and Hill lived next to each other and got into words. Some said it was over a fence that separated the cellars they shared while others said it was over a fence rail at the mercantile. Sarah was called to testify and told the judge that Hill was standing near a large post in the store and demanding to know who tore down his fencing. I guess there were threats made so Gilbert called out to Charles who lived upstairs to bring him his gun. Not long after shots rang out. Gilbert claimed Hill

GEORGE AXIOTIS

shot first and that the bullet almost hit Charles and in response, she said Gilbert shot Hill twice. Hill ran out of the cellar and fell onto the street. Upon hearing the shots a doctor came from across the street as Hill lay there wounded. That must have been the man I saw tending to Hill as he lay there in the street. He not only survived but went before the judge the next day with the papers reporting how strong a constitution he must have had for having been shot the previous day. Dr. Snyder testified that Hill was shot on the left side of his belly, with the bullet passing through his navel and a second bullet had entered the left side of his spine. Gilbert claimed Hill shot first and that his son dodged the bullet thinking it was intended for him. A Police Sargent Newman testified that he examined Vanderwerken's two pistols as well as that of Hill. Charles's pistol had all of its shots fired with Gilbert's gun having fired none. Hill's gun had fired two shots. Sarah must have been wrong or likely talked to by Gilbert himself not wanting to put Charles to task with the authorities for shooting a man.

The judge released Gilbert on a $3000 bail and told him not to leave the District until the trial. I heard later that Charlotte had been the one who had seen it all, having come from school to Gilbert's place, came through the cellar and saw the two men square off and begin shooting. She was never so scared and couldn't bring herself to talk about what she saw for many weeks. His trial came almost a year later and by then so much had happened on account of the war and Gilbert himself being a well-known business man had worked his people so that they ended up in a hung jury. It would not be until after the war that he would be tried again; but I figure nothing came of it, because he lived in the area long after the war.

Papa was late getting to me and had driven the mules hard to get up from the waterfront back onto M Street. He wasn't in too good a mood when he arrived so I climbed aboard not saying much other than what supplies I was able to get for all. He had to stop and water the mules for the drive home further delaying us so it was early afternoon before we got moving. Papa had too much on his mind as we made our way out of Georgetown and there was no time for parlor stops, but that was just the way things happened. We were in a rush to get to the Chain Bridge as our pass across it was only good till sundown. After a while Papa smiled at me and asked if all my chores had gone well and whether I was able to meet up with Sarah. I started talking as if I had not ever done so before, barely catching my breath through it all. Waiving my hands, I asked if he had heard the gunfire and he said yes thinking it was soldiers firing their weapons for practice somewhere along the waterfront. He was so surprised to hear of the shooting at the store, with Charles, Charlotte and Sarah there as parties to it as well; and then Papa was beside himself over my safety. We talked for most of the way to the bridge, but I never even asked him about his hauls. Papa just smiled as he listened to me ramble on and on. It was quite the day for us to that point, but it wouldn't be long before things would change for the worse.

We were in a long line of wagons heading out of Georgetown to the Maryland hills, and after some time only two of them made the turn to the Chain bridge. It seemed odd to me that no one else was headed into Virginia, but come to think of it, we were headed back to the land of the rebels, a place fraught with suspicion and fear. It's almost as if I lived in a land of lepers as we passed each gate and guard stand given the way they looked at us. Some with scorn, and some with pity, saying things like "Say hello to Johnny Reb" or some such thing. Papa paid them no mind and told me not to do so either as we were doing our part for the Union cause. As we were crossing the bridge lined every fifty feet of so with soldiers, I asked Papa if he had gotten all he was asked to get and he said yes and then some. Along with the cloth and canvas needed for the balloon men, the

Quartermaster had given him six barrels of a special liquid almost like water, but not for drinking. These were also to be taken to the Professor Lowe's men at Camp Union. Papa was told to take great care and not to spill the cargo. The chit he was given was nearly half as much more than what was agreed to but Papa was still a bit uneasy hauling some valuable cargo that a stray rebel picket might accost us for. I knew then why Papa was so concerned back in town.

As we got to near the end of the bridge, soldiers began putting boards back on the bridge floor for us to pass over and then took them up when we crossed over. That one thing made me feel so abandoned; left to fend for ourselves until we got to the safety of our home. We began the long climb up the road to Fort Ethan Allen and just as we got to the last two steep turns past the little bridge over the Pimmit Run, the mules got spooked making the wagon lurch and got the front wheel stuck in the culvert. Try as they could, we were trapped and the mules soon began to panic. Papa climbed down to calm them and get some wood below the wheel and help pry us up. Other than a stray soldier in the rifle pits above us there was no one else on the road to help. Papa handed me the reigns to hold with one hand and the brake with the other and told me to hold on good lest we spill the whole load.

The mules were skittish for quite a while and by the time they settled down it was getting past sundown, not a good time for folks to be out while rebel pickets were likely about. Papa began to worry that if we took too long getting the mules free that once past the safety of the fort we would be robbed or worse yet taken as Union collaborators. Either way, it was not a good time for us and I was getting scared inside, but showed none of that to Papa as he worked hard to get branches under the wheel to help pry us up. When ready he yelled for me to get the mules moving, back and forth and side to side we rocked with the mules struggling the whole time and just as I thought we were going to roll over, the wagon broke free. But just as it did one of the barrels slipped free of the rigging, broke through the tail gate and landed in the culvert. Once the mules had calmed down, Papa told me to move the wagon ahead to the next turn on level ground while he attended to the barrel. I was settling the mules and getting the wagon brakes set when I heard Papa yell my name in a wrenching voice. Looking back, Papa was on his knees coughing and wheezing, so I set the brake, jumped off and ran toward him, he desperately waived at me to stop and not come any further.

I didn't understand why he was acting so, but I became scared believing he had hurt himself by the wagon or maybe shot by rebels. He got up real slow and staggered uphill toward me retching and rubbing his eyes. When he got to me, he was pale in the face and his eyes were near swollen shut. He collapsed there and whispered for water. I ran back to the wagon and got my water bottle and gave him some for drink, but he just splashed it on his face. He had a foul stench of rotten egg about him and I kept asking him what was happening as I held back my tears.

After a bit Papa got his bearings and told me something in that barrel had done this to him. What was inside was some sort of elixir that had leaked out on account of the fall. When it hit the damp ground in the culvert it made small clouds like a fine steam and he breathed some of it in. We'd best leave that barrel and be on our way. I helped Papa to his feet and slowly made our way to the wagon, looking back every so often seeing that poison fog get bigger as if it had a life of its own, watching it slowly snake its way down the road toward Pimmit Run.

By the time we got on the wagon and going, it was getting pretty dark and besides Papa's sad state, we had the fort's guards to deal with now that we were out after curfew and maybe rebels to take us prisoner. I rode the mules hard the rest of the way to the guard post at the new military road where we had been early that morning. The guards heard us approach and drew their rifles and yelled at us to halt. I wasn't going to stop and yelled at them to let us through, but they would have none of that. They stopped and surrounded us with their bayonet points staring at us. A corporal came up and looked us over, all the while asking for our pass and why we were out after curfew. I told him something happened to Papa and that I had to get him to see Doc. His questions were all a whirl to me that I could not answer, but he wouldn't let us go thinking maybe were hauling contraband. The corporal told his guards to take us to the fort for questioning and if what we said was true about Papa, maybe we would see the camp doctor.

Papa had gotten a little better by the time we reached the main gate, and after some words with the guards, a lieutenant came up to questioned his corporal on who we were and what happened. Papa was helped down the wagon by the guards, and they commenced to talking. Papa was well known by the officers and a few of the sergeants and they wasted no time getting him to see the camp doctor. I waited with the wagon along with a guard who then started making fancy talk with me, but I had no time for pleasantries, as I wanted to see Papa.

It took some time, but a sergeant came out and looked at the back of the wagon, trying to read what was on the barrels. I asked him how Papa was but he just jumped off the wagon and went back to the camp infirmary in a hurry. I was now bitterly worried and begged the guard to let me go and see Papa, but he would have none of that without orders. I had reached the end of my rope and jumped from the wagon, marching toward the tent where they had Papa when the guard yelled at me to stop lest I be shot. I turned and told him nothing was going to stop me and if he was hell bent on shooting me, then he better do it quick. Before long many more soldiers came over to see what all the fuss was about and began laughing at this guard on his first capture of a rebel. I paid them all no mind and went over to the tent. I saw men tending to Papa on a chair and he was talking to them as best he could. He looked up and saw me and smiled, motioning me to come over. The camp doctor told us that the Papa's lungs got filled with a poison gas from an acid that spilled from the barrel. Papa was lucky in that if he had passed out near the barrel within a few minutes he'd be dead. The doctor ordered Papa to stay put overnight on a cot to rest and let the salve put around his eyes to set in. Papa's lungs were burnt from the acid and would take some time to recover. The *sulfuric acid* as he called it in those barrels was used to make the gas that filled Lowe's balloons and it was dangerous.

I spent a frightful night on a cot next to Papa hearing him wheeze and gasp as he tried to sleep. The next morning we were woken up by the morning bugle call, and after one last visit by the camp doctor, we got aboard our wagon for the last leg home of this strange and frightful journey. The captain asked Papa if we should leave those barrels here at the fort, on account of its danger, but Papa would have none of that. It was our duty to get these supplies back to Camp Union and by golly, Papa was gonna keep his word. So off we went and slowly made our way along the Glebe Road our home, past the Olivet to the fields near the tavern just as the "Union" was being unrolled. It's as if we never missed a step, Papa wheeled up to the wagons gathered about the balloon.

Men came up and unloaded the wagon while Papa went off to talk. I watched as men took one of Papa's barrels and rolled it over to one of Lowe's wagons and pumped its deadly poison into the top which was slowly making this gas filling the big bag. Papa never said what had happened to us saying that he had been stopped at the bridge on account of rebel pickets all about doing his best not to let them see of his ills. He said his eyes were swollen on account of ivy sap getting in and if they believed him or not, it didn't matter. Papa got his pay chit, got aboard the wagon, and wheeled about for home. It was the first time I had seen Papa tell a fib, but when I asked him about it, he said that sometimes we had to do what is needed to help get us through these ordeals. He was right. No one was going to look after us except ourselves. We lived between two hills in the midst of a war.

I got Papa home to Doc and they tended to him for a few days. He had many bad nights and it would be almost a week before Papa was fit enough to continue his rounds. I would lay awake at night hearing him wheeze and thinking of that poison fog snaking its way down that road. Papa was never the same after that day, getting very weak on short runs. Ever since the spill he had gone through severe bouts of the cough and trouble sleeping. It was especially hard in the mornings when it was damp. Papa needed rest, but he could not stop the hauls. There was work to be done, and Papa could not yet bring himself to have me go alone on these runs so I started going with him on long runs and now I had to learn to do all the talking. When he didn't have the strength to go on long hauls, we would stop at farms of acquaintances to rest.

The Union sent out cavalry patrols and scouts from Vanderwerken and Union nearly every day looking for rebels. The burning of three farms, including Hall's at the hands of Virginia militia troops had put these men on alert and they were itching for payback. But they were in lands they didn't know, and their scouts depended on reports from locals to tell them the lay of the land and where the tails were across the many streams and creeks.

That month, the Army decided to press the rebels from the heights much further beyond Minor's and Upton's Hills into the flatlands leading beyond Falls Church toward the Fairfax County Courthouse. Pennsylvania men of the 69th Philadelphia Irish Regiment, who were the only regiment allowed to have green regimental colors, had just arrived that month and the Pennsylvania 71st Infantry regiment of Zouaves, oddly named *Baker's California Men* stationed at Camp Vanderwerken since late July were ordered to pack two days provisions and ready to march that following morning to lands south and east of Falls Church.

Papa had learned of their plan a few days earlier and offered his help to guide these men at least twice but their bluster got the best of them, maybe it was because they thought Papa would lead them to a secessionist trap or because he seemed frail. He said the Union Army felt it had things well enough in hand with their own scouts and their fine maps. Papa did his best to warn them about the hills and steep climbs heading to the springs near the Carlyn farm and on to the turnpike road. But it was not to be and before long their pride would hurt them so.

The Pennsylvania men were readied to march on the last Saturday in September. For Papa and me, it had been a particularly hot week and coming up the Leesburg road from a long day in Alexandria city made for a difficult day for him. By dusk, we were both exhausted with the dust on the road choking us so and a couple of miles from home. Papa had begun coughing something awful and almost fainted on the wagon and it was all I could do to keep him from falling. We had to rest so I drove us to Henry Febrey's farm to see if they could help. Though Papa and John were not the best of acquaintances on account of their secessionist leanings, he and his wife Margaret were friendly folk and seeing his state, welcomed us in. They were well known in this area and had kin who owned land all about this area. Though their name sounded French, I heard tell their patriarch had been left in a basket as an infant at Arlington House on a cold February day and so the servants gave him the name. They lived in a fine home near the creeks of the Four Mile Run on a beautiful stretch of land with hills to one end that set them away from the main road. Papa was too ill to travel so the Febrey's graciously put us up for the night. It was best, as we were both tired from the long day, and it was getting too late to be out on the roads lest militia pickets accost us.

The troops were readied to march at noon, but for some reason they didn't get moving until 8 o'clock. By midnight under a nearly full moon the long column had veered off the Little Falls Road, marching in the trees along the Four Mile Run ridgeline to the edge of their farm. The clanging of equipment and the baying of their horses awoke everyone in the house and the men went to see what all the commotion was about. It was an impressive sight as men with their shiny bayonets glistening in the moonlight, made their way up and about the ridgeline down and along to the run. We knew these troops had wandered onto the steep trails and there would be trouble at this time at night without torches and guides. It had gown a bit damp that night and a light fog had set in closer to the run. The column looked like a long snake slithering across the land. We watched in awe as the men in the lead slowly disappeared into the fog.

Before long the lead column stopped along the trail to clear trees that had been felled by secessionist militia men to halt their march. Our hosts had not said anything about men felling trees near their land seemed odd. Men were brought up from the rear to help clear trees off the road while others were put to guard them against rebel pickets. We heard the sound of axes for a while as they chopped at the trees; and horses, now unlimbered from their cannon, struggled to pull them off the trail. Suddenly there were shots. The men could barely make out the fire spitting from their muskets, thinking militia pickets were firing on them. Some must had been hurt as we heard screams and calls for help. The firing had stopped and within a few minutes we heard someone on horseback yell "take care boys, here they come" and firing his revolver. Men on the road took to firing positions facing either side of their column preparing to meet the enemy. A shot rang out from the woods and within a second, men in the column let go a volley into the woods on both sides of the road. The sound was deafening, startling us all. Before long, firing started all along the line into the woods and from ahead.

A thick cloud of powder smoke filled the area where nothing could be seen but we could still hear noises and shouts from the woods along the road. A few musket balls hit the home, breaking a window as we all ran inside to lay low along the floor lest we'd be hit too. We scurried around trying to blow out all the candle flames lest the Army thought we were signaling the Confederates and arrest us all. There was a loud *"praaat"* of rifle shot as a second volley let loose that spooked their horses, some running off with wagons still hitched crashing along the trail. It's as if all hell had broken loose scaring us all. It went on for what seemed like eternity, but was likely no more than a few minutes. Before long we heard officers yelling at their men to cease fire and after the last shots you could hear all sorts of yells, screams, and bugles with men on horseback galloping to and fro. Less than a half hour later the commotion had stopped and the snake set there until sunup to tend to its wounds.

No one dared go out to check lest we'd be shot by those thinking we had fired upon these troops, but we knew men had been wounded and maybe killed in the skirmish. At sunup, the troops were still about the main road in groups and pickets had been set up to guard them. Papa and the others went out to see if they could help but the pickets closest to us would not let them pass. From where they stood they could see men, wagons and equipment all scattered about. A few wagon and cannon limber were overturned and a field tent had been set up for the wounded. Most were being readied to march back to camp while others were sitting idle. We weren't going to wait much for these troops to clog the road back home, so Papa and I hitched the horses and said our goodbye's to the Febreys, thanking them for their hospitality. We made it home an hour or so later and it wasn't until after supper that those men made it back to their camps. Later on, Papa had learned that the New Yorkers were none too happy.

From the lay of the land, it was clear the long column had no doubt doubled on itself and the fog had hidden the lead men. The Irish Philly regiment under Colonel Owen mistook for rebels Captain Morris's Battery; Colonel Baker's California regiment and Colonel Baxter's Zoaves fired into them killing one sergeant and two California privates as well as wounding fourteen others. The 69th were the same ones that two weeks earlier came to fight off the rebel advance from Munson's Hill. If it wasn't for quick thinking officers ordering a cease fire, the carnage would have been far worse. It wasn't just men that were killed and wounded; there were many horses shot and valuable war supplies lost. Being embarrassed over the affair, not many officers talked openly, but the enlisted were sure grousing about it. A day or so later the Washington papers ran stories about a tragic friendly fire while the official *Affair at Vanderberg's* report talked of a skirmish with heroism shown by both regiments. Everyone here knew this senseless killing was caused by boastful men who had no business marching at night in unknown lands without local guides.

Once the troops had marched on, locals started looking for whatever they could find amongst the many packs, carriages and such left behind. Papa warned them to keep away from such places lest the Union Army arrested them for stealing or aiding the rebels. The 71st would suffer one last injustice that month when one of its Captains was killed by rebel sharpshooters while on picket duty near the Chain Bridge. They would be gone from our midst by October to fight in the peninsulas and we never heard much about them again. The 69th stayed until the next spring when they too left for battles across the state and suffered horrendous losses later that year in Maryland in a big battle at Antietam creek.

The Union Army was slowly making itself felt in the county, every day more soldiers and their equipment were making the camps to our east their home with the newly arrived soldiers leery of us all. Our community found itself in the middle between the Union forts and the rebel pickets and it would remain so until the Union pushed out the rebels once and for all. Until then, there would be many more skirmishes, death and destruction before our safety could be had. Since the invasion, there was uneasiness between those that raised their voices against secession and those who sympathized with the southern cause. Many held sentiments on both, but in nearly four months after the invasion, whatever folks thought in private, they held their tongues when out and about. As far as the Union Army was concerned, you were either with them or against them. There was no middle ground.

The picking of sides took its toll on folks who had been long ago friends; that built the Olivet, which came to Bazil Hall's aid, that helped Mama in her time of need was all but gone. In its place came suspicion and fear. Folks kept their heads down, worked to keep their farms alive and kept thoughts and words to themselves. The days became endless list of chores near one's home, but at least for Papa and me, we were able to move about, seeing with our own eyes what this war was doing to us nearly every day. The risk of arrest, taking of one's property, or worse being injured or killed was just too great. Women started baking bread for camp officers, much finer than those made in camp, but there was still fear. Each loaf had to have the family initials baked into the crust lest any officer got sick, they would know who poisoned than. The only respite we did have was Sunday's when folks would stop by Doc's for a visit and relax. By the end of September, most folks east of the spring had come back regularly, but those secessionists west of it were not to be seen. Since the fires, much bad blood had been spilled and we were not likely to recover anytime soon.

There was always quiet talk amongst the secessionists as they got together, careful as to not be heard lest someone tell and they'd be rounded up and jailed by the Army. Mostly they kept to themselves while others talked to the Union men trying to learn all they could about where they had come from and about their families. But that fear didn't stop the Belles from working their schemes, strolling over to a group of officers attending services and making polite with the officers and the sergeants. They would talk about themselves mostly and get them comfortable enough that these men would boast about their plans on whooping the rebels and how many more troops would be coming in and the like. In those gatherings, Elizabeth and Cornelia were very sweet with all manner of pleasantries to officers and scouts that patrolled along the trails. Little did they know the Belles were none too fond of the Union men and we heard talk that they often told whatever they heard to their ilk in the Virginia militias. It wouldn't be long before their ways would get the better of them. This deceit came to a head on a fateful September day.

Smith Minor was a good man of no particular leanings, but the same wasn't true for his wife or the Belles. He had a two-hundred acre farm with a fine brick two-story house a bit south of the Vanderbergs across the Little Falls Road with many beautiful gardens of yellow rose, snowball and spirea bushes. Mrs. Sarah always spoke on how lovely the house looked at springtime. Smith would talk to Papa often about how unsafe our lands and how he had just bought a boarding house in Washington on account of so many folk had come to the city and there was money to be made.

For a few Sunday's in a row, Marietta, and Elizabeth would take their wagon to Camp Vanderwerken intent on wooing a few officers while Cornelia and Mollie spent time with Eveline and me. Marietta would make all fancy talk while twirling her parasol. It was scandalous as she openly invited them to tea at her Uncle Phillip Minor's vacant home, as he had moved to Falls Church when all this started, that was not far from the camp. The officers politely thanked her but declined her offers on account of a General Order #13 that kept them from visiting local homes unless they were on official business.

Marietta persisted in her invites for tea over the next few weeks telling them that no rebel soldiers would dare burn her home on account of fine Union officers regularly visiting it. I asked her one day why she and the girls were so friendly with these officers on account of their feelings about the Union and that Virginia militiamen visited their home many times in the last few months. She looked at me with a dark look, saying nothing, cracked a smile, and told me it was none of my business and that I best watch myself. Before I could speak, she and Elizabeth turned and walked away. I knew something was in that woman's head and nothing good was going to come of it. Smith Minor now planned to move his family into Washington to run the boarding house, but Marietta was set against it. Why not move to the safety of the city was beyond me, but I suspect it had something to do with Oliver Cox.

It all came to roost that last week in September when Reverend Hoblitzel sent word out of a fish fry up just outside Doc's to raise money for parishioner's homes burned earlier. Everyone turned out and there were a number of officers from Camps Union and Vanderwerken to pay their respects to those that lost so much and to partake in the wide array of baked goods that folks volunteered to make even in these hard times. It was wonderful to see most everyone who had remained in these parts though more and more were leaving and the Belles were next. Marietta and her caught eyes of a few of officers and again plied her invite for tea. After much talk and making eyes at these homesick men, it appears they found a few willing takers so the stage was set for trouble the Minors would not soon recover from.

A few days later six Union men, officers mostly, strolled over to Philip Minor's house taking up the Belles invite for tea. The men came to the door, hesitant at first as they didn't have permission, but Marietta put them at ease. She told them to rest assured, as she prepared the tea and the baked sweets, that Elizabeth would watch from a high window for any Confederates and warn them in plenty of time to take action. The men agreed to stay and made themselves welcome in the parlor. Marietta made pleasantries and prepared the fine china for tea while Elizabeth dismissed herself and went upstairs as promised to look out for Confederates and that she would be down in a few minutes. Her real purpose was to get to the attic window facing Minor Hill and with her white apron signal the militia pickets for them to come over. Elizabeth waited a bit, telling those below that nothing was going on and that she would be down in a bit. She waited until the Confederates got nearly into the front yard when she rushed downstairs and told the officers that Confederates were coming and that they should hide.

Outside the Minor's kitchen door there were rows of

walnut trees that led to a spring a short distance away so the officers at first said they should make a brake for it and hide there. They started for the door in a panic, but Marietta told them the confederates were just opposite the house and that they would be seen running across the yard and would likely be caught and we would all get in trouble, so she urged them that it was best they hid in the cellar through a small door in the kitchen. Thinking all the officers rushed into the cellar, the Marietta and Elizabeth went to the front parlor to greet their Confederates. Unknown to them, all but two of the men reached the cellar with the other two hiding behind the large open kitchen door. Just as the rebels got near the front porch, Elizabeth ran to the front door and yelled "they are in the cellar and have no side arms". With that, the Confederates burst into the house, ran into the kitchen, past the two Union soldiers hiding behind the kitchen door and down to the cellar with bayonets and sabers drawn. Just as quick, the two Union men ran out the door to the spring and then on through the woods back to their camp.

Marietta heard the commotion but stayed in the parlor while Elizabeth went to the cellar stairs. The four Union men down there were trapped and had no choice but to surrender to the eager Confederates. They were quickly taken out the same back door the others had escaped through and were hauled away west toward Minor Hill with bayonets at their back. Now that two had gotten away, they knew troops would be back soon. Their devious plan hoped that all six were captured, but with two escaping the trap, the Belles treachery was now there for all to see.

It didn't take long for those two men to reach their camp and report to their commander that they and some of their companions had visited the Minor girls without permission and that some were taken prisoners. Incensed by the shear treachery of these local women scheming up such a dastardly plan and his men taken prisoner, the commander sounded the bugle call to arms. He ordered four men to go to the camp barn and get as much straw as they can carry and another four to get kerosene from the commissary and prepare to march in force to the Minor home.

Within an hour his force of men was at Minor's home bent on punishment. The Belles came out to the front porch with fear on their faces. The commander told the women in no uncertain terms they had committed a despicable act and while he understood his men had no business coming over, this did not change the fact that they knowingly set a trap with Confederates against the Union Army. Marietta tried in vain to come up with a few words to blunt the commander's harsh words but to no avail while the others began crying. The Belles were all alone without Smith Minor nor any of the other Minor kin to help them.

The commander's decision was harsh indeed, giving them one hour to take whatever they could carry, as he intended to burn the house at the end of that time. He then turned to his men and instructed them to place straw at the four corners the building while four threw kerosene as high as possible on the corners. With a stern look on his face, he said "Young women your time is started" and with a look of horror on their faces at what was to soon be, the two went through the house yelling and screaming packing up the most valuable items they could find and hauling them to the front of the house in a pile. The commander announced every ten minutes how much time had elapsed while his men remained still and silent. Most of the furniture, trunks and food stocks remained in the home as they were either too large or heavy to be moved by just these two.

Neighbors, including Papa, Eveline and me began to gather once we heard all the commotion, but were not allowed by the soldiers to help in any way. Cornelia ran ahead anyway and went to help her sister, but it was of no use. As it got near the end of time, pretty much the whole community was there including Cox who begged the officers to have mercy on these girls. The rest of us sat powerless to do anything, not that many of us felt obliged as many felt they had it coming to them.

We stood there, talking in hushed tones of what was happening to Minor's beautiful home. It shocked us to hear about what had happened to garner such wrath of the Union Army. At the hour point, after watching these two girls frantically build a pile of their most cherished possessions on a heap in the front yard, the commander true to his word called the time, asked his men if there was no one left inside, and once his men confirmed it he gave the order to set fire to the house. The three girls were now a sobbing heap on the front lawn having collapsed near their meager possessions. Within a few minutes the house was engulfed in an inferno that no one could stop even if they dared. The heat was unbearable causing the Belles to crawl away in tears and most to step back from the inferno. Many of us were visibly upset at seeing the destruction before them, while others were less so having seen the same destruction happen to other homes at the hand of the Confederates some weeks earlier.

The soldiers and their commander left soon after, but not before telling all who could hear that no one better put out that fire lest the same happen to them. The girls were left to their new found misery and even with all the visceral talk they heaped toward many of us over the years, I felt pity for them. This war was bad enough for us all, without the added insult of having one's home burned. But the commander's message was clear and it was the same for the Union Army as a whole. They were here to rid the state of its confederates and there was no quarter to be given to collaborators or sympathizers.

Within a few minutes after the soldiers left, other Minor kin had come over to see the destruction and scolded the girls before putting what was left of their things on a wagon. No one said a word as we watched the spectacle. Minor men heaped choice words to those gathered that it was their fault entirely and that the same would soon come to them. This was bold talk and not soon forgotten. The community had been splintering ever since the invasion, but now the break was firm with the spring at the dividing line.

That was the last I saw of the Belles. Smith Minor, his wife Polly, the three younger girls and slave Julie and her daughter, moved into that boarding house. We heard the next spring, Smith petitioned the courts to be paid for freeing his slaves in Washington, as they were rented out to folks which is how they made their money. The whole case became a real story in Washington and George asked to testify on his behalf, but once the court found out about his vote at the tavern, he was turned down. Marietta moved with her Grandmother and Aunt twenty five miles west of us in the old colonial town of Middleburg, smack dab in the middle of rebel country. None of us were surprised when we heard.

Summer of '61 had come to an end and it was not the pleasant one we expected. What started as frets over the secession vote in the spring, gave way to war on our doorsteps. Our community bore witness to rebellious militias scouring our farms threatening those they deemed disloyal to the cause, to whole federal armies living and preparing for war in our midst and to men hell bent on inflicting the most heinous acts on each other. Our families bore the brunt of Federal and secessionist suspicion, keeping to ourselves, trying to keep our families whole in the midst of this evil. I was no more than fifteen years old and had already bore witness to so much and the hardship that came along with it.

I marveled at the many wonders of war, cannon larger than two men were tall, endless columns of soldiers from states I had barely heard of, men soaring to great heights in these new balloons, and the imposing fortresses and roads built seemingly overnight. I had also seen the depths that man could sink to in the name of his cause. How families endured living daily in fear of their lands taken, their homes burned, or put in chains for the slightest wrong at the eyes of these new overseers. Worst was watching how easily men could take another's life without a second thought, remembering that young rebel picket killed at our spring. What hurt me most was watching our community, which had welcomed my family and had come together to build its little house of worship, break apart and not sure if it would ever come together again. Our world had spun too far apart to go back to the way things were. The Union Army would either have to kill us all as collaborators or embrace us. This summer taught me that there was no middle ground. The Union would have to bring us into their fold.

8 IN THE UNION'S BOSOM

That first fall of '61 and into the winter was a curse for most of us trying to keep our farms working, while at night fearing rebel scouting parties bent on punishing those not seen as loyal to the cause. For those west of the spring, that fall was their curse and for some like the Minors it was to be their end. The Union Army had tired of the skirmishes, burning of the bridges and the rails leading from the capitol. It had been shamed with the almost weekly capture of its men, brazen attacks and burring of local farms throughout the summer. Papa caught wind of the Army's plans for a grand push to the county lines, bringing us all within its control. That meant taking all the surrounding heights from above the Chain Bridge, west to Minor Hill and south to Upton's Hill and further a few miles to Mason's Hill.

The rebels were not going to let such prizes, only miles from the Capitol, go quietly with almost daily skirmishing those first two weeks in October. Worse yet, the rebels had now begun to burn the homes of those they thought were collaborating with Federals. They burned down eight or nine other homes, a couple of these belonging to kin of the famous Mr. Mason, just a few miles away at Munson's Hill by the time troops from the 37th New York came to the rescue. These were the same troops who had earned the scorn of all for their pillaging up at Upton's hill and now were redeeming themselves coming to help. The Union Army did what it could, but unless folks lived close to Union Army camps, farms were burnt by the rebels as payback leaving more locals to their misery.

That next week another farm of a widow named Childs was set afire and when men of the 14th New York came to help, ten were captured. The Army now ordered a halt to these rescues leaving civilians to fend for themselves. There were skirmishes all that month with a few rebels killed and some wounded of our own. The Union Army around here was reaching the end of its patience and it would only take one last brazen attack for it to stir.

That came in mid-October when the Union Army, like a bear that had been prodded, began to wake. Our hills, with their commanding views of the Capital, were too valuable a prize not to be solidly in its possession. The rebels tried one last time to keep both Minor and Upton's Hills under their control and looked as if we were going to be in the midst of a fight for one of them yet again and everyone was scared. Papa heard the commotion swirling about the camps and saw troops getting ready. He told me sternly to secure all the horses and gather extra water for the home and to stay there as he took his wagon to Camp Union to complete his last run before trouble started.

Early the next morning, bugles at both camps sounded as Confederate General Beauregard's three Virginia Regiments with their cavalry and six heavy pieces of artillery began their advance toward both hills. Union pickets sent to Minor Hill were reinforced with men and artillery from Camp Vanderwekin and it looked like there was going to be a real fight. By late morning, rebel pickets had exchanged fire with the Union men. One rebel was killed and a New Yorker named Ramsey from the 35th was shot through a lung. Seeing a main rebel force gathering in a cornfield mid-way between Falls Church and Minor Hill, the Union men fired two shells stopping their advance. At the same time rebels took Upton's Hill but the Union soon got it back for good, becoming the new home to the 14th and 84th New Yorkers having come up from Camp Union. The big battle everyone dreaded did not happen that day and by supper the Confederate plans had been stopped. The rebel scouts in and about Minor Hill were gone for good and it seems the guns they left behind were made of logs just put up to scare folks away.

The Confederates left our lands to regroup some fifteen miles west around Centreville. Within a day, the Union Army had, as it did on every piece of high ground it took, built a watch tower that we could see from Hall's Hill less than a mile and half away. Not soon after Union General McDowell moved his headquarters from the Vanderwerken farm to Upton's Hill and troops of the 14th New York, known as the Brooklyn Boys came in to replace those that had moved on. Within a day the 10th Pennsylvania Cavalry made their home there as well in a new camp they called Palmer. The Union Army now had the highlands to the county lines and then some. Although we didn't know it then, that would be the last of the rebel threats to our homes for a couple of years, until Confederate raiders under a Colonel Mosby made themselves known.

The Union brought the rest of our lands into their bosom early in the morning a couple days later when the girls and I witnessed the longest march of soldiers and their equipment in our area. Hundreds, if not thousands of men began to stream up from the camps beyond the tavern to take and hold all the high ground at the county's edges. Hall's

Hill was to be the first as it looked like a swarm of locusts had set upon our hill all the way across the fields and even up to the Hall's burnt out house. Troops from New York, New Jersey, Michigan and others began their march three abreast in an unusually warm October day up the Glebe Road and when reaching the Olivet, turned west into the valley between our two hills. Bazil Hall was arguing with officers outside what was left of his home as it seemed the Union Army was making good its promise to protect our lands by keeping it.

Before long, Hall's land, with its beautiful forests and orchards, from the creek bordering the Olivet to the top of the hill was one of the new camps for the Union Army, and an important one at that. For how long, no one knew, but for Bazil, this was but one more hardship, albeit a profitable one, since this whole business began in May. The Army at least gave some respect to the old Whig Party activist by naming the new camp, Hall's Hill.

On the other end of our hill, hundreds more, if not thousands of men in blue and their equipment marched from the Camp Vanderwerken fields along the Little Falls road toward Minor Hill. The girls and I ran across the orchards to watch this spectacle on the bluff overlooking the road. For what seemed like hours these men marched below two abreast in a long line, boots a stomping and their equipment clanging. There were all manner of wagons, brightly polished cannons and banners and flags of all sorts with their proud leaders on horseback at the front and back of each group. There weren't too many words being spoken as they marched and every once in a while an order would be given from the front that slowly made its way to the end. Some men had worried looks on their faces as if wandering into the unknown others seemingly indifferent to their task.

The long line built for war raised a cloud of dust that

would hide those in the lead from our sight. As they marched, other soldiers with rifles walked along through the woods looking here and there for some unseen enemy in the hills above for any surprise. These scouts skulked cautiously by, sternly staring at us though one did waive and smile at Emily. We were in awe, so many men, horse, cannon and endless wagons; it's as if all of the North had come to our home. The whole thing was a sight to behold.

We made a day of it sitting in the orchard watching this parade men and war provisions. Soon many more folk joined us to watch, as they did when soldiers came to Hall's Hill, lasting until past supper. We decided to follow them closer to Minor Hill where we figured we would watch them as they took the hill. As we approached the Minor Hill property, we realized this army of men and their war wagons were stopping along the gently sloping fields on the south side of the hill on Minor and Febrey lands to make their new home. From the north side of the hill, we saw Minors gathered on their porch staring out in disbelief. Even old Colonel Minor was there, pacing on the porch and raising his fist as if to strike, but his family kept him at bay lest his temper get the better of him and he be arrested.

Most of the other Minor men were gone, some having left with the militia and others went to Alexandria just before the invasion not seen since. Many of their kin had left their homes in this area moving along with the Confederate Army as they retreated out toward the Shenandoah. The Belles, who stayed behind to see over the house, had now shamed their family name by having it burnt not just a week before. They were on the next rise from us standing there with scowls on their faces taking note of men and material as the columns spread out along the fields below as if they were judging the fit of this army. Given their treacherous ways, I wouldn't be surprised if they were making note of the comings and goings for the Virginia militia lest they come by on their patrols. The Minors had been stung by the Union Army's wrath not more than a week ago, and now thousands of troops were on their family's land once again and this time it looked like it was for good.

A day or so after the Union had arrived at Minor Hill on the 9th of October as I recall, the final injustice came to that family. The Union Army was going to make Minor land their own and did not take well to paying them for it on account of their southern leanings. Things must have gotten pretty heated; before long its patriarch was in chains and their land taken as allowed by Presidential Order. A Colonel Black, commander of some New Yorkers sent officers to the home to make their final demands known. Tried as they could, Minor kin could not hold back the old Colonel's wrath, as he leapt to his feet, swinging his cane and yelling all manner of insults to these officers telling them he and his kin could whip them all. Such insults to these officers could not be taken lightly, so the Lieutenant put a halt to all this, had his men put their bayonets to the ready with sabers drawn. One officer loudly proclaimed that Mr. Minor was under arrest for seditious acts against the Union and was to be taken to Fort Ethan Allen and held.

They readied Minor for the long wagon ride while his kin begged them to release this frail 80-year old, on account of his health and not knowing really what he said. The officers and their men paid them no mind and quickly rode off to the delight of all the Union soldiers who had gathered about. They were yelling all sorts of foul words calling him a secessionist, a traitor and such. Little did they know that this little old man, as mean and cantankerous as he was, served his state and country honorably during the second war against the British. He did not deserve this injustice, but such was this war. Once your elders chose a side, good or bad, your whole clan was painted with that brush.

They put the old man in chains and the Army wagon headed back along the Little Falls Road followed soon after by Minor kin to plead their case at the fort. We had come to hear that all their pleading to the camp commander was for naught as this was now an issue for the Provost Marshal on account of him being a civilian. The Army wanted to make an example of Old George Minor to anyone else, especially those who lived near the hill. The Army had tired of Minor and his kin's antics and sent him to the Old Prison in Washington where he was to be held for trial. Old man Minor was gone, their land taken, a family house burned and the remaining kin left to their own to follow the Confederates somewhere else. Though they had made this part of Alexandria County their home for many generations, the Minors had little left to call their own and the wrath of the Union Army to contend with for those that remained.

Within a week, nearly six thousand Union men had made their home on Hall's Hill in the orchards and his fields. Hall couldn't stay there anymore with all that going on so he moved himself, his kin and their slaves, and what belongings were left from his burnt home to his sister's home about a mile away to live out the war until the Army left. Mary Hall, her slaves Miss Gordon and Miss Lucas went back to Washington to be with her "girls" at her fine four story brick "home" to better tend to her business of providing much needed company and relief to the Union Army men. By now there were more than seventy such "pleasant" homes as they called them in Washington, but only a few could be rated as high as hers.

Bazil, unlike the Minors, was to fare much better as he made a business hauling lumber from his lands to the new forts being readied. Yet for us, putting our lands into the hands of the Army had its evils, and more so for our beloved Olivet. When Hall's home was burnt back in September there was no one left to watch over our little gathering place.

Union men had come in and took whatever furniture was there and most of the good wood lining its walls for the floors in their tents. Oliver said he saw our pews and chairs around the camps as our Olivet was suffering a slow indignant death. When the Union had no more need for a hospital to treat the men of Bull Run our Olivet became a guard house, then a commissary and then when the weather got colder, a final injustice as a stable for the officer's horses. By December, there would be nothing left but the stone foundation as its fine wood taken for firewood. Our Olivet which held so much promise and brought our little community together was gone bringing us all to tears, yet another victim of the senseless war.

On Minor Hill enough land had been cleared to make way for nearly ten thousand men looking as if a swarm of locusts had come. From the signal tower atop its hill, one could see both Washington to the east and secessionist troop goings on near the Fairfax Courthouse. Before the month was out, from empty fields grew seven camps, mostly of New Yorkers as well as Pennsylvania and Michigan men called Barnard, Beatie Black, Burnham, Cameron, Carl Schurz, Cromwell, and Owen named mostly after their commanders, with several smaller camps as what was known as the First Brigade of the Army of the Potomac. These were all under the command of a General George Morell, himself a New Yorker who made his command tent not far from the Minor home on John Tucker's land. Their camps were orderly and their commanders strict and forbade contact between them and locals less it was for official business.

With the Union Army now the new masters of Minor Hill and the lands to the tavern, we were safe from rebel fire. Papa didn't waste any time getting to know camp leaders, especially so with Colonel Black commanding the 62nd Pennsylvania who was camped at a station on the

Alexandria, Loudon and Hampshire Railroad a few weeks before they moved up to Minor Hill. It was there where he named his camp after his daughter Beatie. Colonel Black was an affable man, proper in all manners with a large well-groomed mustache. Yet for all things military he was stern, drilling his men endlessly preparing them for battle. He was a stickler for neatness and held inspections every Sunday, giving out awards for the cleanest men and every month a ten-day furlough for the winner. Papa had heard Colonel Black had brought his wife and daughter along to this new home to help arrange things and I think he only caught sight of her once in those early days. For a while they paid him not much mind, but as word got around, Papa got to make runs between this one and the camps in and about the tavern and back along the Little Falls Road to CampVanderwerken which now was home to more New Yorkers, and to men of the 11th Rhode Island and 5th Wisconsin regiments who had replaced those who had moved on to Minor Hill. Colonel Black was to become a leading man around here and with him taking a liking to Papa, made it all the more easy for him to carry on his runs. It seems the good colonel was well thought of by the Generals for success in this war. Camp Beatie Black had also become home to the 3rd Vermont, 9th Massachusetts Irish and the 13th New York regiments who were quickly put to work clearing pine forests, building roads, earthen works, trenches, and officers huts. It was quite a sight to see from the spring up the hill as these thousands of men worked the earth.

Within a week, the Army was making almost daily runs beyond Falls Church. In one patrol, New Yorkers of the 24th under a Captain Barney, whom Papa and I were to make acquaintances later, got into a skirmish with eight rebel cavalry, killing three and wounding others. For most others, there would be fewer affairs with the enemy, but rather endless marching, drills, building their great forts and trenches while others widened the trails to and all about

Minor Hill. The Army widened all the roads between their forts and within a few weeks, the Little Falls Road all the way to Fort Ethan Allen was widened to fit two wagons side-by-side. The same was done for the road leading to Camps Union and Halls Hill as well as the road to the new camp at Upton's Hill. These roads made it much easier for Papa to drive his wagon teams and make his rounds faster amongst the camps now popping up like weeds in our midst. This was good as Papa was beginning to weaken much easier and had not been on long hauls since the spill at Chain Bridge some weeks before.

It was in those weeks we began to see more colored folk in our area. Most seemed to be from farms and rebel army camps further west who had heard the Union Army would free them on sight if they made it across the lines, but we had heard of no such thing. Doc and Papa had strong feelings about these folks, and if it weren't for the laws making folks return these poor souls if caught, we would have helped all those who wandered by if needed until they got well enough and were able to continue. Others in our community felt differently; whatever their feelings were about slavery, property should be returned to its owner and allow the law of the land to settle it. Now in a war, these "contrabands" as the Army called them, didn't know what to expect and when the Army caught them, they were taken to the local camps, then sent on to Washington City or Alexandria to live out the war I suspect in some holding camp. One such man who came over the lines and got taken to Minor Hill was a slave servant of a doctor from a Georgia Regiment camped four miles west of Falls Church. When officers asked him about life with the rebels, he told tales of difficult camp life tending to sick and wounded as well as Union Army pickets captured and now held as prisoners.

This colored man was now amongst us under his own accord wanting to be free, but all the Army did after questioning was to send him to one of the camps in Washington where he didn't want to go, having heard they were awful. While at Ethan Allen, Papa heard of another who was one of Colonel George Minor's slaves named Davis. Davis, while doing the master's business selling wood in Washington, was told by one of General Mansfield's own officers not to go back. When he said he would stay in Washington, they held him in a contraband jail cell, six to a room no more than ten-by-six feet in size. He told them he wanted to go back to the Minor farm as he had not had a change in clothes for six months and that many of these poor souls in this jail were sick. I felt bad for these contrabands and the girls did too as these desperate people risked their lives getting to our troops, only to be sent to camps that were not much better from where they came. Papa told me many times that this scourge of slavery has to be done away with once and for all and that maybe this Union Army would do just that as they marched south, but it seemed that no matter where they went, these poor souls were to have a hard go of it.

Things were now getting a little back to normal. The Army had eased up on some of the restrictions now that the whole county was under their control, so Papa figured he would do one last run south before winter set in. Papa spread word at the camps that he would be heading to Jackson City and picked up a few orders from officers. Doc asked if Papa would take a few things to George at the store. This run was to make for a long day, so Papa asked me to come and keep him company. We made our way down the Glebe road to the wagon road and turned east toward the Aqueduct Bridge, passing the large camps of New Yorkers and Pennsylvanians and finally reaching a very large fort named Corcoran on the last heights before making our way to the river. From the heights, we got a real good look at all the goings on. There were camps, soldiers, horses, wagons and sutlers all about going this way and that with the river filled with all manner of ships and boats. Just how anyone could keep an eye on all of it was anyone's guess. Once on the flats along the river, we turned south on the turnpike to get to the loading docks at the canal. Things had indeed changed. There were two forts protecting the Long Bridge and a few others on the hilltops stretching to Alexandria. I even saw troops, guns and many wagons up on the Lee's plantation that was now the war headquarters for the Union. Somehow this injustice didn't upset me as we had come to see for ourselves how an Army could take over one's community. Between all the forts trenches were dug all about connecting them all like veins in your arm. Most soldiers paid us no mind as we rode by, tending to their marching, digging, hauling and the like. But every once in a while a few men would stop what they were doing and stare, some angry, some smiling, and some playing with their mustaches. It was so unsettling, reminding me of the wagon man so many years ago. I tried not to show any concern as Papa was too busy weaving his teams through the crowded roads.

I spent that leg of our ride looking all about and it was so much to take in. Papa stopped at the docks to pick up a small load for an officer at Camp Union and catch up on the news. Papa found out the Union Army was making plans for a big push to Richmond from the Chesapeake hoping to put an end to all this war once and for all. There was an air of purpose amongst the troops around here hoping to be done with all this rebel business by Christmas. Papa got about his business while I sat there staring downriver at the imposing Long Bridge running the nearly mile into Washington from here. The bridge was being well guarded to protect it from any rebel attack. I saw wagons on tracks being pulled by long teams along its length, heavily burdened no doubt with supplies unloaded from northern trains. It was quite a sight watching that bridge bleed war supplies from its end as if a vein had been cut.

Papa didn't spend much time at the docks and before long we left, making the short trip to Wunder's store. George came out with a big smile to greet us both when we pulled up. Things were pretty busy for him so we just got to getting a few casks of butter off the wagon and into the store while he loaded a few things for back home. This was the first I saw of Doc's store and got to looking around. It was really no more than a shack, but it was filled to the rafters with all manner of goods. He had casks of dried and salted shad, bins of butter, oil, soap, paper, linens, coffee, tea, dried tack and the like and from the many men who came in, it looked like he was doing a good business. Officers who were stationed at nearby Forts Jackson and Runyon would stop by to get things not readily found at the camps or that would take too long to get from Georgetown or Alexandria. There wasn't much time for pleasantries as it was nearly noon and Papa was getting worried about making our way back up-county before dark, lest we be out past any local curfew. George asked Papa if he could do a run for him into Alexandria to drop off to the Quartermaster's place to cash in some script. Papa fretted, but figured it wouldn't take too long and we would go home on the Leesburg Turnpike which was protected by Union troops if it got dark, so Papa agreed. He could never say no to a friend and besides, it gave Papa a chance to cash in some of his own script there as well. For me, this meant we could pass our old home and get to see what happened to the Alexandria since the start of the war.

From there it was a short trip to Jackson City at the Long Bridge. It had been four years since I was here and this place had changed so. Most of it was now pens for horses and cattle or storage areas for supplies for the war. The gambling houses were gone, having been shuttered by the Union Army, and the horse track sat unused and was overgrown. I paid little mind as this area held no good memories for me when we lived near here. We rode along the Ferry Road heading south the five miles to Alexandria City passing all manner of camps and pens. The road was filled with men marching in either direction while others were practicing their shooting skills along the base of the hill near the mills at Roach's Run. We crossed the bridge at the Four Mile Run creek that stretched from all the way up-county at Minor Hill. I stared sullenly as we slowly approached the road that led to the Poor House near our old clapboard house. Although I could see it, the house was now surrounded by all manner of sheds and pens, no doubt used for Army business. The place brought back memories of Cornelia, Jessie and our run in with the wagon man. I couldn't hold back the tears. Why are you crying? It just brings back memories of Mama I murmured. Me too. I do miss that woman so. I held Papa's hand as we went on our way, being comforted as when I was a little girl.

We went through two guard posts as we got just outside the city proper. Things had changed so much in less than a year since the war began. There were large warehouses and many others were being built with holding pens all along the main roads. New railroad tracks had been laid down in an out of the city from the waterfront all the way up through town. There were troops and wagons all about and so much noise it was getting hard to hear. As we made our way along Washington Street getting closer to the town center, it was clear this was no longer a city for regular folk. I only saw a few locals about, no doubt many not coming back since the evacuation days before the secession vote. I saw a few women about, none by themselves of course and oddly avoiding Union Officers by quickly crossing to the other side of the road when they approached. The indignant manner these women, clearly of secessionist leanings, showed to these officers was downright impolite. There were soldiers on nearly every street corner and the roads were clogged with Army wagons. We were now in a far different city from that before the war. Papa had few friends here and needed to keep his wits with the teams lest he upset an Army wagon and get into trouble.

We turned east toward the river when we reached King Street for the last few squares to the Army Quartermaster Headquarters which was next to Meyenberg's. Papa and I knew the city streets and the mercantile well having come here many times, but things were different now. Soldiers were all about and seemed to be leery of anyone not in uniform. Papa set the wagon on a side street and I stayed with it while he went inside to tend to his and Wunder's affairs. I felt uneasy there all alone with strange men all about. I tried not to look at anyone and instead stared at the Marshall House Inn which was across the street. It was here that those first martyrs on both sides were minted during the early morning of the invasion. The place it seems has become a shrine for visitors from the North and newly arrived troops as if on some sort of pilgrimage.

The Inn was festooned with Union colors and mourning bunting on its windows. The porch, some of the floorboards and the stairwell just inside the doorway looked like they were torn apart, no doubt at the hands of relic collectors of this now sacred place. Men mostly in groups of three and four would line up to take a look around. I had wondered to myself if someone was charging admission as if it was a museum. For me such a place held no special meaning as we saw many such desecrations over the summer in the up-county. I saw Union guards arrest a civilian man, dragging him away no doubt to face the provost marshal for one of any number of offenses that could put one in chains in this military city. Papa had said many people had been arrested for selling clothes, alcohol or other contraband items to Union soldiers. One had to be very careful what they said and did and to whom they said it.

After what seemed like an hour, Papa came out looking awful. He didn't say much, but after some prodding, it seems some soldiers saw fit to torment Papa before they would tend to his chits questioning his loyalty and such. Luckily just as he was about to leave in disgust, an officer having heard the commotion, stepped in and vouched for Papa having dealt with him before. I was going to ask Papa if I could go to Meyenberg's for licorice, but I could see just how upset he was and as we had only three hours of daylight left, it was best we made our way home. We went up King Street passing mostly empty storefronts and the many carts plying all sorts for wares to soldiers. At the edge of town just before the climb up the ridge we got to the big military train station that before the war had been a few houses, but now the Union Army had built a marvel of science to feed the war.

The new rail yard covered many city squares with a roundhouse in the middle with eight sets of tracks leading into it and dozens of tracks laid out all about the place. Some headed on Duke Street east to the wharfs, others north to Washington and others west and south to war. This imposing place was belching dark smoke from its middle and large train engines were rolling in and out of it. Tracks were laid within feet of one's home and how someone could stand the noise and smoke at all hours was beyond me. Papa decided to take a different road out of the city to get us to the turnpike faster hoping to cut time off our journey home. He paid the toll with money the Army gave him for his chits, and after two more guard stops we were on our way home. It had been a busy day and Papa was visibly tired. I took over the reins letting Papa sleep in the back while I drove the rest of the way to the Glebe road, then up toward home, past the Wagon Road crossing, the Tavern, and what was left of the Olivet. We made it home past sundown, exhausted, cold and hungry. I gave Papa a wedge of bread with honey, heated some tea and helped him to bed, while I tended to the mules. It was a long day, full of adventure and some sorrow. Things had indeed changed since the war and it seemed everywhere we went, there was misery to go around.

It was in those early days setting up their camp that Papa caught sight of Colonel Black's officers hosting newspaper reporters from Washington touring the camps near the rebel lines. They went up to old man Minor's now empty home for a tour talking about him scornfully as a southern sympathizer who made threats against the Union and got what was coming to him. While rooting through the house like a thief, an officer found Old Minor's orders signed by Secretary of State James Monroe, directing him to the defenses of Washington at Bladensburg during the second war against the British. One officer commented to the reporters that it was a document "he certainly must prize" which was written about in the papers a few days later. Unbeknownst to them, old man Minor was sitting in the Old Prison in Washington with many others accused of crimes of secessionist leanings or outright helping the rebels. We heard his kin were trying to visit him but the authorities would not give them passes to go to Washington likely on account of all their antics in the months before.

That first Saturday in November was real special for the camps around us. Union General McClellan, the new commander of all the forces around here was going to visit Camp Hall's Hill to formally review his troops. Early that morning was quite a sight for all us families as we saw soldiers and their officers from camps Union, Vanderwerken, and Minor Hill and others march to Hall's Hill and form up in neat rows with all their crisp uniforms and banners unfurled in the cool breeze. It was quite a sight and everyone felt proud and hoping we had seen the end of the skirmishes, burnings and such. We weren't allowed in the camp to watch the goings on, but we had a fine view from near Bazil Hall's burnt home. Before noon, the

General came and we saw Colonel Black with his wife and all the other Colonels welcoming him as some amongst us quipped that it looked as if court had assembled for the king by the way they were carrying on. Before long the General finished with the pleasantries and reviewed the troops. It was a fine display and from what we could hear things went well. But this was merely practice for something even bigger.

The next morning, General McDowell marched these men up the pike for an even grander review by President Lincoln himself four miles south of us on the broad fields at Bailey's Crossroads which took all day long and was seen by many dignitaries and reporters from Washington. We saw the men all line up in their crisp uniforms, the officers had polished up their swords which glistened in the sunlight with all manner of bands playing. It all made such an impression on everyone who witnessed it. We came to learn that one of those who witnessed the sight along the Pike was a young author named Julia Howe, relative of a Union General who was so moved by the righteous sight, that when she got back to Washington that evening, she penned a beautiful poem that was printed in the papers soon after. By the next spring, her inspirational words became the rallying cry called the Battle Hymn of the Republic that we heard played many times over the war in camps at special gatherings.

We had no time for such things as there was work to be done, but our lands were pretty quiet that day with most troops away at the review. It didn't take long for more calamity to befall the Minor's. Old Colonel George, imprisoned since early October, was not going to be released to his family but rather as part of an exchange of war prisoners. Smith Minor tried as he did to petition the court to release his ailing half-brother, but it didn't amount to much. They put this frail old man on a prison train and sent him down to Richmond and by the time they got him back, he was a shell of himself. A couple of weeks later Old Colonel Minor was dead. The funeral for him was grand with carriages filled with folk paying their respects at the Springfield plantation stretching almost to Falls Church. Soon after Madame Catherine picked up and moved to Falls Church taking her daughter Catherine Anne and her son Phillip with her thinking they'd be safer there, leaving their home to the care of Marietta. The rest of the Minors were leaving as well. Son John West moved with his family out to Leesburg, while Sarah Ann moved with her family to Richmond.

By mid-November Camp Hall's Hill had become the hub of military affairs in this part of the county being the home to Major General Morell, though Minor Hill was not to be outdone, with it being the headquarters for Brigadier General Porter. At Camp Beattie Black the Colonel, his wife and their two daughters, his second in command, Captain Means and his wife hosting all manner of social events for important dignitaries from Washington visiting the front lines. Their amicable nature and the sight of their wives alongside them made his 62nd Pennsylvania look as if they had everything in hand. And from what Papa saw, Colonel Black was a man in control. There wasn't a day during the runs between the camps that entire fall and winter that Papa or I did not see Pennsylvanians digging, building, marching and drilling in good weather or bad.

Discipline on the Hill, especially at Camp Beatie Black was strict, drilling from 6 to 9 in the morning; then from 10 to noon, each company had its own drill. And after an hour off for lunch, these poor souls would drill for the next four hours until 5 in the evening, when the whole regiment would be brought together for drills. Things didn't let up for the officers either as they would get even more training at night. Papa was not sure what all this training was for. Maybe it was to keep these men on alert and ready given the rebel threat had not died down one bit since they had arrived, or maybe it was just to keep men occupied lest they got into trouble. These men were well trained and well fed. The Union had seen fit to move large herds of cattle into the county across the Long Bridge to feed this army. There were already large pens in Alexandria, but the Army was looking to have another up-country which meant somewhere near our spring. Our beloved special place succumbed to the indignities of a cattle field with a slaughter house tent now set up just down the creek for the grisly business of feeding the Union Army. No one wanted to go there anymore as the smell was awful and the blood in the water brought flies. There were just no more indignities one could bear.

Whatever the reasons, we had little problem with those men on the Hill, unlike some from camps Union or Vanderwerken. The skirmishes around us that summer had now quieted some but those beyond the County lines were coming pretty regular with men captured on both sides. This was dirty war business and it went on quite regular almost as much as it did in September. Confederate cavalry were camped no more than eight miles away coming in often at night harassing and trying to capture Union pickets when they could. Rebels captured nine union men from the 30th and 23rd New York camped near us as they patrolled near Falls Church. Not far from Minor Hill, rebel cavalry skirmished with one of our New York regiments as they went on patrol at a place called Binn's Hill with three rebels killed. Killing had now become almost routine and not a day went by that we didn't hear of Union sharpshooters doing "target practice" as they called it on confederate pickets. How one could call shooting a man target practice was beyond me and God's law!

Even with all the discipline, the Union Army was

still not without its embarrassments as with the California Regiment affair. This time, Union Army leaders were railed by the papers when a large group of General Wadsworth's Brigade was captured by Confederate cavalry with five wagons of supplies and over thirty troops of the 30th New York taken prisoner. To the Union Army, these lands were filled with treason as the capture of those troops was at the hands of locals by the names of Dulin and Bush of Fairfax County who were arrested on giving information to the enemy. Every day, not only those outside the Union control, but also those inside it were being looked on as collaborators and should all be arrested. The Army sent out large cavalry patrols every day in and about Falls Church to make their presence known. It was quite an impressive sight with the rumble of so many hoofs being felt at our feet almost every morning.

That November ended cold and wet which made camp life hard for these men, many accustomed to better lives in Northern cities. There wasn't a week that went by that we didn't hear about another young soldier succumbing to illness or accident. Papa wasn't faring too well either as his lungs were filling with something awful from the scarring done by the acid. He was running his teams less every day. Although the weather was milder than some Pennsylvanians were used to, living in bitterly cold tents took its toll on the volunteers. Camp soldiers mostly kept to themselves and wandered out to forage for wood to heat their campfires which they did regularly. Everything that would burn not locked up or watched carefully was taken as it was with our beloved Olivet and the same for even the small chapel near Taylor's tavern. Papa and I were one of the few folks allowed into the camps besides the special guests who were not much interested in visiting muddy camps.

By December there were reported to be over fifty-thousand soldiers camped in our county, but many were not long to stay. By spring of '62, many were now on the march to fight in the Virginia flatlands on the road to Richmond. The fighting season as they called it was over and both sides had settled in for a long winter. We were merely folks trying to keep warm and stay alive, but the same could be said for those troops living in their cold tents. The county was well in the Union Army's bosom and these men in blue were all about us. When Papa felt up to it, he would talk with neighbors about all these troops from so many states who were organized into three large "divisions" as they called them. One was led by a General Porter who commanded the men from Hall's Hill down to the Balls Crossroads and a General McDowell who commanded the men from Ball Crossroads to Upton's Hill. Porter had three Generals under him; Butterfield, Martindale and Morell who commanded regiments of about a thousand men each mostly from New York, Pennsylvania, Massachusetts, and Michigan.

Papa made me put all the regiments to memory and retell them to him so he could remember their commanders and their officers by name. He quizzed me every so often so as to not offend anyone when he made his rounds. Papa told me never to put such things to paper lest anyone thought we were giving that to rebels. I still remember them as clear as it was yesterday: General Morell at Minor Hill commanding the 9th Massachusetts under Colonel Cass, the 4th Michigan under Colonel Woodbury, 14th New York under Colonel McQuade and the 62nd Pennsylvania under Colonel Black. General Martindale at Hall's Hill commanded the 2nd Maine under Colonel Roberts, the 18th Massachusetts under Colonel Barnes, and 22nd Massachusetts under Colonel Gove and the 25th New York under Lieutenant Colonel Johnson. General Butterfield, also at Hall's Hill commanded the16th Michigan Regiment under Colonel Stockton, the 17th New York "Westchester Chasseurs" under Colonel Lansing, the 44th New York under Colonel Striker, and the 83rd Pennsylvania under Colonel McLean with Rhode Island and Massachusetts men manning the batteries at each hill. The 3rd and the 8th Pennsylvania and 1st Ohio Cavalry were camped on Vanderwerken land.

After all the formalities of the past November, this army set into their daily routine and Papa to teaming his mules between them. We only saw cavalry troops go on patrol two or three times a day. During our rounds, we heard tell that so many men were being captured on both sides that it was getting hard to care for these poor souls that were no longer in the fight. The Gazette reported the Falls Church itself was now being used as a hospital for the wounded and sick, and most were captured Union troops. The Confederate's 1st Virginia Cavalry, led by a Lieutenant Colonel Fitzhugh Lee of that famous kin, harassed and skirmished with Union troops throughout that month in and about the Falls Church. Almost every time hearing of one or two killed and a few wounded and some captured; in one day seven union men, mostly from the 25th New York were captured. That little village had now become the new no-man's land.

At Christmas, those camps at Minor's and Hall's Hills made up of mostly Irish Catholics were in a festive mood, even with all the drilling. Maybe it was on account of them being homesick and such. Their arches over their main gates were decorated with ivy and evergreen. Many of their fences were adorned with bunting and mottos strung here and there. On occasion we could hear their music coming from their camps, many songs I had not heard before and every once in a while a company of men would put on a play of sorts to the delight of many. They had their customs leaving us to our own. Every camp had their customs showing where they had come from and their commander's personal leanings. Some were free of cursing and drinking like their leader's temperance leanings such as for Colonel

Black, while not so much in other camps. There was going to be review the Saturday before Christmas and each of the camps was doing their best to get their camps in order for the review.   Colonel Stockton's Michigan men, with Mrs. Stockton doing her best to keep things orderly, was running a tight ship with good discipline, while Colonel Black was doing his best, along with this wife to do the same.   It seemed as each Colonel was competing for prized compliments from their commanders.

That Saturday at Hall's Hill was to be a splendid one as everyone gathered to see troops marching here and there in fine formation.   Many of the troops wore fancy trousers and leggings looking as if they came from some foreign land.   Papa told me that Black's men were wearing French style uniforms and called themselves Chesseures.   The 44th New Yorkers, known as the Peoples Ellsworth Avengers regiment for the slain Colonel Ellsworth that first night of the invasion, had their own style of colorful pantaloons.   For Papa and me sitting on the ridge, it was another marvel of men with many Generals there along with dignitaries from Pennsylvania to see their men and reporters from Washington for the event.   While there I caught sight of Eveline who had come as well to get out of the home for a spell.   It was nice to see one of my friends after these last few months.

We spent much of the time on that ridge catching up on all the news and gossip, mostly about the Minor's misfortunes while the regimental bands give us all quite a respite from the cold and the war. After much marching, and when all had come to order, Colonel Black walked smartly up to the stage that had been set up and took his place amongst General McClellan himself and Secretary Cameron to receive flags presented to his 62nd and 83rd Pennsylvania regiments.   It seems Colonel Black's regiment was also especially noted for having much esprit-d-corps with a neatness award going to his own 62nd Pennsylvania and a Private Fahnestock of Company "K" winning an award of his own and a ten-day furlough. This was an honor not easily had as they made such fanfare over it with speeches by many of the important men there. Colonel Black gave a long speech about his men and the task that lay before them much to the delight of the reporters there.

After the formal talk, Colonel Black and his men left, marching right past us back to Minor Hill where he was to host his own festival at his quarters in honor of receiving his flag at the review. Papa was asked to bring up supplies for the celebration so we were able to get in at camp to see it all. It was a big celebration in a large tent with the food brought in special from Washington. By the time we got there, the reception was already started with Colonel Black, his wife and daughter Beatie hosting Generals Porter and Morell, Congressional Speaker Grove and a foreign Royal Prince d' Joinville, son of the king of France who has been watching Union operations in these parts. We saw Mr. Brady take their likeness in plate together and another of Colonel Black in front of his signal tower. It was quite a sight to see this much gayety from men who would likely see more battles in a few months. For Colonel Black it was to be his last Christmas as he was to die in Gainesville leading the 62nd six months later while his second in command, Lieutenant Colonel Sweitzer would be captured. Both men we had come to know well. With the Olivet in ruins within Camp Hill, we held Christmas Eve prayers at the Wunder's home with many of locals there. We sang and ate biscuits amongst friends to celebrate the birth of our Lord, then folks went home before it got too dark lest the patrols accost us.

On New Year's day of '62, we could hear music coming from Camp Hall's Hill and Eveline told me later she saw grown men of the 83rd Pennsylvania dressed as infants running around while others were dressing in long robes with horse hair beards pretending they were father time and dancing all about to music played on squeeze boxes, fiddle and the flute which must have been quite a sight. That was the only happy day in January of 62' as most days were cold and like many others spent the hours trying to keep warm and tending to Papa's breathing ills. From what I saw, it wasn't pleasant for many of the men in those camps and they were suffering more than many of us were. Soldiers did what they could to stay warm in their camps foraging for anything that could be burned and to keep boredom away. Papers reported a soldier foraging while on picket duty from the 14th New York went to the Minor house and found an order book belonging to General Washington, dated March of 1776, that was signed by him and many of his generals. But those were just stories to keep men's minds busy as men were dying of many things, illness mostly. We heard of a senior officer at Minor Hill from Massachusetts who died of paralysis to the distraught of all his men. Every month or so, there were more reports of men succumbing to illness without ever so much as seeing a rebel. It was a sad state of affairs that first winter.

There was some good news on Valentine's Day that year as one of the Donnelly girls by the name of Leddy was getting married to a young artillery man named James Barry from New York camped at Minor Hill. I didn't know her too well having only spoken to her briefly at the oyster fry and a little bit after the invasion on account of her farm was further north of the Glebe just off the new Military Road. She and her young suitor had met at the Olivet the year past while he was at Camp Vanderwerken and they would see each other there when he had the chance. Once the Army made its big push to Minor Hill they began courting. So much to everyone's surprise, they couldn't wait until spring and decided to get married in the District that day. We heard they got up early that morning and traveled on foot from Minor Hill all the way to the District across the Chain Bridge with a one day pass given by his commander.

When they came before the judge, he told them to wait as there were too many cases to be heard that season. The two were beside themselves so private Barry begged the judge to reconsider on account that his pass was to expire. The officers in the court must have felt some compassion for these two on account of the day and gave the young man a license then and there. They came back to camp that evening to celebrate. Leddy later went home to be with her family and would come by wagon to see her new husband every day in between all the drilling. In some ways I was jealous that I had not yet seen any man yet worthy of courting but mostly in awe of these two for doing what they did in the name of love. It seemed to me rather odd that in the midst of all this turmoil that one would even think about getting married.

Winter turned to spring and it had gotten to be nearly a year since the invasion. In that time we had been witness to thousands of men making our lands their home, protecting the capitol and us, I suppose, from the *rebels* and preparing for war in faraway lands. Most of these troops, who had spent the winter in up-county, marched off to war in March. Some would return here to rest after their long campaigns thinned by disease and musket fire. But for us here it was still months of fear and ordeal as rebel militiamen would ride in and burn homes of those thought to be traitors to Virginia. We were still under curfews and there was always the fear of capture by rebels or being killed by an errant musket ball. We were tolerated, but not fully trusted as women still had to put their family initials on the bread crust before camp men would buy it. How could our community that only a year ago had come together to celebrate building the Olivet, split asunder so with one vote. This war had uprooted our families, seen our farms decimated to feed our new guests and pitted neighbor against neighbor.

The only bit of news besides the endless talk of war was that Mr. Lincoln had been prodding states to begin putting an end to slavery and promised them money to help do it, while in Washington, Congress voted to free the slaves being held there and pay their former owners for their loss. We had no such help. The hardship took its toll on the locals and in early April, George, Gilbert, Robert Donaldson, John Birch and other landowners met at the Tavern to talk about the bad farming conditions and the livestock missing since the Union occupation. They took stock of all the losses and laid out their grievances hoping to get to talk with General Porter. We heard that aids close to the General were sympathetic to their plight but had told them that these matters would have to be taken up after hostilities ended. There wasn't much we could do and as the first anniversary of the dark period in our lives approached, it seemed as if there might not be an end to our suffering.

By the end of the spring of '62 with most troops gone to fight, things at Camps Hill and Beattie Black quieted a bit and although Papa had shown himself to be a trusted teamster hauling goods and supplies between the camps, the runs were getting fewer. He had a few of the boys working for him and even asked me to join him on the longer hauls. But as far as we could see, this war wasn't leaving our midst anytime soon and our community was breaking up. Anne and Apbelia had reached their wits end and couldn't sleep, both worried that rebels would rush in and take Doc, or that brigands would rob George on his way to the store or that Army men of ill sort would accost them. By mid-summer Doc, Anne, George, Apbelia, Barbara and little William left to live just north of Georgetown across the river in Maryland believing it would be much safer behind the protection of guns that ringed the city and living there allowed George to be much closer to the store on Mason's Island. Danny was going to stay behind to watch over their farm and with Papa and me at the cottage keeping each other company.

The same was true for many others, seeing no end to it all decided they had had enough too and were leaving, even Eveline was sent by her Pa to the District to be with her sisters at their boarding house and go to school in Georgetown with the Vanderwerkens. Reverend Lemen was making daily trips to Washington to find a house to rent to get away from the war, but everywhere he went, it was all full and folks were paying up to $100 a month. How anyone could afford such prices was beyond me. It took him the better part of six months to find a place and they too moved into Washington. Everyone I had grown to know was gone as we were never that safe even though they told us we were in the Union's bosom, far behind the lines. We heard that Polly Minor became ill of typhus and soon succumbed much to Smith Minor's sorrow. Though I loathed how those girls treated us, no one should suffer such loss. For Marietta, life must had been real hard in the countryside for even a staunch secessionist such as her had come back to live with her family in Washington once the blockades were lifted on the main roads.

For others like John West Minor, the war would paw at them endlessly. His wife would be arrested for carrying Confederate mail and wouldn't be released for some time leaving her children without a mother. Everyone was gone or tending to their own affairs and for me, I only had Papa and Danny. The troop comings and goings was endless and by the summer, some like the 62nd who had spent that first winter in up-county had returned to Minor Hill, without their beloved Colonel Black, to rest up from their long campaigns in the south before being sent out again to fight somewhere else. It was sad to see as they no longer seemed as eager for war as they did when Papa and I first saw them.

By the beginning of '63, the war had moved on to other lands and most folks had tired of it with so many men dead and wounded. For us here folks were able go pretty much about their business without needing all the passes yet mindful of the rules that controlled us. Things weren't at most stores and the prices were so high. Because we weren't making as many runs, we cut back on things. Instead of candles, Papa had me boil lard into a bowl and put a muslin wick in it to light the cabin. It reminded me of the poor days in the clapboard house, but at least the cabin smelled like bacon, even though we didn't have much of it to eat. Every few months a new regiment would make our lands their home for a bit and then move on to wherever the Army sent them throughout the south. We would read about some of these men in the papers when they reported on battles fought, wondering aloud if we recalled any of the names of their commanders.

By the summer of '63 Papa was so frail, all he could do was get up in the morning, have his coffee and a biscuit and sit outside the cottage watching folk ride by on the Glebe road. They would wave and yell pleasantries; and he would do his best to return the favor. He now spoke in a low raspy voice barely able to be heard and would cough something awful when he was winded. I did what I could to keep the hauls going between the camps as Papa had done, but by the last of July most of that work had gone to Tucker and when he left with George for Washington, the Army no longer had a need for us locals. I spent most of my days tending to Papa, working the garden that kept us fed, tending to the mules and selling whatever we had extra to neighbors who were generous; I guess feeling pity for Papa and me. It pained me so to see Papa this way, but the war had done so much to so many.

9 WELCOMING

Those three years of war had hardened me but now those memories were now washing over me as our wagon made its way to Minor Hill. I could see up on a small ridge where I knew of another spring to be and the home of James Tucker, but what was there now looked nothing like the old log home when I was here last. Tucker's land was where General Morrell had his headquarters amongst all those camps and who took over most of Papa's runs when he got ill then left with George for Washington when things got bad. He must have done well for himself by the looks of the two story home. I asked our driver if he knew anything about the home, and he said it was called Bloomindale and one of a few having been built after the war. He knew of it having hauled lumber and brick for it himself. He said a lot had changed, and I was in for more.

Once around the east side of the hill, for the first time I could see the lands of my upbringing and of those firebrands in up-county. I strained my neck looking about trying to take it all in. The driver paid no mind to me as I whirled my head about though I did notice he just smiled. I woke Tommy up to tell her all that I was seeing in front of me, not that she would know right from wrong either way. I caught myself talking but to no one but myself of what I knew from those days and what I was seeing today. I could just now make out Colonel Minor's farmhouse on the North Slope. It's odd, seeing it alone on that slope when last I remembered it was surrounded by Union Camps, Beatie Black in particular, and troops using his home to store war stuffs. No one seemed to be milling about but there was some laundry hung on the lines. It looked like the land had not been worked in some time which seemed odd. The Minor's would have not given up such a prized parcel so I suspect one of their kin was working it, or maybe the land was sold after the war.

On my right was the long graceful expanse of Minor, Tucker and Febrey land which in those days made up the seven Union Army camps, mostly of New Yorkers, now barren of all such trappings and being now hay and oat fields. I turned back and spoke to Tommy who was getting up from her nap, telling her to take a gander at Minor Hill. She stared for a bit and then looked at me strangely not seeing anything magical about this place. There wasn't much to see on this treeless rise, except remains of a few walls and trenches and the bottom of a signal tower where the Union spied on the Confederates. But here I was at one of the two hills that made my lands, of my home. Just thinking of the thousands of troops that were here with their tents all laid out in neat rows grouped by the flags of their regiments filled my mind. Even after 63' when most of these men went off to fight throughout the south, some camps still remained until I left in 64'. From what I saw then it's as if they were going to be here forever, but now it's as if a giant broom had swept them all away.

We were now on Little Falls Road heading down the gentle hill into the valley of the spring and the Little Pimmit creek, now about a mile from my home. Tommy had nodded back to sleep and that was for the best. These were my memories to tell. Off in the distance I could see what was left of Birch's farm that had been burned down by rebels those few months after the war started. I didn't see anyone out and about. I was so looking forward to hearing from them remembering how he and his wife had been good to us and one of the few that lived west of the spring who helped Papa. Maybe I would learn more from George or Miss Barbara once I got home.

At the bottom of the valley we reached the trail that branched off the 100 yards or so to the spring nestled amongst a few trees where I spent many a day during the summers hauling its fine clear tasteful water home. I stared at the spring house a bit as the wagon slowly made its way along the Little Falls, a bit beat up, no one there to tend to it, I guess. Before the war, it was where we played when we could, where folks would gather to get away from the hot sun and boys would go to court young girls away from sight of their folk. It was also where the Belles would meet their militiamen at night until the Union Army made its push to new camps at Minor Hill. This little insignificant creek, halfway between Minor and Hall's Hills in many ways was the dividing line between both sides of the war that split asunder so, and like so many nice things around here, it did not escape the evils of war. It was where I saw a confederate picket fall to Union sharpshooters, now all but forgotten, but in an instant it all came back to me. Looking a bit more I saw a large pile of cattle bones down the rise just a bit away along the creek, bleached white from the sun, still there, no doubt reminding anyone of the slaughter house that turned our special place into something awful. The whole place was now quiet with the rustle of a gentle wind across the grass of the hills.

I saw more open fields with few, if any of the trees

had grown back, and I remembered just how barren things were when so much of the timber was cut to feed the building, heating and cooking the Union Army demanded. The place was nearly picked clean in those days. Now with much less folk around, it seems nature was trying its best to come back. I saw a few folks tending fields as we rode past the creek, seeing farmhouse but recognizing no one. Had everyone left this area? Thoughts kept coming into my head as we rolled slowly up the rise on how I was going to find men to speak on Papa's behalf before the Commission.

Finally, the last rise before home reaching the hill at Vanderberg's home, marveling at the place, still a pale blue in color and the orchard of fruit trees. I was hoping Eveline would be there, or at least her folks would know where she went. I strained my head looking for signs of life. Just then a woman came out the back door, the same one I recall seeing with Eveline and her mother there that night of the rebel burning and shelling. I asked our diver to stop. He, seeing my excitement, said he would wait, but only for a bit. I stood up and yelled to catch the woman's attention recognizing it to be Charlotte. I waived frantically until I caught her eye and she strained to make out who I was. I yelled it's Cecilia Payne and she screamed for me to come over. Tommy sat up and just watched the spectacle of grown women yelling across a field at each other. I got off the wagon and ran toward her with Tommy not far behind me. We hugged for what seemed like an eternity.

It had been so long and the memories so deep, that by the time we separated, we both had tears streaming down our faces. She was as surprised as I was to see me and the smile on her face was priceless. I introduced Tommy as Charlotte leaned down and said how she was such a beautiful little girl. I told her there was so much to talk about but I only was in town for a few days to settle Papa's affairs. Charlotte stepped back and it all came back to her.

Up until then it had all been pleasantries, but when I mentioned Papa, she got all choked up. Things had changed so much since before the war some ten years ago when she was just a girl herself, not much older than Tommy.

Charlotte was now married herself, living in local lands near Chain Bridge and stopping by to tend to affairs at her father's house. I smiled as I listened to her story, then asked her if Eveline was about, and she said, gosh no, Eveline got married some three years ago to a fine young man from Washington and now they live in New York. She has a young boy named Jack, though we don't see her much except holidays and such. Eveline a mother? I guess it was to be expected, as we were all in our twenties; it was time to start raising families. Maria is still at home and seeing a man from Washington who makes measuring tools for the Government surveyors. Little Maria? Why she was only nine when the war began and now courting a man. Charlotte said her Ma and Pa survived the war fine and are doing well. She kept staring at Tommy and smiled. She asked me to stay a bit and wait for her ma and pa to get back from Rosslyn where they went for supplies. There was so much to talk about but I didn't want to keep our driver waiting as he had been so polite to this point. I told her thanks but we had to get moving on to Wunder's but that I would stop by. She asked if I knew that Doc had passed on in '66, and I told her that I had heard the news from Barbara, but most of the family was still there with George still politicking. She said a lot had changed with many more folk having moved here from Washington after the war.

I had to hear more and Charlotte offered to take Tommy and I in her surrey to Wunder's after a bit, but I had so much to do, so I told her I'd be back to talk more. With that Tommy and I got back up on the wagon with her now at my side and off we went for the last leg of this long journey. I must have apologized a hundred times to our driver and he just smiled. I saw you talking to those folks and it reminded me of the hardships and friends lost during the war myself living in Drainesville during those years. He recalled the Army cavalry forays and later on when Mosby's raiders came a looking for traitors and collaborators. Those were dark days he recalled. I just sat there and listened as he went on. The war it seems touched everyone I met and mostly in bad ways. So off we went, now with renewed excitement, as I began to recognize more and more of the area and the memories pouring over me. We were soon abreast of what was left of John Minor's place that had never been rebuilt since that awful night in September of '61 when the Army burned it down for the Belles' treachery and used the bricks to line Camp Union's baking ovens. I began to wonder what had happened to them, not that I meant them any pain, but those girls knew their ways would get them in trouble. And it did. I'm sure Barbara knew what became of them, but for now, all I knew was the story already told of their place being left as a stone base covered in vines and its beautiful rose gardens and bushes long gone.

We took a side trail to the Fairfax road and from there I could see Hall's Hill. From there it was only a quarter mile to the Wunder Farm. I was surprised to see that old man Hall had rebuilt his fine home, no doubt with the money he got renting his place to the Union Army. Things had changed a bit though, gone were the lush forest of trees that were cut down to house soldiers and officers. Gone was the large frame and gate the New Yorkers put up for those many months and from where we saw generals reviewing their troops and giving awards to Colonel Black. I'm sure Barbara would know what became of Bazil and his land, his family and who was now on his land.

The Olivet was where I was to find out what became of our neighbors and with God's help get their support for the hearing with the Claims Commission. Our wagon had just approached the high point in the county at Minor's Hill, when I realized Tommy and I were now less than a couple of miles from home. A feeling of dread came over me as memories of our community strife began washing over me. The hill and its surrounds sat on old George Minor's property, himself a hero of the second war with the British commanding a Virginia Militia sent by President Madison to defend the capital fifty years before this war. This hill was held by confederate spotters watching Washington from its heights and a sought after prize by the Union Army early in the war. Colonel Minor's farmland surrounding it was taken by the Union Army becoming a camp for nearly ten thousand men by the fall of that first year and remained so for most of the war. An ardent secessionist, Colonel Minor, and many of his family, fared badly for those leanings having land taken and even his own arrest never to return while others had their home burned for treason or others who picked and left with the Confederate Army as it moved deeper into Virginia.

As our wagon rounded the hill along the Little Falls Road, there was little, if any reminder, of the big Union camps along the poorly tended fields stretching eastward. The Minor home somehow seemed unkempt now as I wondered what became of them. I was not about to ask my driver. Looking up at the hill one could still make out the remnants of those old fortifications and the tower. These broken ramparts and tower were the only reminder that while the war had all but been erased in Alexandria City, there were to be many reminders of it here. I started thinking of the dozen or so families in our community spread mostly between those two hills that Papa had been acquaintances or had business dealings with leading up to and during those war years. I was soon to find out what became of them.

My stomach was all a flutter as we crested the hill just off Hall's place when I saw Wunder's place. The smells became rich and the colors of the fields brighter.......I was home. I told Tommy to look up, pointing at the farm on the hill and just off the fence our cottage that was our home those many years ago. Our driver stopped at the corner of the Glebe Road and the fence line where Papa used to tell the news to all who gathered. I could make out someone working the farm in the distance but couldn't see who. Our driver asked me where to go, but I was caught up all in emotions and sat there speechless. Again he asked and I told him the farmhouse if he didn't mind. By now he had gotten used to my ramblings as if he were with a three-year-old and said with a smile that it would be his pleasure. He had come to know Doc and his fine works around here and his son who was now one of the county elders and it was the least he could do given all the fuss I made since we left the station. As we turned in the gate, it was all I could do to keep from jumping off the wagon and running the hundred yards or so to the house. Tommy, sensing my excitement, asked if we had arrived and I told her we were home.

Not a minute later, the soul from the barn I had craned to see was Danny now staring at us coming down the road. I began waiving my arms then screaming, it's me, Cecelia, I said over and over. He dropped his haul and began running toward us, screaming himself like a child. He stopped just shy of the wagon, with his hands on his knees gasping for air breathing something fierce with tears in his eyes. Oh my dear, God has brought you back home to us. I knew you'd be here soon enough. With that I jumped off nearly catching my petticoat on the rail and falling over into his arms. We hugged each other for what seemed like forever. Cecelia my dear, you are a sight as I wiped the tears from his eyes and he of mine, but neither of us could stop. It was fitting that my partner and protector was the first to greet me home. Tommy climbed down and came close. Danny, this is my little girl Tommy. He looked at her and put his hand to his mouth like he always did when he was surprised. So yooooou're Cecelia's little girl, he asked. I'm no little girl, Tommy snapped back, much to Danny's surprise, and I thought, mine too as I scolded her. Oh that's ok Danny quipped; I have been hoping to meet you for a long time. Your Mama and I go way back and are sort of the best of friends. Sort of!; Tommy looked quizzically back then properly introduced herself. Oh this will be fun as Danny smiled looking back at me.

Charles interrupted us and said he had to get to the Glebe House before it got too late. Danny quickly grabbed our bags and thanked our kind driver for bringing our Cecelia home after all these years. She is a special woman, a real gift from God he said. I don't know about that I quipped back to Charles as Danny took Tommy with him to the house. I cannot thank you enough for your kindness. I had not much to give him, but I offered him five dollars for his troubles. That won't be necessary; it would seem un-Christian for me to take money from such a fine mother and her most precocious girl. Your kindness and wonderment entertained me the whole way here and brought back many memories of my own kin and hope to see my own someday as well. The war, he said, did much to take from everyone and the reconstruction even more so. I wish you the best in your fight to right the wrongs of that war. May God be with you and your daughter and with that he wheeled about and went on his way. Charles was right, I at least was home, and soon to be with my kin. But for many, those were luxuries not easily had.

A loud scream came from the house just as Danny got to the front porch,...they're here! They're here!.... came from inside the house. The door burst open and there stood Barbara, a little older and a bit greyer, but there she was. Widow Anne had come to the door with George just behind when Danny reached them holding Tommy's hand with everyone crowded around and hugging her. I just walked up slowly trying to soak this all in. I was home and these kind folk were welcoming my little girl just as I had been by this kind family when Papa, Mama and I first arrived on that porch, tired and cold and needing a home all those years ago. Then it was my turn, and I got no further than the first step when they rushed to hug me. There were tears and smiles from all and most of all from Barbara. Anne, said with a smile I had not ever seen on her, said I knew you'd be back my dear and we have missed you so and wish my Henry was still alive to see you. Barbara was fussing with her hair and dress as if she was ashamed of her looks having aged a bit, but we hugged for a good while. I said it was wonderful to see you all and that everyone looked the same, maybe a little greyer, as everyone laughed. We made our way inside and it all looked so much the same. Anne apologized for the color and decor as things had been a bit hard since Doc's passing just before Christmas of '66, but my visit was already cheering her up by telling her it was just lovely and it was good to be home. Things were still hard and though some in the area were doing well, many had lost much and the riches in Washington City had not yet spilt over this way. We all sat down in the parlor and everyone just started talking through each other asking questions, barely got a word out before another was tossed my way. Danny took Tommy to show her about the house, while George, Barbara and Anne sat to take it all in.

I told them about our journey here, the stop in Alexandria City to see a few sights and figure out where the Courthouse was and the like, the Marshall Home, the Mercantile and the Sickles barracks. I told them about the old man, Caldwell who I met just outside the train station. George was surprised at that as he thought he had passed on account of a whooping cough some years back. I told him about his family and such as the talk got more serious. There were lots of stories to be told and not all of them pleasant. Talk soon got to the Olivet. My dear, the good

Reverend Hoblitzell stayed almost a year after you left, and for a while had no one here. Oliver Cox is still around, living with Reverend Lemen closer to Freedom Hill and still not married. He is working in Washington once in a while clerking for the Quartermaster. When you left, there was only a stone foundation remaining of our nice gathering place by the time the Union Army left. But after the war, we all felt it was time to put it all to right and the new Reverend Ames tried his best to bring us all together again. By '66 we had twenty five members in the Olivet and this time there were far less folk chipping in to help but the spirit was no less dampened hoping to rebuild if we raised the money. We finished putting together God's little house last year. I think it would be fitting for us to go there tomorrow morning to see the place and give thanks to God for your return.

I came to learn that some of the families had gone on and especially those west of the creek but some were back. Matriarch Catherine Minor and much of that clan had returned, but now leased their farm to a man named Crimmins of Ireland who had served in one of the Irish Brigades when they were camped there. What an odd thing that a Minor would give their land over to a Yankee, I thought. Smith Minor and the Belles lived in Washington after his wife Polly died, and are still running that boarding house. Marietta had gotten married to a man from Washington while Elizabeth, Cornelia and Mollie were living together as spinsters with Oliver Cox on the Minor place. Elizabeth was working in Washington for the Treasury Department.

It all seemed so strange to me. I told them about the spring, seeing how the whole area had come back a bit after being taken over to graze and butcher Union Army cattle. It took many seasons and much rain Barbara said to cleanse away the ruin of having so many cattle in that area and asked if I had seen the bones all bleached white and still in a large heap. Not many folks go down there much anymore, except to cut hay for the winter. It's too bad; the spring had been such a refuge for us young folk. I asked what was happening at the Hall place as I remembered him staying at his sister's place when the Union Army took over his land. Well, chimed in Barbara, it seems Bazil had a good change of heart staying with his sister as he is much more hospitable to the freed coloreds. Madame Mary still owns that *pleasant* house in Washington near Capitol Hill, but she is letting her sister Elizabeth run things now. She now spends her days at Maple Grove while Bazil rebuilt his home and still lives there. He started parsing out some of his land, giving some to his girls, and other kin. He made a claim himself for thirty-thousand dollars for all the timber lost and use of his farm and I think he got almost eleven thousand.

The Vanderberg's came home in '65. Gilbert is now quite well known and respected here as he was appointed to the County Board of Supervisors and when the County got its constitution back a year ago, he was made Registrar for the Arlington District while John Minor is doing the same for the Washington District. Maria is living at home, now seeing some man named George Saegmuller, and getting pretty serious. I think he is an instrument maker from Washington making a good name for himself with the surveyor's office. Eveline married a friend of this fellow named Rudolph Reichmann a couple of years ago and moved to New York with their son. In her letters she is always asking about you. You saw Charlotte, and if she didn't tell you, she married a young man named Lockwood on New Year's Day a couple of years ago and now lives in a nice home nearby close to the Titus farm.

George came in the room, eager to talk about Vanderwerken as he always did and said that he is still running his businesses in the District spending most of his time at his home on M Street in Georgetown. If you remember, after shooting his neighbor, he went to trial but got off on account of a jury split vote. Most said he paid off some folks to have the whole thing go away. Gilbert still owns Falls Grove that General Hancock used as his headquarters, but is now going to sell it to some businessmen from Washington. It seems the war was rather good to him. The Army closed Fort Ethan Allen in '65 selling the timber at auction and giving the land back to Gilbert. Now he is making claims for lost timber, the same he was paid for when they cut it and asking me to testify on his account. He had boasted of his petition for over thirty thousand dollars for his "losses". He also made claim to losses from the land Fort Marcy was built on, that was claimed by the Frey family. Had he no shame?

It seems everyone is putting in a claim for something lost during the war. Well, I guess, if the government is willing to give us money for the hardships they caused, then maybe we should all get a piece of it. Gilbert had so much going on that he hired a criminal as captain of the guard for his place. When the guard robbed him, Gilbert couldn't figure out why. His daughter Jane met a young Union Lieutenant in '65 named Grunwell on her porch when he got lost on his way from Minor Hill to Chain Bridge, and when the war ended they got married and are living near the Donaldson place in a fine home Gilbert built for them with the timbers from Fort Ethan Allen. Emma and Ella are still living with Gilbert in Washington, though they do spend the summers at Falls Grove. We see them some times for a wedding and such at the Olivet.

The talking went on for hours through supper and well into the night. Tommy was playing outside, but I wasn't afraid, certainly not the kind of fear we felt back in those days of cavalrymen riding though our lands. If Danny looked after Tommy half as good as he did me during those days, then she was in good hands. Barbara sipped her tea slowly, and with a low voice spoke about Papa. Cecilia my dear, I am glad you are here to help settle Papa's affairs. I do miss that man so. He was good to you and did what he could under the most trying of times. So what will we do about the Claims Commission, she asked? My date with them was still three days away, but we hadn't found others to help attest to Papa's losses other than maybe George. I had brought a purse of chits written by camp commanders that Papa had hid when things got bad and never got to cash them at the Alexandria Quartermaster when he got sick. We pored over them and made a good accounting of what we felt the Government owed us and they came to nearly $700. We did more storytelling and made plans to see the cottage tomorrow, but for now it was time to turn in for the night. The day had drained me, but the sight of these folks filled my soul. George opened a bottle of sherry, something on account of this being a special occasion, while Barbara got the special glasses out of the cupboard and poured each a taste, but Anne still wouldn't have any of it as it seems she had not mellowed any with age. George raised his glass for a toast: Cecilia, it is good to have you home, to your mother and father, may they rest in peace and let God help you in your journey to right some wrongs of this war.

The next morning, came and went as I didn't wake until pretty much near noon. We let you sleep as long as you needed to, Anne said as I made my way to the kitchen. Tommy was up early and is out in the fields with Danny who is just smitten with her. We have some things to talk about when you have something to eat. I stood at the window looking out across the field leading to the Glebe Road. I was back home, but things were different, as I expected they would be, but I had purpose to do what I could to bring some justice to our family. After supper, George went to tend to things while the women talked around the table of the war. Barbara and Danny told stories on how things were after I left in the spring of '64. One horror was the murder of a Mr.

Reid whom Papa knew from his runs. Confederate raiders, *guerillas* they called them, under a Colonel Mosby from the Shenandoah Valley started making runs on the lands about the Falls Church and the Ball's Crossroads. The stories went wild and how folks were scared of evil men riding in the night, robbing and even killing those suspected of Union loyalty. We didn't pay much mind to those stories as it looked every time something bad happened or something went missing around here, Mosby's men were being blamed. But it didn't take long for us to fear them for real.

Danny told the tale of the kidnap and killing of Preacher Reid at the hands of these Raiders in early October of '64. Reid was a well-known local farmer who was one of the leaders of the Falls Church Home Guard and a pastor's assistant at the Baptist Church there. He had spoken out many times of it being the right thing to do, teaching the colored how to read and Papa too when he went on his runs through his area. Mr. Reid would hold class on his front porch when the weather was good and welcomed anyone to sit. He even brought his wife and two daughters to a fish fry or two at the Olivet and they had made quite a name for themselves, but some were none too fond of his views on the Negros.

On an October day, between fifty and seventy-five of these Raiders crossed the Federal picket lines pretending to be 8th Illinois Cavalry looking for vengeance. These Raiders rode up and to everyone's horror they held Reid at gunpoint for trial, convicting him of crimes against the state of Virginia. They warned that if anybody interfered he would be shot. They took Reid and his farm hand servant named Jacob Jackson as well as four Federal pickets that had been captured along the lines. They went to a farmhouse near Huntersville where they shot the four Federal pickets as enemies of the state of Virginia. As it had begun to rain, Reid and Jackson were taken into the barn for their *trial*.

The Raiders demanded that Jackson admit that Reid had taught him to read but before he even answered the Raiders who were so whooped up with rage, shot him in the head. Only god knows why, but the bullet only grazed him, tearing his ear off and feigning death, he collapsed on the floor. Through it all, Jackson could hear the angry Raiders yelling as they accused Reid of high crimes against state by teaching the colored man to read, by cavorting with coloreds and by supporting the Union cause in the invasion of Virginia. They asked Reid how he could justify such heinous things while Reid accused them of murder in the eyes of God. The Raiders had enough of him and became so angry that they stripped him of his clothes, chained him naked to a post like some animal, and shot him in the head.

Jackson stayed still for what seemed like hours fearing return of these evil men. He then escaped in the night slowly making his way back to the Falls Church. When he got to the Federal picket lines he showed them his horrific wound and the pickets allowed him to pass to tell his story to the officers at Minor Hill. To add insult to this grievous deed, Mosby sent word to Mrs. Reid that she could pick up her husband's body without fear. Jackson was treated for his wounds and went with Mrs. Reid and a posse of eight men to the farm. In the barn they found Reid's body, still chained to the pole, and brought it back for burial in Falls Church two days later with many County folk there to pay their respects. This kind man who taught Papa and others to read was no guiltier than any of us. We all had tears in our eyes listening to Danny's tale, reminding us of how much was lost during those hard days.

George went on and said that all throughout '64, we heard tales of battles fought in Maryland, Virginia and even as far up as Pennsylvania with many of the regiments that lived on our lands with horrendous losses. The war came to an end in the spring of '65 and just when we thought it was all over, the leader of this great nation was shot by a southerner named Booth as Mr. Lincoln sat with his poor wife in a Washington City theater. The papers went wild of a plot by Southerners to kill or capture all our leaders and things got pretty heated around here as the papers talked about revenge. No place on this side of the Potomac was safe as the Army believed Booth had escaped into Virginia. Troops at Ethan Allen and Marcy and the camps all the way to Minor Hill were on high alert and they sent out patrols every day searching every house and barn and rounding up County men on suspicion of being collaborators. Anybody who had seen anything that day or had any ill feelings toward Mr. Lincoln was rounded up and threatened with having their property taken. In Washington, anyone with a drop of Southern blood was suspect and the many County folk riding out the war there lived in fear. Our County was in turmoil and would not ease up until this Mr. Booth was brought to justice.

A few days after Mr. Lincoln's death, Danny said, a company of cavalrymen rode up to Vanderwerken's farm. Gilbert was asked by a young Captain if he had heard about Lincoln's assassination and was told yes, as word had spread quickly. He said that they had had orders to search all the buildings close by. Gilbert, being the man he was, said that Booth was not there and that a search would be made over his dead body. The incensed officer drew his revolver and immediately ordered his house surrounded then told Gilbert that they would now go through his house searching every closet, every room, the sheds and the barns. Soldiers took pitchforks running them through the hay and others with sabers drawn at every door to see if anybody was hiding. After almost an hour or so Gilbert turned to the captain and said gleefully, "See, I told you he wasn't here so put away your swords." To which the Captain sternly put his finger in Vanderwerken's face and said, "I know that, but I wanted to let you know who the boss was." Like Georgetown in '62,

Gilbert's hot temper almost got him arrested again.

The Troops then remounted, forming into columns ten feet wide and rode through Gilbert's fields. It looked like a cyclone came through nearly destroying the whole crop for the year. Danny said Gilbert was shaken by what had happened and he seemed no longer the brash man he once was. The Union Army was letting everyone in the county know they were serious and knew that word would get around. For two weeks as the searches went on, we sat near our homes afraid to go far lest we be arrested as collaborators. The Potomac was filled with every sort of navy ship that could be found searching for the assassin. Two weeks after the dastardly deed, the Federals caught up with Booth and captured his accomplices. There were six conspirators altogether, even the mother of one of the men, and they were tried and hung at the Armory in Washington City. In those two weeks, the Federals rounded up seventy County men and if there was any doubt about their motives or if they caught the eye of the Union Army, then they were sent to the District's Old Prison to be sorted out later. Many sat in that wretched place for days until someone came to vouch for them, while others stayed for months.

I had had enough of war talk! Then things got quiet. I know you all are wondering why I picked up and left in that spring of '64. You probably figured that I had had enough; Papa's passing and the endless fear of this war took much out of me. I thought back years ago to Mama's talks with Papa about moving back to Pennsylvania, so I figured I might do the same. I thought about leaving in 65', but the death of a dear friend made me leave earlier. Who was that Barbara asked? I never heard that any of your girlfriends died. We will get to that in a bit, I said. About a week after that horrible day I was sitting alone in the cottage when it all came back to me, the injustices, Mama, Papa, the war, losing the Olivet and my friends and seeing no end to the misery.

The next day I gathered what few things I had, enough to fill only a small bag and the papers Papa had from his dealings with the Army and told Danny that I was leaving and that the old wagon and mule were now his to do as he wished. He was beside himself, but I had to go and he understood, and then gave me twenty dollars that he had saved up for the trip. Barbara and George were surprised to hear that Danny knew all along. The next day Danny and I set out for Washington and when we reached the bridge and said our goodbyes, I begged him not to say anything to anyone and he swore he would never tell. I told the guards in a sweet tone and smiling, as only a young lady could do for a man, that I was visiting my uncle Gilbert in Georgetown, and without much mind, they let me through. From there it was a short way to the depot and soon, Washington was nowhere to be seen. I watched the countryside pass me in a daze as the train headed north to Baltimore, then Philly, and with every mile the burden on my soul eased.

But who was your friend they asked? I stared at the floor for a bit. Barbara seeing my discomfort asked Danny to take Tommy outside to tend to the mules. I couldn't hold it any longer and just wept into Barbara's arms. Of all the things that befell me during those times, it was Thomasine who became my rock and the best thing that ever happened to me. I wasn't going to hide her in the shadows any more, feeding idle gossip. She was my girl, and I was proud to be her mother, blessed to me by a man I had come to know in the midst of war. Though the Union Army took him away from me, this young girl was my salvation, conceived from love, when there was little around here. Almost no one knew about John, but it was now time to let my closest friends know the truth. It was a story that needed a bit more tea to get through and after making a fresh pot, we retired into the parlor to let them hear the tale of a young cavalryman..

10 A DASHING CAVALRYMAN

On a Sunday in October of '62, Papa told me to go on ahead to Camp Union to finish off a run he was to make the day before being tired on account of his coughs. I bridled the mules, hitched the small wagon making my way past Camp Hill and was no further than a few yards off the side gate when out in a hurry came fifty cavalrymen. They rushed by so fast that it spooked my horses, wheeling the wagon and throwing me off onto the muddy ground. I was so angry at the nerve of these men and that none paid me no mind. I stood up and screamed at them over their rudeness, that we were not rebels and deserved better. All of a sudden one of the last two cavalrymen wheeled his horse around, came back and stopped right before me to scare me no doubt, but I didn't move a bit. He looked down at me and I stared at him something fierce. I was just about ready to give him a piece of my mind when others around me tried to hush me lest I be arrested.

This man started his yelling to me that he was a soldier of the Army, but before he could say more I pointed my finger right at him and told him to stop then and there.

He was so surprised that he stopped and we just looked each other. This young man was a bit thin, his jacket didn't fit well and his belt was tied well past the last hole. He had a chiseled chin and blondish hair and wonderful blue eyes. He wheeled around a couple times finally stopped and said sorry ma'am, we didn't mean to startle you and the horses and I apologize on behalf of my cavalry troop. It took all that I could muster for me to just not keep yelling at him, but something in his eyes made me stop. He didn't dare get off his horse risking the ire of his commander who by now was now a hundred yards away. He tipped his hat again said "ma'am you just met Private John H. Thompson of the Ohio 1st Cavalry, Company C and we are here to fight the enemies of the Republic". I put my hands on my hip and told him to never mind that "Private John H. Thompson". Around here you show courtesy when you pass a woman in a carriage and that you take care not to startle the horses. It pays me no mind what *Army* you are from as we have many regiments come and go through in this war and never had any of them been so rude. This Private Thompson was taken aback, then paused for a second look and said, "I'm sorry, Miss."

I've seen you around these camps riding in the company of an older man he said. My Papa is a teamster helping get supplies to and from the camps and is well-known by the commanders, so you best pay heed and watch what comes out of your mouth next time. This now sheepish soldier was taken aback again by my fiery tongue, but said he must attend to his mission but that he would keep his eye on me. I doubt you will, I said, and with that he wheeled around and rode off to catch up with his men. That was the first time I had met Johnny, and I was blushing so from the emotion of it all. Maybe that young man might be something kind in all that is hateful of this terrible war. I thought about him much, but told none of girls about this young man.

Three days later I was riding with Papa and as we entered Camp Hill I looked over and saw the standard of that 1st Ohio Cavalry just inside the gate and over at the horse pen, I saw him again. He glanced up and we both caught a long glance at each other, the way a proper girl shouldn't do in public not wanting to seem meek. Papa had wheeled over to the quartermaster's tent to get his chit for the supplies we brought. Private Thompson tied off his horse and walked on over quickly, more sheepishly this time. He held his hands nervous like a young boy and looked at me and said, "Miss, you know we were not properly introduced in all the fury last time and I again wanted to apologize for my behavior." So again, I'm Private John Thompson, Ohio man born and bred. As a good Christian man, I am atoning for my sins that day when you fell out of the wagon. He asked if I was from around these parts. Certainly I said, Alexandria County is my home and my Papa is a teamster making the rounds in these camps nearly every day. Johnny said that he had seen us and was happy to catch my eye, of course not meaning to be so forward in front of Papa. I looked at his dusty uniform and said "it looks like you've been on patrol". Why yes, we had just come back from riding all day and the Union Army did well not losing any troops to rebel fire as he tried to impress himself upon me. Well, Private Thompson, we all have work to do in this war.

We just stared at each other awkwardly in silence until his men, seeing him talk to me began to razz on him. He turned and looked sheepishly at them as they said, her Papa won't be one to put up with the likes of you private, so it's best you leave that nice little girl alone. They were laughing as Johnny looked at me and I looked at him. I told him that as a good Christian man, he would have no trouble seeing what he could do to find the furnishings that belonged to the Olivet that were taken last winter, and maybe get what was left of the church returned to the congregation. He said he would try, but he was being boastful, but our Olivet was nothing but footings on the corner of their camp, while horses were stabled out back behind the burial grounds.

The following Sunday Johnny rode up to the Wunder fence and stayed there a bit, hoping to see me. Danny saw what was happening with this young man and yelled for me to come out. Johnny was taken aback when Papa and I came out, but like a gentleman, he introduced himself properly to Papa. After some pleasantries, Johnny asked me to come to the Olivet where they were to bury yet another young soldier friend of his who had died the night before, having withered away from a chronic stomach as so many others had. Of course, I said, and together we watched a fine little service for a young man so far from home. I knew then that everyone was feeling the pain from this war. Johnny led me back out to the gate which gave us a chance to talk, trying to understand what this war was about. He was far from home getting $13 a month to do the nation's bidding, but he had nothing in his pockets to show for it as everything was on account with the Government. He spoke softly about the horrible conditions in camp and how many men were sick with diarrhea or scurvy and what they gave then to eat wasn't much. When they could, to ease the boredom, soldiers would sneak out of camp and forage for things to eat.

That talk was to be one of many as we found ourselves finding excuses to run into each other about the area and along the fence line. A couple of weeks later, I was driving the team past the camp with a small basket of vegetables from the garden when Johnny came riding up. Before I knew it, we got to talking about the vegetables and I asked him outright if he would join me in a lunch sometime? He was taken aback, but eagerly agreed as I suggested we meet the next day noon at the spring lest we attract too much attention and I didn't want him to get in trouble. I was so nervous and my heart was beating a mile a minute, and he must have seen me blush. "Well, Miss Payne, I would be honored, and since I don't have duty until well past supper, I would be happy to join you." With that I wheeled my wagon around and he his horse eagerly awaiting our meeting.

It was a beautiful day without a cloud in the sky when I made my way along the Little Falls Road to the spring, basket in hand day dreaming. I didn't tell Eveline or anyone else what I was up to, not needing any of the girls to start gossiping. Johnny came up riding hard behind me. Not wanting to look too eager, I didn't turn until he was just on my heels. He quickly jumped off, not saying much, but with the biggest grin on his face. We got to walking together talking about things and just as we topped the ridge, I saw the unthinkable. In the two weeks since I had come here last, the Army had found our spring. Dozens of soldiers were sitting there, talking, some cleaning and some relieving themselves, it was horrible. Down a ways along the creek, a hundred head of cattle were grazing and just beyond them a slaughter house. I was shocked, turning to Johnny, angrily asking him when did this happen? He said the Army had moved its beef cattle here a week ago and were likely to stay. He was sorry, but the Army had to be fed and someone figured this was a good place with the creek and all being between both camps.

I just broke down and began crying, Johnny standing there not knowing what to do. You don't understand, this was *our* place, where we got away from the war. I wanted this to be special. They had no right. We just sat there on the ridge off the Little Falls, letting me rant for a bit. I know a spot I said, let's go. We went back up a ways to the grove behind Eveline's place, set a blanket near the tall oaks, and had a fine meal of bread with jam, tomatoes with vinegar and pepper, cucumber with salt, all from my garden. Johnny didn't say much at first, but as he ate he looked like a little boy savoring food not tasted in a while. You don't know how awful the food we get is, so this is a treasure, he said. We got to talking, getting to know more about each other. Johnny enlisted the summer of '61 for three-years, riding for the 1st Ohio. By the next March, his Company and another had been in skirmishes all throughout the Shenandoah Valley and even a big battle in Winchester, Virginia. Things cooled down a bit for them in June and July, but picked up in August with a major battle at Cedar Mountain, and then after that came the second battle at Bull Run. Johnny told me of long marches, cannon fire and seeing men consumed by it to their deaths. As he spoke, I looked and saw the horrors in his eyes of friends from Ohio now gone.

It was only this September when the 1st was assigned here, far away from the killing they said. War was not the boastful adventure they had once thought it was. Johnny needed the rest and it showed in his face. In many ways I need the rest, too. 1862 was as much a mess for many with the war raging, as much as '61 was such a surprise with all the troops coming here. It was a trail of tears that we didn't know where it would lead. I told him about Papa's problems with money being tight and all, and being a terrible burden on everyone. We talked about everyday things and where we thought we would be if this war didn't happen. We met every Sunday by the back corner of the camp along the ridgeline where we first saw Lowe's balloons. He got permission to leave his post to see me from his Sargent by the name of McMasters. Though he was a tyrant of sorts, McMasters had seen what this war could do to people and that everyone needed somebody to talk to. He even did what he could to make life easy for us when Papa came to the camp. I needed Johnny and he needed me. Our meetings by those trees were like medicine for tired souls. But something was happening; Johnny was not the brash young cavalrymen like when I first met him, and things only got worse in November.

Johnny told me about his best friend Jacob Conklin. He along with George Williams and Ethan Hall were from the same county and enlisted together, becoming close friends. While in camp a man nearly twice their age by the name of Fred Walker took them all under his wing and worked to keep them alive. But death came anyway, as George died early in the campaigns out in the Shenandoah, and Jacob died in August before they were posted here, felled by a musket ball at Brandy Station, being in agony until he died. Ethan was struck down by sickness before getting posted here and was taken to a hospital in Washington, where he later died. Johnny said that all of this loss was hard to take in as they had gone through so much together. These boys were no longer on a grand adventure, being used up doing the Federal's bidding, all the while trying to make a good account of themselves. Johnny and I were now close friends and by late November '62 my feelings for him were pretty strong with him telling me that had it not been for this war, he'd ask for my hand in marriage. No one had ever treated me the way Johnny did with his kindness and tenderness. He was looking at me like he knew we were beginning a love for each other.

At Christmas, Camp Hill held a big festival with the fence lines and the main gate decorated with fir tree branches and ribbon. You could hear music and psalms coming from the camp as men tried their best to make the special holiday bearable. Johnny earned a pass and came a calling to our home; as it happened, Papa was at Doc's being treated. Johnny came to the door, scared a bit not knowing what Papa would say, but he had nothing to fear. I opened the door and there we stood staring at each other. I don't know what came over me but I hugged him hard then we kissed for what seemed like forever giving me such a rush of warmth and excitement that every bad thing I felt that day just melted away. Seeing that we were out in plain sight of anyone on the road, I led him in and shut the door. I was in the arms of a man who was kind and gentle, caught in a whirlwind of war like I was. It was as beautiful as it was frightful; and we spent many an hour together in each other's embrace. This was the best Christmas I had in a long time.

January of 63' was a particularly cold month. Johnny told me that his friend Fred Walker was none too good, as illness struck Company "E" hard and men were dying. A few days later I got word that Johnny's friend and guardian had died as well and he took it real hard. It was one thing to die in battle, but it was another to watch a man die of illness, no bravery, no tearful memorials, nothing. Men withered away, delirious from sickness, lying on soiled bedding unable to control themselves. Men who died in camp rarely got much remembering, their things were packed away and sent home quickly as if they never were. I couldn't see Johnny that day as he was on patrol, but I did send word to Sargent McMasters to let Johnny know of how sorry I was to hear the news.

I didn't see much of Johnny in February as the 1st Ohio went on even more patrols, getting in skirmishes all throughout the lands west of Falls Church. I worried all the time hoping nothing bad happened to him. With the loss of his friends George, Ethan, Jacob and now Walker, Johnny got into a terrible malaise. Walker's death had struck Johnny unusually hard and he was no longer the same young man I had come to know. The war was taking away too many good folk and it was weighing heavy on him. On those days were we caught a quick talk at the fence line, he would rile about the rebels cruelty, but also said he understood about defending one's state. I hushed him as best I could as these sorts of words could get a regular man arrested, and a soldier like him shot.

Johnny showed up at our door one cold March night and I almost didn't recognize him without his uniform.

Thank goodness Papa was sound asleep, heavy from the laudanum Doc had been given him before he moved to Washington. He looked nervous, saying he wasn't in uniform on account of a pass he got, but I knew better as any soldier caught wearing civilian clothes would be put in jail or worse, shot. Johnny said he had permission from Sargent McMasters, but I didn't believe him. He had a worried look, so I let Johnny inside and tried to talk some sense to him, but he admitted he was hell bent on deserting that night. I begged him to stay with me for a while as I missed him so, but we knew he had to leave before roll call as patrols would be sent by sunup. We sat there together in each other's arms in a dark corner thinking how our time together would put an end to his plans and he would soon get back to camp, but instead he looked me straight in the eye, and said he was taking a horse. I was shocked, as this would mean trouble for Papa's hauls, but that wasn't important now. My young suitor was about to leave for good, and worse yet be on the run from the Army. Cecelia, I'm coming back to see you when I can. I'll tie a blue handkerchief on the fourth fence rail along the Glebe and that would tell you to meet me at sundown the next evening in the woods where the Little Falls Road met the creek. Johnny gave me a long kiss goodbye, and walked out the door. I just stood there, numb from what had just happened, but before I could gather my thoughts and run outside, Johnny mounted and rode away. I was shattered not knowing when I'd see him again or what to expect. This was yet another injustice for me and I cried the rest of the night.

The next morning, it came over me that Johnny was a deserter from the Union Army and it was best that no one knew about it, but I had to tell Papa that one of his horses was gone. When I did, he was beside himself as we were now going to be one wagon short for our hauls and with the debts we had from last winter, we weren't in a good spot as he had made many commitments that he now couldn't meet.

In a low voice of a man shaken to the core and weak from illness, he told me to hitch a wagon so he could go to Camp Hill and report that thieves got to his horse. Johnny didn't set out his kerchief that month as I knew he was probably long gone from here. By May, rebel Colonel Mosby was leading a group of raiders making trouble in the rear lines and word was he was in our area. Folks were scared not knowing if their farms would be burned as they were in '61. Making the rounds some weeks later, Papa and I were at Camp Ethan Allen when we heard talk from a Lieutenant Moore about a cavalry Private from Ohio who deserted to the cause of the South and was now marauding with Mosby's guerillas.

Major Doubleday, the Provost Marshal at the fort, had gotten so many reports of marauding and robbery up this way, that he gathered most of the key landowners and told them in no uncertain terms that this traitor must be found and brought to justice. Should they not assist in the capture, under his authority as commander in the area, he would arrest them all and put them in the Old Prison in Washington as collaborators. His order had put the fear of God into folks in this part of the county, so a big manhunt was now on. Papa told me that they hired the likes of the seedy Trummel brothers who lived just a few miles above Great Falls to hunt him down. My heart sank, as I knew that the hunted man was my Johnny.

It was an unusually hot day in June and I had made the rounds through all the forts that was just coming home with little to show for it. Papa was weaker than ever and set to sleeping most of the day. As I was putting away the horses, I stopped in my tracks staring at a blue kerchief that was tied on the fence. My heart was racing and I looked around hoping to catch a glimpse of him, but nothing. I eagerly waited for the next day to get to the woods by the creek and just as we planned when I saw him that last night.

We embraced, kissed and cried as we were both scared that at any time someone would see us and call the troops. I told Johnny that a bounty was on his head and that the Tremmel brothers were sent to hunt him down. The Army said you were doing some awful things, robbing folks and stealing horses, is that true? You pay them no mind as I'm just riding with some other men just trying to set things straight around here. He said that I shouldn't worry as he was doing just fine and soon the Union Army would get tired of looking for him. Johnny was an honorable man and would do what was right. I told him that Papa's debts were mounting up, well over $100 and that he was in a poor state. Johnny told me not to worry, that everything would work out. We embraced and held each other thinking maybe it could be the last. After staring at each other in the dark for what seemed hours, we got spooked by noises in the woods, so I hugged him one last time and off he went into the night.

Three weeks passed before I saw another kerchief on the fence. Things had gotten pretty hard as Papa was pretty much bed ridden now and the runs now given to others. My days were spent keeping us fed and caring for Papa, the only respite was thinking about Johnny and how I missed him so. When we met, he said he had been all around these lands, way past Fairfax Courthouse seeing all kinds of things without a care as in his mind he had done his duty for the Union Army now it was time for him to do little for himself. I told him things were terribly hard for Papa and he told me that things were now getting real hard for him, too. Johnny had met up with other like-minded folk looking out for their homes and that he had done some things that he was none too proud of. He got real close to me, looked at me serious and took out a pouch from his jacket with nearly $200 in it. "This is for you and your Pa, he said as I sat there just staring at it all. "It's my way of taking care of things just as you and Papa took care of me," he said. "Where did you get this," I demanded. "It's best that you not know," he said. I knew something terrible happened and this money was ill-gotten, but he assured me he was just gambling and had a lucky streak; I knew better.

At Fort Ethan Allen, Colonel Banks had reached the end of his patience as there was not much to show in finding their traitor. He was now sure locals were hiding him and now threatened to stop us from doing business with the camps unless Johnny was found within two weeks. Sure enough, I learned from Sargent McMasters that troops arrested Johnny and brought him back to Fort Ethan Allen. It had been four months now that Johnny had been on the run and word had gotten to all the camps of his capture. He was hurt, and I hoped that once he recovered they'd give him a stern admonishment and return him to duty.

I was being naïve. McMasters said Johnny was in serious trouble and there wasn't much we could do; and I couldn't speak for him lest I'd be arrested, too. The Union Army had become emboldened by its victories on the march and there was no room in this man's army for deserters. I made my way to Fort Ethan Allen a day later asking Sargent Baker if he knew anything more. He told me Johnny was marauding around Great Falls and was captured on the 21st and has pled guilty. He was being sent to the convalescent camp at Sickles Barracks in Alexandria city to tend to his wounds before his trial. The charges against Johnny were grave, being accused of deserting the Union Army, and of serving in the guerrilla band known as the Mosby's Raiders. This was terrible news as my Johnny was now a criminal, imprisoned and may even be executed. I couldn't tell anyone, not even Papa of what I knew and that I've been seeing a deserter. That would surely kill him. But things got worse, McMasters told me a week later that Johnny had escaped from the guards as he was on his way to the convalescent camp and was now on the run again. I was beside myself with grief. The Union Army would likely show no mercy once he was caught. The manhunt for my Johnny was back on.

Weeks went by and I heard nothing. Mosby's men had made themselves known in these parts all summer long. It's as if they were ghosts and folks were scared. By October of '63, we were hearing about battles all throughout the south, Maryland and even just over the border into Pennsylvania with such horrific losses on both sides. Folks were just numb from the war and hoped that it would just end. Papa was now worse than ever having lost a lot of weight, finding it very hard to sleep, coughing something awful. Danny tried to help where he could, but without Doc, I didn't know if he would survive the winter. Although I paid off most of Papa's debts over time using the money I got from Johnny, I had to be careful lest folks became suspicious of where it came from as I was no longer hauling. To pay off the rest and to get Papa the medicines he needed, I sold one of the wagons and another mule to other teamsters and I was pretty much set to living on the hill. Finally, in late October as I was getting to the garden, I saw the kerchief on the fence. I just stood there staring at it not knowing what to do. It wasn't for me to get any more involved as many were on the lookout for him, it just wasn't safe. So I made up my mind that I wouldn't go to meet him the next night and that would be the end of it. I had shed too many tears for him, and I was now empty. Besides, I had other things to worry about.

That next night, I was cleaning up after supper while Papa was sleeping, there came a quiet knock at the door. Thinking it was Danny coming to check up, I said to come on in and just kept on doing chores. When I looked up, my heart almost burst from fright, I was so startled that I almost cut myself with a knife. Standing there holding his hat in his hands, looking all broke and dirty was my Johnny. I was hoping we would meet by the creek he said, but when you didn't show, I had to risk coming here to see you. I just ran to him and began crying so, touching his face and staring into his eyes. We sat over by the far wall away from the fireplace not wanting to wake Papa. We stared at each other for a while not saying much. We knew that if anyone saw him coming here, that the Army would soon be here. I wanted to spend as much time as I could with him, asking if he was still hurt as I had heard. Johnny said he was fine, but scared; we both were. He was in real trouble and was going to make his way to Dranesville in the dark as the Army was after him and maybe he could meet up with others out there, but he had to see me one last time. All he kept saying was how things had gotten so bad, but that I was the best thing that ever happened to him. He loved me and maybe once the war was over he'd come back to get me and we'd live out a proper life together.

I just sat there listening as he spoke and as he did, my fears just melted away. I wanted Johnny and he wanted me. Before he could get a few more words out of his mouth, I kissed him so; and before long we were in a passionate embrace. We made love to each other in such a tender way and spent the rest of the evening locked in each other's arms. All thoughts of the war and the like melted away. I didn't care if the Army came in the morning, burst through the door and took us both. For now it was us this night. By midnight or so, Johnny knew he had to go lest early patrols catch up with him. It was bitter sweet after such a night, but things were going to get very hard for him, so I packed some food and gave him a couple of Papa's old shirts to wear. We embraced one last time, repeating our pledge to come together after the war. And with that, he was gone. Not really knowing if we'd ever see each other again, I barely got any sleep the rest of the night thinking of our wonderful night of passion and yet worried what was next.

Papa's condition took a turn for the worse a few

days later, with him not being able to breathe right and the days and nights being so cold. Danny and I did what we could and even sent for Reverend Hoblitzell a few times, but there was nothing anyone could do. Papa was nearing the end; his eyes had not opened in a couple of days and he lay in the throes of a death rattle, moving his jaw as if trying to speak to the heavens. I held his hand, thinking how strong it used to be, holding me safe. He would murmur for Mama and say things I couldn't understand. It's as if I was with Mama all over again years ago when she succumbed to the grip. I sat for two days watching as this shell of a man was being taken from me. Papa had been so strong, but now he was as frail as a child, coughing up something awful and breathing in a loud rattle.

On that final night, Danny sat there with me as tears rolled down both our faces. Papa's breathing got real weak and I leaned over, holding his hand, and whispered in his ear that I would be alright, and it was proper that he now go see Mama. I saw his last breath leave his body and just sobbed on his chest as the grip from his hand loosened. Danny hugged me then went off to get the Reverend while I stayed with Papa. He was gone and I was now all alone. We buried him next to Mama the next day under that tree on the corner of the Glebe Road and it was fitting. Many folks came by to pay their respects and remind me of how good of a man he was. I spent the next few days alone, not wanting to talk to anyone. So much had happened these past few years, and this war had taken yet another good soul.

Johnny was captured by the Trammel brothers in late October and taken again to Fort Ethan Allen. The charges against Johnny were many; deserting, riding with Raiders, and now horse thieving, robbing a man at gun point and marauding. This couldn't have been him, not my Johnny I said to myself. I pleaded with Sargent Baker to let me see him when I went over there a few days later, but there was nothing he could do except maybe let me know what was going on as best he could. The Union Army was going to purge its ranks of such criminals and Johnny was going to pay. He was going to stay locked up at Fort Ethan Allen until his trial later that month. Could I see him, I wondered. But such was nonsense as it wouldn't take much for them to figure out if I was involved. I wanted so much to testify at the trial on his behalf, but I was well aware of the terrible suffering that would befall folks around here. Whether Johnny committed these heinous crimes I wasn't sure, but the Union Army had seen fit to accuse him and likely wouldn't do so without proof. I went home feeling so weak from all the worry, and even threw up twice along the way. There was little I could do.

The military court martial happened a week later in early November. I came to find out from Sargent Baker who was there that they held court in the mess tent. The names of the Officers that were to judge my Johnny were read aloud. Johnny was asked if he objected to these men, to which he answered no. To many gathered outside the tents, the charges were read aloud, accusing him of desertion to the enemy in March of '63, escape from the guard in July while on his way to the hospital camp and marauding with a certain band of brigands known as Mosby's guerillas. To those charges, Johnny looked down and pleaded guilty to escape but not guilty of being in a guerrilla band. He was also accused of robbing $239 from a James Trammell, citizen of Great Falls, but I knew that to be a shady character that likely made it all up.

Trammell was one of the witnesses for the Federals with another farmer named George Jackson that I remembered having done work with Papa some time ago. Jackson testified under oath that he saw Johnny in Dranesville as part of Major Legate's Confederate Raider command nearly all the way through since March '63, saying that Johnny had been living with the Trammel's. He said they captured him and took him to Major Young at Fort Ethan Allen in November of '63. The young man told me he stole horses and robbed citizens saying Johnny had stolen from Daniel Gordon and Albert Anderson. He said Johnny told him personally that he joined the company by permission of Mosby himself and I saw him ride with a raider name Karp, known to be with Mosby. James Trammel testified that Johnny was riding with Mosby's men nearby and had a bad reputation. He said Johnny admitted to them that he was a deserter and rode with Mosby's men all throughout the spring and summer of 63' and that he stole my money. It looked like Trammel just repeated what Jackson said.

I almost collapsed when I heard that the Court-martial deliberated for a short time and the next day found my Johnny guilty on all charges and recommended he be executed. But there was hope as a reprieve was given by the General in command of the area that the execution be suspended until the pleasure of the President is known. If there was to be no execution, then he recommended a dishonorable discharge and five years of hard labor. There was hope that Mr. Lincoln would show some mercy and not allow a 19-year old that had served well and gone through so much loss to be shot. They told me Johnny was going to be held at the Fort all through the winter and I tried so hard to see him or leave something for him over the next few weeks, stopping by almost every day in my black mourning dress, but the sergeants would have none of it. It was draining me so and I was sick nearly every morning.

To my surprise in early December, they transferred Johnny to the Sickels Barracks in Alexandria city, the same place they took him before when he was hurt. Maybe he'd be too sick and the Army would have mercy on him, forgiving his conviction. But regardless, I was going to see him there if I could in February when the roads were more passable. Maybe Johnny could be freed, I thought, as I heard that one of the Trammel brothers who had testified against Johnny, had been arrested with some other man named Barns and were both in the county prison. Both men were accused of associating with the Mosby gang and had been taking money themselves. To me, this was all nasty business and no one's hands were clean. Johnny must have taken their stolen money and given it to me. I knew those Trammels could not be trusted and my Johnny was now to be executed for their dastardly deeds.

Danny and I made our way to the Sickels Barracks Hospital a week later after a dry spell when the roads got better. The place was just off the Fairfax Road as you came into Alexandria and I had watched the camp being built when I was in Alexandria last with Papa. It was a large camp with a large three-story hospital and a barracks that went on for two city blocks. Surely he was being cared for there and it might be easy for me to see him. I talked to the camp guard to see if he knew anything about a Private Thompson who was being treated that had been accused of desertion. Sadly he said, we have many Army deserters and thieves here and he had no time to look for just one Private cavalryman from Ohio. I begged him to please look at the log book as he was sent here in early December. The guard took pity and asked around, coming back after a bit saying that a Private Thompson of Ohio was being held in the camp prison to await his sentence being carried out, but the prison was no place for a woman to be unless I had an official pass from Fort Ethan Allen's commander. Angry and scared, I was so close to him, I could feel it, but alas it wasn't meant to be. I made my way back home to see what I could do.

I was feeling quite ill most every morning as the week went by when the unthinkable happened. Sergeant McMasters got word to me through Corporal Jackson that

Johnny's pardon was not to be and that he was to be executed. Lincoln himself saw no reason to question the court's ruling to stop the sentence from being carried out. Corporal Jackson told me that Johnny was to be executed the following Monday and they weren't going to let anyone see him. I thanked the corporal for the news and closed the door, sobbing as I fell to the floor. Yet another injustice was heaped upon me. On that first Sunday in February of '64, Danny came by with Reverend Hoblitzell who no doubt had been told about Johnny. We spent a few hours saying verse and singing hymns as it helped ease my mind a bit. I told the Reverend that I had to see Johnny and that Danny and I were planning to take the wagon in the morning. My dear, the good Lord will be with Johnny that day, and a woman in your *"condition"* shouldn't think about such a hard wagon ride. You could have heard a pin drop. Was it that obvious, I said in a low voice? My dear, you can't hide what is there for all to see. You have to see to the health of the child in you and while I will not pry in your affairs, it may be best you do not go to Alexandria tomorrow. I thanked the Reverend and told him I would take care of myself, but that Johnny needed to know and that I was going to go there regardless. Fine he said, but I can't have you risking your health, so you will take my buggy as it will afford you a much safer ride than your wagon and here is some money to use the turnpike, as it will get you there faster. I gave him a big hug and thanked him so.

Danny and I got up hours before sunup to make our way to Alexandria before many folks on the road. It had dried up a bit and the Glebe road was more passable and since I wasn't feeling well, Danny did most of the driving while I ate some biscuit and chewed on some mint and chamomile leaves to soothe my stomach. We headed south for a few miles and then took to the turnpike road into Alexandria for the next five miles or so to a checkpoint just this side of Sickles Barracks hours before noon. There were many more Army places about than last year, but there weren't as many troops around as I had recalled, likely on account of the war had moved on up into Maryland and further. We told the soldiers gathered there that we were here for the Private Thompson affair and could they point us to where we could see him. "Affair? My dear, this ain't no *affair!* We are going to shoot the traitor known as Thompson today and he can't be seen now as he is getting his last meal and rights. So, if you want to see justice done with everyone else, I suggest you leave your buggy in that field and walk over." My teeth were clinched and it was all I could do to keep from screaming at the guard. Danny held my arm, knowing how mad I was, but he thanked the guard and we made our way to the fields.

There were many soldiers and civilians standing around, I suspect waiting for the spectacle. We asked around and some soldiers told us that the execution would happen at noon on the far field along the hillside. I was scared and weak from fear and a morning of sickness more than I had ever been. When we got to the field and I just stood there hearing folks talk about the war and Johnny, a man they knew nothing about. Oddly, I saw many women, colored and white, there to see this, even reporters from the National Republican there talking to folks gathered. I wanted none of that and stood there quietly with Danny at my side.

The church bells startled me as they told the noon hour. Soon after, a drummer began a somber marching cadence as a line of a dozen soldiers from the 1st District Volunteers led by a Sargent Summers, who Papa and I had known from our trips into Washington. They formed up and at the end was a man in chains wearing a white shirt. I could barely see his face as he looked down, but I knew it was Johnny. My heart sank as I grabbed Danny's arm. The soldiers marched slowly as they came closer to us and formed a line facing the berm that now had a pine casket set on the ground with its lid set aside. Johnny stood next to a preacher and an officer. I struggled to see, but there were just too many men standing ahead of me. Danny grabbed me and led me to one side so that I could catch a glimpse of Johnny and maybe him of me. The drumming stopped and the field got quiet. A sergeant read aloud the charges: John H. Thompson, Private, 1st Ohio Cavalry deserted in 1863 in the vicinity of Chain Bridge and Fort Ethan Allen. He has been jailed six months for robbing and plundering alone and with Mosby's Raiders. Private Thompson was found guilty by the court in a sentence that was upheld by none other than President Lincoln himself.

I wanted it all just to just slow down, but things were now moving in ways no one could stop. The reverend faced Johnny, raising his Bible in one hand as he put the other on Johnny's shoulder, and whispered to him. Johnny then began singing a hymn at the top of his voice, all the while with a smile on his face. My Johnny was accused of crimes by treacherous men and about to die for them. Danny struggled to hold me as my knees got weak. The militiamen lined up and got their rifles at the ready. They walked Johnny over to the wooden casket and sat him down on the edge while they covered his face with a hood. I yelled out for Johnny, seeing his head rise a bit as if he recognized me, when at that moment the Sargent yelled *fire!* The loud rap of rifle shot dug deep into my soul as four musket balls tore into Johnny's chest. It was eerily quiet and blurry in my mind as I watched his body fall into the coffin. I collapsed to my knees as others around me stared. After a bit, the militia marched off and the crowd began to clear. Soldiers carted Johnny away in that coffin to be buried later in the local cemetery. The war had consumed yet another soul and I was alone yet again..

11 JUSTICE

I needed a break from all this talk, so we made our way to see the new Olivet. It was a bit smaller than the one before, only one story, but it had a nice front porch to welcome the new flock of parishioners who now came to call this area their new home. The burial grounds were much larger than before and there were a few crosses set there for soldiers who died. These poor souls were never sent home and I thought of how their families must feel not knowing what happened to their sons. Danny and George took me out back to the hitching post where back in '60, Eveline, Ella and I had carved in our initials promising to be friends forever, bringing tears to my eyes. The Olivet had gone through a few pastors on the circuit with Reverend Ames now tending this flock, but Barbara and Danny both said he was not the firebrand, or the character that Oliver Cox was. Although not quite what it was, it was beautiful to see this little church back to being the center of our new community.

Later, folks stopped by when they heard I was home, welcoming me and the like. It was especially good to talk with Charlotte telling me the latest on Eveline and her infant son. We spent hours repeating stories and reminiscing about summers at the spring, tramping for berries, sharing what we knew about whom. The men talked about the war, of battles and what became of those regiments who lived with us that first winter. Most all the men that were camped at both Halls Hill and Minor Hill went off to fight valiant battles in Richmond, Fredericksburg, Antietam, Gettysburg, and other places as the names of the officers they knew kept rolling off their tongues. Most of those we got to know real well on Minor Hill were killed by that next summer in the Peninsula Campaign: Colonel Black of the 62nd Pennsylvania, leaving behind that lovely woman and those girls, Colonel Cass of the 9th Massachusetts, and Colonel Woodbury of the 4th Michigan. Commanders at Halls Hill suffered their losses too as Colonel McLane of the 83rd Pennsylvania was killed and Colonel Kerrigan of the 22nd Massachusetts was severely wounded. Just about all the Regiments camped amongst us suffered horrendous losses all through the war, including men from the 14th New York under Colonel McQuade, who came so gallantly to our aid in that rebel shelling that first fall. After four long years, what was left of many of them were shells of their former selves as they marched proudly in Washington in the week-long Grand Review that May of '65. This talk of war was more than I could stand, but I sat there politely and listened as best I could, thinking a bit on whether those commanders were kind to Papa or not.

The women talked about friends lost and who had moved away. It was wonderful to see faces and get reacquainted with past neighbors and Papa's friends. After they left we got to the business of preparing for the Commission, now only two days away. George said he would come with me and testify to the rightness of the script for services Papa rendered to the Union Army. I was also gonna petition a claim for Papa's horse and his good wagon too. It was not much money, maybe $700 in all, but it was the principal. But sadly, none of the many folk were eager or willing to speak on my behalf at the Commission, as most thought the whole thing seemed seedy, asking for reparations when tens of thousands of sons and husbands never came home. It looked like all folks wanted to do was put the war behind them, and here I was trying to kick it all up again like some common beggar. It had been seven years since the war ended and it looked like the country wanted to move on. I had returned not because I wanted to but because I had to for Papa and I'd spent nearly a year preparing myself for this day of reckoning.

George said the Commission started their work in March and it didn't take long for some to see it as a way to dismiss wartime wrongdoings and get what they now thought was their fair share of the spoils. Some were putting in big claims that few were willing to argue against, but most didn't put in any claims at all. George heard from some of those who had already gone before it and said the whole thing was crooked. It seemed after so many years, men who didn't speak to one another during the war, now got together to support each other's claims and get their share of what they thought they were due. Bazil Hall and Smith Minor had all testified and petitioned the commission for wages lost for road work near Minor Hill done on behalf of the Army that neither I nor George remembered any such work done.

The Federals must have caught on to these ploys as we heard they were now only paying about ten cents on the dollar for most claims. Even those that had their land taken from them for the building of a fort, like Fort Smith, were having a tough go at it. Those with questionable claims and without testimony from old Union Officers found it hard for to get their due. The Douglas's, Birch's and the Donaldson's all made claims and Samuel Ball who owned the Tavern at the crossroads put in one too. Some had more luck than others depending on who vouched for them. I wasn't going to be as lucky as Papa didn't own land, but what he lost was done at the behest of the United States Government and if anybody had a right to a claim, it was me.

George said that Minor kin petitioning for $5000 and the Commission gave them over $1000. They had asked Charles French to testify on their behalf, telling the commission that their six room home was burnt by the Union soldiers and his wagons were taken and fixed up by the rebels to look like canon when they occupied their Hill in those early days of the war. Other Minors claimed that Old Colonel George didn't vote for the ordinance and that Confederates never were allowed on the Hill and that she was owed just compensation for the Union setting up camp on her family's property. The Commissioners asked about George's secession vote at the tavern and he said it was all under duress and that General Scott himself asked him to spy for him at Minor's Hill. How could this be for a man who was arrested for sedition?

Philip Minor and his wife Elizabeth, who lived in the District during the war claimed roughly $4000 for their brick two-story home that they claimed was burnt during an attack and that Union soldiers use the bricks from the ashes to make baking ovens at nearby Camp Union. They had a lawyer testify that the Belles and their mother were truly loyal, saving Union men there during a raid by the Confederates, placing herself in between them to save their lives. That was a lie! I spit out, as we all knew that those treacherous girls invited those Union soldiers over there where they were captured. The Union burned their home for their treachery and here they were petitioning for Union wrong doing! Had they no shame?

Samuel Ball testified that they cut six acres of wood for the corduroy Military Road and that New Yorkers camped and stabled their horses on his property. The Birches were questioned about their vote when they filed a claim for food and wood taken but got nothing when their leanings were learned. A Madame Ager claimed $15,000 and was only allowed $3000 even though her place was used as a hospital by the 3rd and 8th Pennsylvania, that were camped there early on in '61. If anything, she should've been allowed more. Those with much smaller claims like the Donaldson's for $2000 had a much harder go of it due to their kin's past deeds. They lived near Halls Hill on 16 acres claiming lost timber to build Fort Ethan Allen. Donaldson had some testify on their behalf, but as he had two sons in the Confederate Army, he too was denied. Neighbor Malcolm Douglas claimed nearly $4000 and was allowed $1300 for a place he had near the Balls Crossroads that the Union Army took over when he moved into Washington to work for the Quartermaster. He told the commission how a neighbor named James Roche made threats at the polling place and had pulled a revolver on those like himself who leaned to a "no" vote.

It was not going to be easy, but George said he'd come with me to the Alexandria courthouse though he did not have much to offer the commission as he had spent most of his time those days either in Washington or at the store. But George did have standing in the community and that would help with my claim on the unpaid chits, three mules, a horse and two wagons that we tallied up at over $700 dollars. I figured it was a small price for all Papa had done for this country, supporting the Union cause, delivering his goods all throughout the county. The next day we got up before sunup to make our trip to Alexandria. I left Tommy with Barbara and Danny so she could rest, and besides, it wasn't likely they would allow her to appear anyhow. We arrived at the courthouse side door, signed in and nervously waited outside for our turn to meet with the commission with the few scraps of paper to account for Papa's sacrifice.

TWO HILLS

When I heard the clerk yell out "Payne", my heart sank. This was it, my time to make amends and to give Papa's good works a voice. We walked into a large room that had flags on both sides and pictures of Lincoln and Washington high up on the wall. We both sat down and a clerk read out my name and the petition for the amount of $700. The three men sat there and looked quietly over my petition as all I could hear was the tick-tock of the clock behind me.

After a bit they looked at us and asked who was speaking for the family. I lifted my head and leaned toward them, letting them know that I had come from Pennsylvania, spending what little money I had to seek justice for my Papa. I told them of how he came to help the Union as they were first getting settled in our county hauling supplies and teaching many sergeants about the trails in the area. The commissioners were taken aback by my tone but then asked more questions on who I was, our leanings toward secession and asked to see any papers that would corroborate my story. George just sat there and didn't say much except that Papa was an honest man, only charging the Army half the cost of others to haul goods to all parts of the county. Papa said it was his duty to support the Army as best as he could. Only one of the commissioners seemed sympathetic to my plight seeing that I had gone through all this trouble.

Before long, they ruled that the chits had no standing as those were to be paid then and that Papa had erred in not cashing them in at that time. As for the wagon and the horse, nothing could corroborate my story as George was not there when it happened and no proof the Union Army was to blame. I was nearly in tears by this point but I refused to let them beat me. I leaned in again and looked the most cantankerous of the three in the eye and explained the story of how Papa and I struggled through the war and could barely make ends meet. I was now getting pretty angry telling them that Papa did his part for the Union, standing up

227

to men at gunpoint to cast his vote against secession and it was people like us that the Army was there to protect. We were caught in the middle of the war zone for a year just trying to survive and that Papa had helped the Union cause by delivering supplies almost daily between Fort Ethan Allen, Camps Union, Hall and Beatie Black and even making long trips to Washington and Alexandria City for the Army. For all intents and purposes he had served the Army and had done so and done so valiantly. When they asked why Papa wasn't here to testify, I told them that he passed away in '63 of grave illness after his lungs were burnt by acid he hauled for Professor Lowes balloons which were important for the war. I was not seeking a pension or any such thing from the Government, only a bit of justice as a testament to a man who gave so much.

The commissioners seemed in no mood to listen as they had no doubt heard many stories with people twisting the truth of how loyal they were and how their property was unjustly taken. We weren't the only ones to testify how we supported the Union Army and did so at great peril to ourselves at the hands of people like Mosby's guerillas and rebel pickets and raiding parties. The commissioners seemed little interested in digging up old hardships as many had suffered during the war and all folks wanted to do now was put it behind them. The commissioners thanked George and me for our time and that they would soon give their ruling. We waited in the hall for what seemed like an hour , but was only about ten minutes. The clerk came out, waving only to me to come in for the ruling.

The commissioners asked me to sit and just stared at me. Miss Payne, we have already spent too much time on this petition, but we all sympathize with all your Papa did. That being said, the U.S. Government cannot fully back your claim for lack of proper papers attesting to the losses. These men seemed sensitive to my cause. Miss, we have ruled for a $200 compensation in exchange for your signature on a promissory against any future claims against the Federal Government. I sat back and thought to myself whether $200 was all Papa's life was worth for the hard work over three long years, his suffering, and thefts. This paltry sum was less than the $13 a month a soldier would get paid and from where I stood, Papa was just as much a soldier for the Union as anyone else around here.

They were getting impatient and the head commissioner barked out, "Miss you don't understand, we have lots of work to do and already spent enough time on your claim. I highly recommend you take this settlement and sign acceptance or you will be back before this commission to even less satisfaction." I sat back, paused for a bit, then looked them in the eye and smiled as I knew then that the Government, in offering what it did, had officially acknowledged Papa. I agreed to their terms, took their chit and thanked them for their time. I walked out, smiling at George as we went to see the clerk.

To the Federal Government, my signature was just one of many to close the books on the war. For me it was the last scene to this sad tale; seeing Papa wither away serving the Union cause, living in fear for those years, losing friends and having my Johnny taken from me. It was more than any young girl of seventeen should have had to endure. But, my trip here brought meaning and closure to Papa's life; so in a sense I felt victorious. We stepped out onto the street, stopping to let the sun shine on my face. "I think it's time for Tommy and me to get on with our lives." "Where would that be," George asked? "Do you know of a nice place in a county nestled between two hills where a mother could raise her daughter?" "I think I do," he said with a warm smile.

EPILOGE

Alexandria (now Arlington) County was granted its charter back from the military in 1870 after five years of Federal control during the Reconstruction Period following the Civil War. At that time it formed a County Council with Smith Minor and George Wunder as members. In 1900, the County restructured its lower border as Alexandria City became part of Fairfax County. The county changed its name to Arlington after "Arlington House, the residence of the Lee-Custis plantation overlooking the Long and Aqueduct Bridges. Arlington's population is now over two-hundred thousand, a far cry from the 1500 or so in the county areas at the time of the war. Arlington maintains a strong link to its Civil War past and many of the sites in this story remain.

Alexandria remains a vibrant city on the Potomac in the Washington Metropolitan area. It too maintains a strong link to its Civil War past with much of its Old Town made up of mid and late 19th century buildings. Streets, such as King, Duke and Washington remain as key thoroughfares throughout Old-Town with a monument at the intersection of

Washington and Duke Streets where Alexandrians first volunteered to fight with the Confederacy shortly after the secession vote. The large railroad roundhouse erected by the Union Army to move war supplies up from the wharfs to all points south no longer exists, but was bordered by Duke, and Henry Streets. Historical markers exist where key fortifications were and the city maintains the remnants of Fort Ward a few miles up from Old Town just off the Leesburg Pike. Within its museum is a piece of the flag that Colonel Ellsworth gave his life to tear down that first night of the invasion as well as his cap.

Places:

Aqueduct Bridge – The Bridge from Georgetown to Virginia that spurred off the Chesapeake & Ohio Canal system that was drained to allow union Troops to invade Virginia no longer exists, though the stone landing on the Georgetown end can be seen just a few yards up river from the current Key Bridge built in the 1930s for automobile traffic.

Bloomindale – The lovely home built on Tucker's land just after the war that Cecelia first saw on her trip home remains today just off Tacoma Street and Williamsburg Blvd and fine example of a Post-Civil War period home.

Mount Olivet – A second, but smaller church was finished in 1870 which lasted until 1895. In 1904, the U.S. Government settled a claim for $3400 to cover the losses suffered in 1861. Those funds supported the construction of a third, much larger structure and meeting house which remains today as a leading United Methodist Church in Arlington with a very proud 150-year legacy. Its burial grounds contain many prominent Arlington family members. A stone marker attests to the Union and Confederate soldiers buried in the graveyard. The church resides on the corner of the Glebe Road and 16th Street North, (then called Brown's

Bend Road). Reverend Drinkhouse died in 1903 and Oliver Cox continued to work as a clerk for the Army Quartermaster after the war and died in 1912.

Ball's Crossroads – The lands on which Camp Union stood were used by the Union Army up until the end of the war. Some of the original Regiments that were camped there in 1861 returned to participate in the Grand Review of the Army in 1865. The tavern which stood there through the war later became a general store and an annex to the Georgetown Post Office. The land around it returned to agriculture after the war and today is the site of Arlington's Ballston commercial district at the corner of Glebe Road and the Georgetown Ferry Road, now called Wilson Blvd.

Chain Bridge - The sixth bridge was destroyed by the Potomac's high waters in 1870. The seventh, a wrought iron bridge, was built by the US Army Corps of Engineers in 1874 on the original foundations and remained until 1938. The bridge has been rebuilt two other times since then and remains a key connector to suburban Maryland and Washington DC. The paper, flour and wool mills and warehouses at the Virginia side of the bridge at the mouth of the Pimmit Run remained through 1890. The Columbia Light and Power Company used the waters flowing from the run to generate electricity for the community and remnants of it remain on its shores.

Court House and Quartermaster Headquarters – The old courthouse meeting rooms where Cecelia petitioned the Commission remains today at the intersection of Columbus and Queen Streets in Old Town Alexandria. The buildings where the Quartermaster Headquarters and Meyenberg's Mercantile across from the courthouse no longer exists. Both were located at the intersection of King and Pitt Streets.

Falls Grove – The Vanderwekin home and its surrounding

lands used by General Handcock as his headquarters and camp early on after the invasion, then later the house and grounds as a Hospital for retreating Union Army troops after the Battle of Bull Run remains. Locals said the home is haunted by the spirits of soldiers who died there. The house sits today at the northwest corner of Glebe Road and Little Falls Road.

Fort Ethan Allen – The fort was shuttered in 1870 and the land returned to Gilbert Vanderwerken and others, though it remained on county maps as a fort site well into the 1920's. Today, Fort Ethan Allen Park stands on some of the grounds of the original fort where remnants of its ramparts and bombproofs remain. The fort is located near the intersection of the Old Glebe Road and Military Road.

Glebe Parish Home – Known as the Glebe House today has a distinctive, octagon shaped addition. It later became the home of the famous Virginia Senator Ball of the original Ball Family. Glebe House remains as a private home off the Glebe Road at 4527 17th Street North, a historical marker attests to its significance.

Glebe Road - The Road to the Falls or sometimes as the Road to the Glebe, which ran the length of the County, up from the flats near mouth of the Four Mile Run creek to the Chain Bridge was renamed Glebe Road. That part of the road that passed by the Balls Crossroads Tavern, Glebe Parish home, Mount Olivet, the Wunder Farm, Maple Grove, Falls Gove and Fort Ethan Allen remained a barely passable dirt thoroughfare until the 1920's. Today, Glebe Road is the key north-south thoroughfare through the county.

Georgetown-Fairfax Road - The East-West road that passed by the Wunder, Hall and Smith Minor farms to the Falls Church was renamed Lee Highway in the 20th century as a tribute to Confederate General Robert E. Lee.

Little Falls Road – The road to the Little Falls connecting Minor Hill, past the Titus, Minor, Vanderberg and Vanderwerken lands and then on to the mouth of the Pimmit Run at the Little Falls on the Potomac remains today pretty much along its original path, though its eastern section joins at the Glebe Road and takes on that name to the Chain Bridge.

Long Bridge – The wood trestle bridge that was once a world wonder that troops used to march over from Washington to Virginia was augmented in 1863 with a stronger bridge about 100 ft down river from the original that could support railroad engines and cars. Eventually those bridges were replaced with a single Iron bridge on the original pilings of that second bridge. Today, a railroad bridge exists on those original foundations while three other automobile bridges of various names lie up-river from where the original stood.

Marshall House Inn – The place where the first Union and Rebel martyrs were made in Alexandria no longer exists, having been demolished in the 1950's. A plaque attesting to the Inn is on the wall of a hotel which resides at the site on the corner of King and Pitt Streets.

Military Road – The corduroy timber road built in three days by the Union Army to connect Fort Ethan Allen, past Mary Hall's and Donaldson's lands to Fort C.F. Smith, then on to the Aqueduct Bridge remains, is now a modern paved road of the same name. It is likely that some of the original logs used to construct it remain below the asphalt.

Minor Hill – The fields around Minor Hill that were home to the seven Union Army camps are today surrounded by housing developments along North Sycamore Street near the intersection of it with Little Falls Road and Williamsburg Blvd. Surrounding its Northeast face is the small Sharp

Park. Its summit was leveled a bit to build a county water reservoir. From atop this reservoir, one can still see the top of the Washington Monument five miles away attesting to its importance during the war. Lumber from its fortifications was used to construct Freedman's Village which was the first dedicated housing development for African Americans after the Civil War. A Virginia historical marker is the only reminder of its relevance to the Civil War. The Minor "Springfield" two-story brick-sided home stood at the corner of Virginia Ave and Nottingham Streets was torn down in 2015. John Minor's Home was said to be located at the 5600 block of 35th Road North, while Fairfax Minor's home which burned down in 1920, was located at 3026 N. John Marshall Drive.

Old Dominion Trail to the Falls – The road which spurred off the Little Falls Road across Vanderberg land to cut a shorter path to the Glebe Road at Mary Hall's farm was expanded in 1900 with tracks laid down for trolley service from the Cherrydale section of the County all the way to the Great Falls. This service continued through 1934 until the company went bankrupt and the tracks were removed. Today this old track bed is known as Old Dominion Drive.

Price & Birch Slave Traders – The Alexandria house where the Price & Birch Slave Traders, later the Contraband holding place, Confederate Jail and later a hospital for Negro soldiers still exists, though without the walled courtyard section with the holding pens. The home is currently the location of the Alexandria Urban League and is open for tours with displays relating to the slave trading period before the Civil War and its use during the war. The home is located at 343 Duke Street, Alexandria.

Sickles Barracks – The imposing Hospital and prison where Private Thompson met his end in Alexandria City was torn down sometime before 1890 as it does not appear in later maps of the city. The Hospital site is today bordered by West, Fayette, Oronoco and Pendleton Streets.

Spring – The favorite place for Cecelia and her friends which was in the valley between the two hills is now buried below a non-descript clump of trees which splits today's John Marshall Drive just north of the Little Falls Road. You can still hear water rushing from this underground spring in the storm sewers that run to the Little Pimmit creek. Longtime residents recall an old springhouse that sat amongst the clump of trees well into the early '90's. The springhouse is mentioned in some of the source books and Arlington Historical Society Magazines. In 2014 a large trove of cattle bones were found just east of the spring in the rear yard of a private home on 33rd Street North near where the creek bed sat attesting to a large slaughter pen that was there.

Wunder Farm – The farmhouse and cottage that were home to Doc and Cecelia and the others no longer exists. The corner of the Georgetown-Fairfax Road (now Lee highway) and the Glebe Road where men gathered to hear the war news was called Wunder's Corner many years into the next century. Today a sign in a lot attests to the Wunder's Corner and the family contributions to the county.

People:

Cecelia Payne – This story hopes to give her some life as there is little in the records. She is listed in the 1860 census as a white 15-year-old female living with Doctor Henry Wunder. She does not show up in the 1870 Alexandria County Census, nor the County Marriage or Death records through 1896.

Bazil Hall and Family – Of all the families on either of the two hills, one could rightly argue that he and his family suffered the most in the war. Bazil filed with the Commission and did get some redress, but it was not enough to cover his losses over four years of war. He rebuilt his home, burnt during the war, in 1870 nearby when he served as a Justice of the Peace, naming it Cherry Grove. Bazil had five more children since the start of the war according to the 1880 census. One of those daughters was named Francis who married a Birch and lived in the community. Their eldest daughter Elvira, who was five at the start of the war worked as a government clerk in her twenties. Bazil died in 1888 and his wife did so the same year of pneumonia and both were buried in the family cemetery at Halls Hill. In 1939, Hall family members in the family cemetery were re-interred at Oakwood Cemetery in Falls Church. Bazil, his first wife Elizabeth and second wife Francis are buried together. In 1870, Bazil subdivided some of his land to family members after Alexandria achieved self-rule and then in 1880 began to sell one acre or so plots to free blacks at discounted prices. Given his treatment of his slaves and death of his first wife by his slave, the reason for this change of heart is not known. His legacy remains today as the Hall's Hill Highview Park neighborhood in Arlington with some families descended from those original African Americans. The Hall's Hill neighborhood and Arlington's hospital reside on his lands. Locals say Bazil's original home was located where an electrical appliance company currently resides on the 5000 block of Lee Highway while Cherry Grove was located on a rise at the west side of the 1800 block of George Mason Drive North. Cherry Grove was sold to Gaillard Hunt, a prominent national archivist and businessman who was the son of the Secretary of the Navy under President Garfield to use as a summer home. Hunt's relatives used the home until 1997 when it was demolished for a housing subdivision. Bazil Hall is spelled differently in various sources (Bazil, Basil).

Mary Hall – Mary returned to the large two-story farmhouse

at Maple Grove after the war and purchased twelve more acres of adjoining land. Later on she let her sister Elizabeth run the brothel in Washington that she had built in 1839. In her later years she returned to Washington DC where she died in 1886. The brothel was sold in a bitter family dispute involving Elizabeth, Bazil and his brothers. The Washington DC four story brick home with 25 rooms and its contemporary furnishings was sold to become a women's health clinic, then a school for colored youth until 1916 when it became the home of the Washington Animal Rescue League. The building on the 300 block of Maryland Avenue was demolished in 1920 for the renovation of the National Mall. The National Native American Museum currently occupies that site. Admiral Rixey, Surgeon General of the US Navy and friend of Teddy Roosevelt, purchased Maple Grove after Mary Hall's death and used the farm as a respite from District life until it burned down in 1907. In 1908, Rixey sold 70 acres to the Washington Golf and Country Club where it exists today. After World War I, Rixey built a larger house on the foundations of the earlier home. A station stop off the Old Dominion trolley was named after his place. In 1948 he sold the land to the Sisters of the Sacred Heart who opened a college for girls. The foundations of Mary's original home and Rixey's stately rebuild is today the main building at Marymount University. Mary's home at Maple Grove stood at what is now the northeast side of the intersection of Old Dominion Road and Glebe Road North.

Minors – Phillip Minor petitioned the Commission to compensate him $4115 for his beautiful brick home that was burned, testifying that the home was burned in a shelling with their daughters valiantly saving Union soldiers lives. He was awarded $1275. Little did the Commission know the house was burned as punishment for the Belles's misdeeds. The home was said to have been located at 27th and Florida Street North near the present Yorktown High School in

Arlington. Smith Minor was deemed by history to be a loyal man. His county home burned down in 1877 while he lived in Washington. He returned to his 190 acre farm the following year. Catherine Minor survived the war and returned to Minor Hill to live out her days. Over the years, the land was subsequently parsed out to relatives, leased, or otherwise sold. The Minor "Springfield" two story brick-sided home sat on the corner of Virginia Ave and North Nottingham Street until 2015.

Vanderberg Family – Gilbert, wife Sarah, daughters Eveline, Charlotte, and Maria remained in their home after the war. In 1872, Eveline married a watercolor artist named Rudolph Reichmann and then moved to New York. Rudolph brought a young George Saegmuller, designer of survey instruments, back to the Vanderberg home to meet Maria. They were married in April of 1874. Charlotte met and married a man named Henry Lockwood who worked in the Treasury Department on New Year's Day 1868. They lived in their home called "Easter Spring Farm" which remains today at 3722 North Glebe Road. Saegmuller and Lockwood formed a partnership to set up the electrical display at Philadelphia's 1876 exposition. George became quite renowned for his instruments going on to design the equatorial telescopes for Georgetown University and several U.S. cities, as well as gunfire spotting optics for the U.S. Navy. In the 1880's he purchased the Vanderberg home and surrounding lands renaming it Reserve Hill after the Union Army stationed there in the war. Saegmuller was a strong advocate for educating children of that part of the county, so he used his own funds to build the original Saegmuller School on the grounds of Fort Ethan Allen in the 3800 block of North Stafford Street. The light blue Vanderberg farmhouse that had been the girls refuse during the shelling burned in a fire in 1894, only to be replaced with a beautiful stone home with twenty-one rooms that is today the meeting house for the Arlington Knights of Columbus. The Vanderberg name is spelled differently in various sources (Vanderburgh, Vandenburg, Vandenbergh, Vanderburg).

Vanderwerken Family – Gilbert, wife Jane, sons Charles and John, daughters Jane, Emma and Ella, nieces Cornelia Golden and Sarah Oaks lived through the rest of the war in Washington D.C. The family went back at Falls Grove after 1870 where Gilbert continued to run his businesses including the Potomac Blue Stone quarry that stretched along the Potomac from the Chain Bridge to the Aqueduct Bridge. Its stone was used to build many prominent Washington landmarks including St. Patrick's Church and Georgetown University buildings. Gilbert died at Falls Grove in 1894 and his wife Jane and son Charles shortly after in the same year. Daughter Jane met and married the young Union Army lieutenant named Alfred Grunwell, who got lost crossing their lands from Minor Hill, in April 1866. Their home by the name of "Bellevue" is today located at 3311 North Glebe Road built with timber reclaimed from Fort Ethan Allen. Emma married a lawyer named Thomas Jewell in 1883 and lived in Arlington. Ella married the Reverend George E. Truett in 1878 and lived at Falls Grove until her death in 1947. Falls Grove is located on a hilltop at the Northwest corner of Little Falls Road and Glebe Road. Many of the family are buried in the Vanderwerken Circle section of the Oak Hill Cemetery in Washington DC. The Vanderwerken name is spelled differently in various sources (Vanderwerkin, Vanderverkin).

Wunder Family – Dr. Henry Wunder died of pneumonia in December 1866. George continued to remain active in county government in many elected and appointed positions as well as a delegate to Richmond. He was involved in all manner of county affairs, but best known for successfully lobbying to tax residents to fund good schools. This tradition remains today. No county court, marriage or death records were found for Barbara Blogger or Daniel Turner.

SOURCES

Arlington County Courthouse Records
- Land Transactions 1814-1875
- Alexandria Court Cases 1855-1866

Arlington County Public Library:
- Virginia Room. Testimony of Southern Claims Commission – 1871
- Marriage Records of Alexandria County Virginia – 1870-1892
- Death Records of Alexandria County Virginia – 1853-1896
- Slave Schedule, 1860: July 1860
- Civil War Oaths of Allegiance

Arlington Historical Society Magazine:
- Vol 1#1- 1957
  - Chronology of Actions on the Part of the united States to complete Retrocession of Alexandria County to Virginia – Harrison Mann
  - History of the Potomac Bridges in the Washington Area – George Schwabel
- Vol 1#3 – 1959
  - Ballston's Beginnings – Eleanor Lee Templeman
- Vol 1#4 – 1960
  - Ball's Crossroads – Percy C. Smith
  - In the Beginning - Eleanor Lee Templeman
- Vol 2#1 – 1961

- o Civil War Military Operations on Northern Virginia, May-June 1861 – William H. Price
- Vol 2#3 -1963
  - o Notes on Two Arlingtonians: Bazil Hall, Robert s. Lacey – Paul Covey
- Vol 2#4 – 1964
  - o The Arlington I have Known – Frank L. Ball
- Vol 4#3 – 1971
  - o The Glebe of Fairfax Parish – Ludwell Lee Montague
- Vol 5#3 – 1975
  - o Civil War Reminiscences – John L. Saegmuller
- Vol 6#3 – 1979
  - o Bazil Hall of Hall's Hill – Donald L. Wise
- Vol 7#1 – 1981
  - o Some Civil War Letters - George E. Pettengill
- Vol 7#4 – 1984
  - o Life in Alexandria County During the Civil War – Ruth Ward
- Vol 8#2 – 1986
  - o U.S. Balloon Corps Action in Northern Virginia During the Civil War – June Robinson
- Vol 8#4 – 1988
  - o Springs of Arlington – Eleanor Lee Templeman
- Vol 9#3 – 1991
  - o Chain Bridge – A History of the Bridge and its Surrounding Territory 1605-1991 – Jim Fearson
- Vol 12#1 – 2001
  - o Early History of the Mounty Olivet United Methodist Church – Hank Hulme
  - o From the Hill: Civil War Letters From Hall's Hill Virginia – Scott S. Taylor
- Vol 12#4 – 2004
  - o Mary Ann Hall: Arlington's Notorious Madam – Willard J. Webb
- Vol 13#3 – 2007
  - o The Bazil Hall House/Cherryhill, - Willard J. Webb
  - o The Photograph of Bazil Hall – Willard J. Webb
- AHS 1860 Map of Arlington Land Owners – Draft

Alexandria City Public Library
- Map files; Various 1850-1870

Books & Reference Publications

- A Historic Resources Study: The Civil War Defenses of Washington, Pt. 1. Interior Department, National Park Service, National Capital Region
- Arlington Heritage – Eleanor Lee Templeman - 1959
- Civil War, Northern Virginia 1861- Willan S. Connery - 2011
- Cloud of Witness – The Methodists of Mount Olivet – Kirk Mariner - 2004
- Mount Olivet Methodist, Arlington's Pioneer Church – Frank L. Ball – 1965
- Mr. Lincoln's Forts: A Guide to the Civil War Defenses of Washington – Cooling and Owen, 2009
- Once Upon a Time – Mary Williamson Lemen Mellor – 1929
- The War of the Rebellion. A Compilation of the Official Records of the Union and Confederate Armies - 1880-1901

Library of Congress - Chronicling America: US Newspapers: 1690-Present. http://chroniclingamerica.loc.gov
- Alexandria Gazette: 1861 - 16-26 July, 1 August -27 September
- Alexandria Local News: 1861 - 12, 21 October, 11, 13, 18, 19, 20 November, 5, 6 December
- National Intelligencer: 1861 - 29 August,
- National Republican: 1861 - 16 May, 10, 12 June, 8 July, 6, 9, 18, 23, 26, September, 2, 16, 18
    - October, 30 November, 10, 18, 21, 24, 28 December; 1862 – 2, 30 January, 3, 14, 18, 19
    - February, 8, 15 April, 15 July, 5 September, 6 October, 13, 28 November; 1863 – 3 June, 27 June, 16 October, 4, 6 November; 1864 – 29 September; 1866 – 16 January; 1867 – 2 September
- Richmond Daily Dispatch: 1861 - 10, 12, 18, 19, 29 July, 29 August, 2, 4, 11, 13, 16, 17, 18, 20,
    - September, 9, 14, 16, 29 October, 12, 13 November, 4, 10, 18 December
- Staunton Spectator: 1861 - 3, 10, 14 September, 8 October
- Soldier's Journal Publication: 1864 – 26 October, 21 December
- Washington Evening Star: 1864 – 16-17 August; 1864 – 10 December

National Archives:
- United States Census: 1850, 1860, 1870, Alexandria County Virginia
- Court Martial Proceedings of Private John H. Thompson

- Record Group 77 – Civil War Maps; F99-1 through 65, Alexandria, Virginia G483 and DR 127, 171-210, Topographic Maps 1862 F102, Defenses of Washington Maps 1-12, DR171 91 through 102, Defenses of Washington Maps, 1864 Z238 and 445, Folios F99-1, F100-1, 2, 3, F102, F103, F104A, F118; Survey of Roads and Defenses, Publication 1862, No. 7; 12th Regiment Camp – G443 Vol 2.
- Maps: 7445 of 4 April 1864, 265A, 210L 14-16 (Fort Ethan Allen and Fort Marcy)
- Post and Reservation Maps: 1820-1905, NARA 305818
- General Orders: May 1861 – August 1863, NARA 4706691
- Special Orders: June 1861-April 1862, NARA 4706693
- Records Concerning the Conduct and Loyalty of Certain US Army Officers, Civilian Employees of the War Department and US Citizens during the Civil War: 1861-1872, NARA 642808
- Record Group 92 – Records of the Quartermaster Group: 1.158 installations 1861-66, 158-C-1 DC Prison; Quartermaster Accounts 1861-63, NARA 5860048
- Prisoner Files – RG-393 Part 2 and Part 4
- (NM-68) Preliminary Inventory of Records of Commissary General of Prisoners (Record Group 249)
- Record File 1528 – Register of Prisoners in the Alexandria County Jail (1862-65)
- Record File 2132 - Prisoners of State – Old Capitol Prison – Sep 1865 source: monthly acct records of the Prison

Online Regimental and other Historical Histories:
- http://www.civilwararchive.com/
- http://dmna.ny.gov/historic/reghist/civil/infantry/civil_infIndex.htm
- http://www.firstbullrun.co.uk/index.html
- https://archive.org/details/importantevents00franrich - Frank Leslie's Illustrated History of the Civil War - 1895
- http://www.sonofthesouth.net/leefoundation/the-civil-war.htm - Harper's Weekly - 1860 -1865
- http://www.civilwarindex.com/
http://civilwar.com/

ABOUT THE AUTHOR

George Axiotis raised his family in between the two hills that Cecelia and her friends called their own, in what is now Arlington, Virginia. A desire to know what happened in those early days of the Civil War sparked interest in researching and later writing this book. What he found were wonderful stories of happiness and despair, of friendships and fear during a calamitous time in our history. George wanted to write a book on local history and sacrifice as seen through the eyes of a young person for non-historians. This is his first book.